The Idol of Mombasa

The Idol of Mombasa

Annamaria Alfieri

FELONY & MAYHEM PRESS • NEW YORK

All the characters and events portrayed in this work are fictitious.

THE IDOL OF MOMBASA

A Felony & Mayhem mystery

Copyright © 2016 by Annamaria Alfieri

ISBN: 978-1-63194-100-9

Manufactured in the United States of America

First edition, October 2016

Library of Congress Cataloging-in-Publication Data

Names: Alfieri, Annamaria, author
Title: The idol of Mombasa / Annamaria Alfieri.
Description: First edition. I New York : Felony & Mayhem Press, 2016.
Identifiers: LCCN 2016032291 (print) I LCCN 2016038766 (ebook) I ISBN
  9781631941009 I ISBN 9781631941016 ()
Subjects: I GSAFD: Mystery fiction.
Classification: LCC PS3601.L3597 I36 2016 (print) I LCC PS3601.L3597 (ebook)
  I DDC 813/.6--dc23
LC record available at https://lccn.loc.gov/2016032291

For Barbara Fass Leavy, Ph.D.,
precious friend, literary scholar,
and lover of crime fiction

The icon above says you're holding a copy of a book in the Felony & Mayhem "Historical" category, which ranges from the ancient world up through the 1940s. If you enjoy this book, you may well like other "Historical" titles from Felony & Mayhem Press.

For more about these books, and other Felony & Mayhem titles, or to place an order, please visit our website at:

www.FelonyAndMayhem.com

Other "Historical" titles from

FELONY&MAYHEM

ANNAMARIA ALFIERI
City of Silver
Strange Gods

DAVID STUART DAVIES
Forests of the Night

FIDELIS MORGAN
Unnatural Fire
The Rival Queens

KATE ROSS
Cut to the Quick
A Broken Vessel
Whom the Gods Love
The Devil in Music

CATHERINE SHAW
The Library Paradox
The Riddle of the River

TYLER, LC
A Cruel Necessity

LAURA WILSON
The Lover
The Innocent Spy
An Empty Death
The Wrong Man
A Willing Victim
The Riot

The Idol of Mombasa

Acknowledgments

I am grateful to:

Adrienne Rosado, my agent, whose belief in my work keeps me going.

Maggie Topkis, my publisher and editor; and Julia Musha; both of Felony & Mayhem Press, who have given Tolliver, Vera and Kwai a new home.

Stanley Trollip, who shares my love of Africa and helps me to get it right.

Kannan Srinavasan, my fellow writer-in-residence at the New York Public Library, who graciously pointed me at period books in English by Islamic scholars. Any errors in that regard are mine, not his or theirs.

My tribal brothers and sisters of the New York Chapter of Mystery Writers of America and my blogmates at Murder Is Everywhere— writers whose mutual support brings joy into what is essentially a lonely process.

The caring, affectionate people who take care of David and make possible the peace of mind it takes for me to do my job.

The staff of the New York Public Library. Without its splendid collection, I could not write the books I do. SUPPORT YOUR LOCAL LIBRARY!

Thou shalt not make unto thee a graven image.
The Bible (Exodus 20:4)

Yet some men take idols beside God, and love them as with love due to God.
The Quran (Surah 2:165)

The Sultan's sovereignty (on the Kenyan coastal strip)...led to slavery dying out more slowly than elsewhere, for the status of slavery was legal within the Sultan's dominions, whereas in the rest of the Kenya Protectorate, it was forbidden by law.
J. Spencer Trimingham
Islam in East Africa

On the Indian Ocean
Off the East African Coast
Early January
1912

Prologue

As always, the dhow approached Malindi harbor under cover of darkness on the night of the new moon. A tall African man stood in the bow of the boat. He wore a *kanzu*—a man's long gown, ubiquitous on this coast, but not in the traditional white. His was midnight blue, so that with his dark skin and dark garb, he—like this boat and its crew—was nearly invisible in the African night. Being seen would mean prison. Death.

Miraculously, the Zanzibari at the tiller found their way on the inky sea. He followed the stars, he said, and the ocean currents, feeling them through his scrotum as he sat upon the deck.

The tall man in the bow found pleasure in being on the water. It was cool and smelled clean—unlike the sweltering streets of Mombasa with its sweaty throngs of hurrying men. These sorties were dangerous. Required constant vigilance. But these missions also gave him satisfactions that little else offered. On this boat, he stood in the place of his master. He could command these men, even the captain. He craved this sense of power.

But he would also be the man to die if something went wrong.

As they neared the port, he easily recognized its old Portuguese pillars and dockside warehouses, silhouetted against a million stars. With the sail lowered and the boat powered only by the oarsmen, they approached the reef that separated the harbor from the open ocean. Phosphorescence in the breaking waves showed them the gap where they could make safe entry.

Once through, it was a simple matter of steering to a spot between signal torches stuck in the sand just north of the docks. A pair flickered to the left of their destination, and about fifteen yards farther to their right, a group of three.

The surf was blessedly calm tonight. The Arab captain of the boat lowered the anchor. "As fast as you can," he said in a harsh whisper. "I'll put the small boat out to ferry the children."

The man in the dark *kanzu* answered only, "Yes." He hated being told every time what he had known for years. It was his decision how fast or how slowly they would go. He was more than a slave. He was the Master's overseer. And the boat's captain knew that. Still that Arab always pretended his word ruled.

The overseer reached into a canvas bag at his feet and took out a saber in its scabbard. Holding the weapon over his head, he put his backside on the gunwale, thrust his legs over the side, and slid waist deep into the water. Its chill struck his privates. No matter if he knew it was coming, it still shocked. He waded ashore and then strode with difficulty across the sand toward the trees, his bare feet sinking in; it was slow going.

There should be, he had been told, eighty-six people hiding a few yards away. Over the past two months the captive men among them had carried twenty-two elephant tusks from the base of Mount Kenya to the shore of the Indian Ocean. Tusks that the porters would load onto the ship.

Now that they had reached the sea, they too would become cargo on the Arab ship bound for the slave market in Muscat.

This was the master's secret. And no one must know.

The British, only lately arrived in this part of the world, had made slavery illegal. His master had laughed at the folly of such a rule. The change in the law had, as the master had predicted, only pushed up the profits to be made.

The overseer-slave, his *kanzu* still dripping seawater, approached the trees. He strapped on the sword and put his hand on its hilt. What price, he wondered, might he himself bring today, knowing what he knew, capable as he was?

He drew the sword and knocked it against the trunk of a mangrove. Two beats. Then a pause. Then three. He counted to ten. And repeated the signal.

A rustling in the undergrowth brought the ivory caravan's captain to his side. "I have only sixty-one. Thirty-one died along the way," he said quietly, without preamble. "The usual number from disease and snakebites. But the rest became rebellious. I had to kill six who tried to run off. To make an example of them." He was attempting to excuse the dreadful performance of his duty. Excuses to a slave, to be repeated to his master.

Such defenses were useless. "The master will be angry whatever your reasons for delivering so few."

The caravan captain swore in Arabic. "Yes, and he will be even angrier that almost all who perished of illness were girls and young boys." His voice had turned bitter. "Almost all who survived are grown men."

"You needed them to carry the ivory."

"You know as well as I do that buyers don't want grown men. We won't be able to sell this many. We will have to kill the ones who don't find a buyer. And your master will take the difference in profit out of my pay."

At least you get pay, the man with the sword thought, slipping it back into its scabbard. "We must move now."

"*Malo,*" the captain said in a sharp, whispered command.

Suddenly the area not two feet away was alive with movement. "Push them onto the beach," the caravan captain ordered to his assistants, unseen in darkness.

The porters began to move. Once they were out on the beach, the elephant tusks they carried on their shoulders appeared ghostly in the starlight. The men themselves were all but invisible. Only metallic noises gave away their location. They were bound together in groups of six, with rings around their necks joined by a length of chain. That clanking meant fear to the man in the *kanzu*. He had heard it for the first time as a child holding his father's hand during the long, miserable trek from his pleasant birthplace in the highlands to the edge of the ocean and a lifetime of servitude.

It was the only sound any of the people made. The porters—*slaves* he should call them—had certainly been warned that their throats would be cut if they tried to call for help. They followed the caravan captain's barely visible white turban, moving toward the edge of the water.

Again with sword drawn, the overseer recrossed the sand at the rear of the column. The caravan captain's assistants were fanned out a few steps before him on either side. As the most valuable cargo, the young women and children were kept at the head of the group, so they could board first. In the old days before the British had taken charge of this part of the Sultan's territory, it had been the ivory that went first. But since the British had forced the Sultan to outlaw slavery, the prices for people had gone higher and higher. The young because of their scarcity and the pleasurable uses to which they could be put, fetched the highest prices of all.

As always, a few of the assistants had to carry the children to the small boat waiting to ferry them to the dhow. The women went docilely behind them at first but balked in terror at entering the water. They struggled. Calm as the surf was tonight, they had never seen it before. One of them started to scream. The entire column froze. If she raised enough of a ruckus, the policemen from *boma* down the beach would be on them. Then there would be hell to pay.

More women began to wail. The assistants pushed forward to help their fellows muffle them with hands across their mouths.

The man with the sword hung back. He could not do this again—forcing people into boats. He had done it so many times before. It should have been easy by now. But each time it hurt him more. He was turning them into him. Not a man, but a possession. To be whipped until they bled. To be violated for the pleasure of whoever owned them. Or whoever their masters gave permission to use them. As he had been used.

And when they grew too old to be wanted in such a way, they would be relegated to whatever work their masters wanted of them. The boys might be castrated and used to guard the harems. Or slain to avoid the expense of feeding them.

The overseer feared for himself. If the police came and caught him. If he failed in his duty. He had grown to be a trusted servant, to enjoy privileges and powers beyond those of an ordinary slave. To command these men as if *he* were the master. To plan, to deal with any emergency that came up. To use his mind and cleverness, to enjoy his master's cohorts' admiration for his ideas. These things he was allowed, provided he served as if willing. But he had no will to do this, the taking of others into a life like his. Not again.

Suddenly, while the captain's assistants were struggling to get the terrified women into the boat, one of the chained men before him grunted and whispered a word in their language. And they turned and ran—six bound together—north toward the dark place under the trees. He stood and listened to the clanking of their chains receding.

"After them, you fool," the caravan captain spat out. He was holding two of the girls, trying to impel them into the water toward the waiting boat.

Reluctantly, the man gripped his sword and pursued the runaways.

They were only a few steps ahead of him. He could have reached them. He could hear them breathing. And the chains clanking.

Stop them, his master's voice called in his head.

Kill one, he thought, and the others will not be able to move with speed. They will be easily recaptured.

Run, run with them, the inner voice he could not silence said. *Go and be free. Be what you cannot remember ever having been.*

The caravan captain was approaching behind him. "Stop them. Stop them," he said in a guttural whisper. "This noise will raise the guard."

The man with the sword caught one of the chained porters around the neck. The captive struggled. The others all started to resist, beating the overseer on the head and back. If he used his sword, he would have them all.

The captain was closer. "You will die for this, you stinking savages."

The man stopped fighting them. "Go quickly," he whispered. "Go free."

The instant he was loose from them, he sliced a searing cut into his left shoulder, dropped the sword, fell down, and cried out in agony.

The six disappeared into the trees.

By the time the caravan captain reached him, the clanking of the chains had stopped. The wounded man writhed in real pain, the sand stinging the wound.

Why had he not gone with them? He should have gone with them.

Mombasa
British East Africa
Late January
1912

From the deck of the Union-Castle steamship *Galacian*, the sight of Mombasa brought tears to Vera Tolliver's eyes.

Her husband, Justin, who stood beside her with his arm across her shoulders, drew her to him. "I can see how moved you are by its beauty." He offered it as a statement of fact, not imagining that she wept for any other reason. "So am I," he said with all his heart. "So am I."

She nodded, took the handkerchief he offered, and used it to suppress a sob. Truth be told, seeing the East African island port city brought her pain. Mombasa's panorama was certainly splendid seen from the sea and shining in the morning sun—as vividly green as any English county in June, but with tall palms jutting above flowering flame trees and mimosas, enormous baobabs towering over whitewashed buildings with red roofs.

But Vera was all but blind to the beauty. The last time she had looked upon this bustling, exotic city from the water, her parents had been standing on the dock to greet her, her father waving his straw clergyman's hat, her mother—the proper missionary's wife—standing decorously at his side. That was six years ago. Returning from a visit to her granny in Glasgow, fourteen-year-old Vera had been holding her younger brother's hand as their ship neared land. The moment her mother had caught sight of them, she smiled and waved.

On this occasion, no one watched for Vera from the shore. Her father had not come to the port to meet her and her husband. He had remained up-country, at the Scottish Mission just south of Nairobi, where the demands of his work made it impossible to travel here to meet them as they returned from their honeymoon. At least that was what his last letter had said. As for her mother and brother—well, her mother was no more, and Otis had disappeared last year in the aftermath of their uncle's death, leaving Vera and her father with only each other.

She put her arm around Justin's waist. He had been there through it all, had investigated her uncle's murder, had protected her and her family as best he could. And since then, his love had repaired her heart after all that sorrow. He was her family now. The trip they had just taken—all the best parts of it, the days in Italy and Yorkshire—had proven to her that she was no longer alone. Her soul and her body knew in him all she longed for.

She had become infatuated with Justin when she first met him and danced with him at the Nairobi Club socials. In retrospect, that girlish attraction felt juvenile. The more she knew him, the more she admired his character. Oh, she was still moved by the golden brown of his hair, his bright eyes, the beautiful shape of his mouth. She had despaired that he would ever do more than dance with her. She had longed for him despite her certain knowledge that he was too perfect ever to take an interest in a missionary girl with unpolished manners and a habit of blurting out embarrassing opinions. But he did. Well, not always. Sometimes their differences came between them. But he admired her enough to press all that aside and be her husband. And it thrilled her to be his wife.

Still, images of her past haunted her: her uncle lying dead in a coffee field with a spear in his back; her lost mother and brother. She longed now to see her father. She craved the reassuring clasp of his hand, the understanding of their shared grief, no longer spoken of, but present nonetheless.

The hubbub of the port drew her attention. To their right, men wearing white mechanics uniforms were ferrying American motorcars down the ramp from a tramp steamer. Emblazoned across the men's backs were the words *Mombasa Motor Garage* in bold black lettering large enough for her to see twenty yards away. Vera and Justin had seen such machines, Model T Fords they were called, in London and Rome. She had found their speed thrilling. Justin had complained about their fumes and worried they would foul the African countryside.

The crowd waiting on the deck to disembark pressed forward, but then, before the gangway was lowered from their own ship, a great noise arose from the vessel docked just to their left. Onshore, a military band, augmented with native drummers, struck up a tune Vera did not recognize.

"Oh, look," Justin exclaimed, "someone of note is arriving on that Deutsche Ost-Afrika boat. I believe that is District Commissioner Hobson-Jones and District Superintendent of Police Egerton waiting near that bandstand to greet him, whoever he is." A white canvas marquee had been erected in front of the corrugated iron shed that housed the Customs Office. Justin recognized Egerton only by his uniform, but in a few days he would be reporting to the D.S. as his assistant district superintendent. There would be a row with Vera about that. Tolliver had been an A.D.S. when he and Vera fell in love, but during their honeymoon she began to express a hope that he would leave the police force. Try as he might, he could never get Vera to properly explain why she felt so strongly about it. All she would say was that deep in inside her something told her it was wrong for him to be a police man.

She was not alone in that opinion. Many in the British Protectorate looked askance at the likes of Justin Tolliver—the son of an earl—serving as a police officer. The aristocrats, who made up most of the settler population, regarded such work as "not really the done thing, my dear." To them, an assistant district superintendent barely rated above a butler or a shopkeeper. But Tolliver had been a second son, with too little capital to develop a farm, even at the low price for which one could be bought in British East Africa.

Vera was no snob. Her desire, he was sure, was not to raise his social standing by turning him into a cattle rancher or a coffee grower, what he had wanted to become in the first place. Now, with her granny's wedding gift, he had the means to do so.

But he was not ready to. Not yet.

Vera stood on tiptoes and tried to see who was descending from the other ship. "Very likely a German count of some sort who's come on a shooting safari." She spoke with a bit of the dislike most British settlers harbored against their neighbors to the south.

"You are quite mistaken, my dear." This from a nearby portly Englishman in a sun helmet, who sported a drooping ginger-and-gray mustache. "It's the Grand Mufti of Egypt, don't you know."

"We didn't know," Justin answered before Vera had the chance. "Quite an occasion."

Vera giggled. "I knew the band and the bunting were not for us."

Their neighbor on the deck harrumphed. "All humbug! Great lot of folderol over a heathen, if you ask me. You'd think King George himself were arriving, what?"

The ship's boatswain came up behind them. "Sorry for the delay, ladies and gentlemen. Captain had hoped we would be ashore before the ceremony began. I am afraid it will be the better part of half an hour before all the formalities are completed. I apologize, but we must wait."

The grumpy Englishman's ears turned red and he bit on his mustache. Vera smiled to herself. The man was holding in a string of swearwords, she was sure, and it was costing him dearly. She hoped his sun helmet would not catch fire with the heat of his anger.

"At any rate, we have the best vantage point from which to observe the festivities," she said as soothingly as she could.

The big man then pushed forward, completely blocking the view of a girl of about ten standing nearby with her nanny.

Silently, Vera invited the child to stand in front of her.

"Oh, look," the girl exclaimed, pointing at a man disembarking from the other ship. "He looks like Father Christmas."

The stately figure descending the gangplank of the German steamer did indeed resemble Santa Claus. He was tall and broad, with a beautifully groomed long white beard. He wore a black robe and a white conical hat that flared out and up and added to his considerable height. As he reached the shore end of the gangplank, they could see that the crown of his impressive headgear was bright red.

"Father Christmas, my foot," the man beside them grumbled. "He's here to get gifts, rather than to give them." No one nearby had the nerve to contradict him.

A great deal of tiresome and largely inaudible speechifying ensued by the district commissioner and then by various white-turbaned Arab dignitaries dressed in beautifully colored, elaborate brocades. As predicted, many gifts were presented to the Grand Mufti, among them a long, curved gold-mounted sword, its scabbard encrusted with precious stones.

Justin leaned over and whispered in Vera's ear: "Exactly the kind of thing a devout Anglican would give a visiting bishop, wouldn't you say, darling?"

At that moment the ship's first officer made his way through the onlookers at the railing. "Mr. Tolliver, sir," he said. "This letter just arrived for you."

Tolliver took the envelope the man offered. "Excuse me, dearest," he said to Vera with a bow, and made his way to the back of the crowd.

By the time Vera arrived at his side, the band on the shore had begun to play "God Save the King." Justin was standing at attention and singing in his lovely baritone voice. She wanted to pry open his fingers and fetch out the letter, but she dutifully stood and sang the anthem.

"What is it?" she asked as soon as the music stopped.

He shoved the now crumpled paper into his pocket. "I'll tell you once we have disembarked. Nothing to worry over, really, darling."

She did not believe him, but she had no choice but to move with the mass of passengers now pressing forward down the gangplank to the wharf.

Early that same afternoon, at the Wesleyan Mission on the mainland at Nyali just north of Mombasa Island, Joseph Gautura stood with his back against the missionary's house and listened at a window covered only with mosquito netting. The loud voices of the men arguing in Swahili inside made it easy for him to hear. Robert Morley, the missionary, trumpeted his angry words. The ivory trader Khalid Majidi shouted back in kind.

"Bwana Majidi, I have nothing but respect for your religious beliefs," Reverend Morley said in a tone that seemed to Joseph anything but respectful. "I must remind you, though, that you have been keeping Joseph as a slave, which has been against the law in this country for over five years."

"I remind you, *Mchungali* Morley, that you British can say what you like. We Arabs have been trading on this coast since before Christ was born. The Sultan of Zanzibar has said we may not trade in slaves anymore because he has given you British charge of this place, but you cannot tell me what I can and cannot do in my own house. By keeping Joseph from my service, you are stealing my property. Whatever you say, that is what my law tells me."

Joseph knew that neither man was being completely honest. He had lived in Majidi's household for nearly thirty years, starting when he was taken into slavery as a boy of nine. Since then he had served Majidi every day of his life, was his overseer until six days ago, when he ran away. Majidi was selfish and hardly ever honest in his dealings, especially with the British.

Father Morley had been kind to Joseph, and only this morning, at breakfast, Joseph had heard him tell his sister, Katharine, how he hated slavery so much that he found it nearly impossible not to hate people like Majidi, who insisted on practicing it.

"I have an assistant district superintendent of police who is going to help me with this," the missionary now said to Majidi. "Then we shall see what your rights are."

Father Morley said the words as if he truly believed them, but Joseph knew that the missionary was not as sure as he tried to seem. Joseph had heard both Morley and his sister complain that, in this part of the Protectorate, the British Administration did not care about the fate of Arab household slaves. Given a choice between freeing the slaves or turning a blind eye to what the local traders were doing, their countrymen preferred to keep the peace between the English and the Muslim populations. The brother expected the A.D.S. to be helpful. The sister doubted anyone would help them.

The brother and sister had spoken of this in English, which they thought Joseph did not understand. Bwana Majidi also imagined, when he spoke Arabic to the men who bought ivory from him, that Joseph did not understand. Joseph had never let on that he could speak and understand both languages. He could have been more useful to Majidi if he had admitted this fact, but he did not care to be more useful to a man who valued nothing but money.

Beyond the window, within the missionary's parlor, the scrape of a chair against the bare wooden floor and the rustle of silk brocade signaled that Majidi was getting ready to leave. "I came here to claim my property," he said. "You will give him to me immediately."

"I will not!"

"If you refuse, I will find a way to take him back."

There was a crash that must have been a chair overturning, followed immediately by the missionary's voice booming out, "Over my dead body!"

"Yours or his." Majidi's voice was quiet and cold, and Joseph knew that when he used that tone nothing would stop him from having his way.

Joseph did not want to be the cause of harm to the kind English priest. But neither did he want to die himself at the hands of the master whom he had feared since he was taken as a slave. Now that Majidi had found out Joseph was here, this British Mission could never be the safe haven he had hoped for.

There was no choice. He would have to steal away in the night. His only trusted friend was his tribesman, Juba Osi. But Juba had refused to let Joseph stay with him. Juba had only recently bought his own freedom, and he still feared his former master. Harboring a runaway would draw attention to Juba and might give his old owner an excuse to take him back.

Joseph knew a British man, Carl Hastings, who had been away but was supposed to be returning to Mombasa this very day. Hastings had dealings with Majidi. Joseph understood that in his heart the Englishman despised the Arab, who paid him too little for his ivory. Hastings lived at the club where the British went to drink alcohol and play games with balls and sticks. Joseph would appeal to Bwana Hastings to save him from Majidi, a man they both knew to be evil.

After dark that night, Carl Hastings waited, hidden at the base of the battlements of Fort Jesus, the historic citadel on the edge of the sea. He longed for a stiff gin and quinine. He scratched at the mosquito bites that tortured him and imagined that any one of them could bring him malaria, which would lead to blackwater fever and a horrible death. Bloody savages who lived here never seemed to get anything.

Joseph Gautura, that bastard Majidi's servant, had sent him a message and chosen this benighted place to meet. The blighter had said to come after dark, the hour when an army of insects went on the attack.

The only good thing about the time and place of this meeting was that no one would know of it. If Gautura had come to see Hastings at the Mombasa Club, the entire membership would have been wondering what dealings they had and nosing about in Hastings's private business. And certainly Majidi would have gotten wind of their meeting. Miserable as the Arab was, Hastings needed him. He had debts that would land even an Englishman in prison. Without the income from his arrangements with the ivory trader, Hastings would drown in what he owed.

In his message, Gautura said he had bolted, and he begged Hastings's help. Much as he would have preferred to ignore the plea, Hastings could not. Now that Gautura was out of Majidi's control, he was dangerous, knew far too much—not only about Majidi's dicey deeds, but also about Hastings's part in them. Besides which, the letter had been written in English, which in and of itself had taken Hastings's breath away. The slave, who knew no English, must have dictated the message to someone who wrote it for him. That scribe now knew that Hastings provided more to Majidi than just elephant tusks.

Hastings paced along the wall of the bastion. Vasco da Gama had built this great pile to keep invaders out of his harbor. Now Hastings's own countrymen had made it into a prison, and it was here he could end up if he did not gain control of his situation.

He reached into his pocket for his watch, but there was not enough light to read it. He could not go out into the street, where there were electric lamps. Out there, trolleys clattered along, full of his countrymen. He could not risk being spotted in the wrong place at the wrong time. *Where was that bloody nigger?*

Hastings wiped his forehead with the back of his hand. His sweat came not only from the heat, but also from the horror of rotting in jail because he could not overcome his money problems. He was sure the moisture attracted the mosquitoes. A picture dropped into his head of that poor English chappie— what was his name?—who had been caught passing bad checks. No doubt that sod was somewhere behind these walls being eaten alive by insects at this very moment. Hastings imagined himself sharing that cell.

A rustling of the weeds along the wall spun him in its direction. Two figures approached. They were practically on top of him when a girl giggled. They were silhouetted against the pale light out on the street. Clearly, neither of them was Majidi's slave. Just two blackies here to fornicate.

Hastings pretended he had come out of the light to relieve himself. He marched off and left them to their sin. He would have to find the slave, wherever he was, and deal with him before the night was over. And he would also have to find whoever had written that note in English and take care of him too.

But first he needed to stop in a bar. At this moment his survival seemed to depend entirely on a double dose of quinine water with a triple dose of gin.

The following morning, in a cottage isolated in a charming cove, under the bare, twisted limbs of an enormous baobab tree, Justin Tolliver awoke as soon as the pale first light of dawn entered their room. He blinked and wondered—not even a gentle rocking of the ship? This bed? The stateroom was—and then, fully awake, he realized where he was: back in Africa at last.

He turned to Vera, asleep beside him, her dark hair half covering her face. She hugged her pillow as if it were a child's teddy bear. He took her in his arms and breathed in the warm, spicy scent of her skin. She stirred. Her lashes fluttered. As soon as her eyes opened and looked at him, she smiled and kissed his mouth. "Good morning, my love," she said, and he marveled. She spoke as if a woman's passion for her husband were the most natural thing in the world.

Tolliver had been raised to believe that good women would barely tolerate the act of love. Indeed, Vera had told him, during their recent visit to her granny in Glasgow, that that ultra-traditional lady had told Vera that as a dutiful wife she must bear his needs as best she could for the sake of having children. Yet Vera hungered for him nearly as much as he did for her.

Last month, during their sojourn in Yorkshire, Justin's brother had remarked on Vera's "affectionate nature." He had bounced his eyebrows as if he were talking about a music-hall actress. Justin had been torn between offering to punch his brother's nose and pretending not to know what he meant. Typically, John had taken his momentary silence for permission to go on. "I suppose," he said, "having had a native nurse, she drank in the tendency with the blackie's milk."

Then John blithely put some chalk on the tip of his cue and took his shot in snooker, as if he had just made some bland remark about Vera's dark eyes or small stature.

Justin had not responded. Frankly, he had not known what to say. He and John had both been brought up to regard an attitude like Vera's as the sign of a dreadful character flaw, but he refused to believe that. Vera loved making love. To her it was natural. And joyful. And he had learned to long for the thrill of her. He could not imagine that John got any satisfaction at all from that chilly, aloof wife of his.

Very likely John, like their father, visited the higher-class brothels of London.

For all that John, or his father for that matter, might feel superior to him in his choice of wife, making love to Vera made him feel more of a man than they were.

He began to kiss her warm skin, her neck, her shoulders. "These will be the last days of our honeymoon," he said. "I want to make them wonderful for you."

She laughed, a silvery sound. "That is a policy I heartily embrace." She began to run her fingertips over his chest, his shoulders, his back.

All other thoughts left him for a while.

Later, when he and Vera threw aside the mosquito netting and arose, they drew on bathing costumes, went out the back door, and crossed the veranda to the beach. Justin ran across the patch of fine white sand and dove into the tranquil blue sea. Out beyond the reef, foamy white breakers were sending up rainbows. A dhow under an orange sail made for Kilindini Harbour. To their right, atop a rocky cliff, rose the black-and-white-ringed lighthouse.

Vera, not knowing how to swim, waded in hip-deep and splashed water over her shoulders. As always, after making love, her skin felt extra sensitive. The cool droplets sent little chills down her back. She licked the salt from her lips and watched as Justin rose and shook sea water from his hair and arms. Droplets gleamed in the light of the sun behind him. The sight of him moved her and not only because of his physique. Unlike other British settlers, Justin loved Africa very much the way she did. He did not understand it as well as she, but he wanted to. And he was learning and growing to respond to it with something very like the passion she felt. Married to him less than four months, she still found it hard to believe that he was hers.

She was about to shout a demand that he teach her how to swim when he ran toward her and with the palm of his hand sent a splash of water that drenched her hair.

"I will make you pay for that," she said with a giggle as she raced him back to the house, her sopping skirts flapping against her thighs.

She got her revenge. Standing behind a screen of vivid greenery, they had rinsed away the salt with buckets of fresh water. Just as Justin finished drying off, she emptied a full one on him. He scored his own vendetta by embracing her and getting her wet again in the process.

It was not until they were seated at the breakfast table that they took up again the difficult subject of the message Justin had received yesterday.

Last evening he had revealed the contents of the letter delivered to him just before they disembarked. She had been dismayed, tried to get him to see reason about continuing to serve on the police force. All she wanted was for them to collect their belongings and take the next train up-country to her father, away from the wet heat and the sour smell of the crowded streets, and from the other administrative wives, who would shun her for being the daughter of a missionary—the clergy, with their staunch defenses of the natives' rights, being a thorn in the sides of the king's empire builders. And because of Justin's flawless accent, his Harrow-Cambridge education, and his ancestry, most of the administrators and their wives, she was sure, would do what similar women in Nairobi had done just after their wedding—call her "My lady" in the archest possible tone of voice and apologize for the plainness of their tea service.

So she had spent most of yesterday pleading with Justin to quit the police force. She had tried to speak sweetly, like a proper English wife, but she had lost her temper and raised her voice. They ended up in a row. Before bedtime, she had burst into tears with remorse over her shrewishness, but still his good-night kiss had been perfunctory for the first time since their wedding. She was determined that, this morning, she would control herself. There would be no histrionics.

Miriam, the Swahili maid who had come to them with this rented cottage, served a second round of tea and withdrew. Justin buttered a third piece of toast and looked across the table, fully expecting Vera, forthright as she was, to resume the argument that had ended with her in tears the night before.

"I understand that the Protectorate needs more men for the police force. But is there really no one but you?" she said, as if the discourse had not been interrupted by hours of sleep and delightful early-morning lovemaking. "Why can't they bring over more of the men who are living posh lives in India?" At least her tone was a bit more subdued with the light of day.

"As I have tried to explain, my darling, there *are* others coming along, but most of them know nothing of Africa. And the force is dreadfully understaffed. My service will not go on forever. Just a tour of a year or fourteen months. They won't keep a chap here in Mombasa for longer than that."

She sighed. "That's another thing. If you must continue, why does it have to be in crowded, smelly Mombasa? Why can't you go back to Nairobi, or to Naivasha, where I can be close to Father, and we can have the chance of a healthy life?"

"You read the district superintendent's letter," he explained, holding his patience by a thread. "How this is a particularly delicate time here because of the Grand Mufti's visit. How critical it is to have proper leadership on the force."

Her eyes told him she remained unconvinced. He supposed he ought to be grateful that she had not reminded him of her grandmother's very generous wedding gift. Some wives might bring up the money as a way of demanding their own way. Even if she did not say it, he suspected she was thinking of it.

His father had taken a similar stance. *Stop this policing nonsense*, was how his father had put it. *Not proper for the likes of you. Really, my boy.* Justin had not responded. No argument would have convinced him; the Earl of Bilbrough never strayed from opinions appropriate to a man of his rank.

In a way his father was right. But he was not yet ready to leave the police force. Vera's granny's money would still be there in a year or two. For now he wanted to earn his own way, support his wife himself. British law certainly gave him the right to all she possessed, including that sizable gift. But Vera would not go along so easily. She had not grown up in some stuffy Scottish parlor. With one foot in each of two worlds, she had absorbed neither the British mores of womanly behavior nor the customs of her African playmates. She was neither a docile Kikuyu wife nor a compliant British matron. She rebelled against rules on both sides. He sometimes feared that one day he would lose his tolerance of her unconventionality. But then he would think about the two of them alone together on safari, united in the glory of their surroundings, their souls fed by the majesty of the wilderness, watching the sunset, and knowing she would be in his arms, both of them feeling the wonder of love in the surpassing beauty of the African night. His love and desire for her and for Africa overwhelmed his doubts.

He had his own misgivings. All his life he had chafed at the shackles of his prim and proper upbringing—having to be friends with "the right" people, regardless of how boring he found them, how odious he thought many of their opinions and much of their behavior were. Having to stifle his own ideas. Never telling his father the Earl that he was wrong and the servant he had just chastised was right. He felt suffocated.

Life with Vera in Africa would never go stale. He was certain of that. Still, he wanted some time to establish himself as the head of his family. She was not the sort of girl to automatically follow tradition and let her husband make all the decisions. He must keep calm and convince her that, for a little while longer, he needed to do his duty.

"They need an experienced man right here and now," he said gently. "There are only six European officers in this entire province. The other three hundred policemen are all Asiatics or Africans. That is why the district superintendent sent that note on board before we even disembarked. We must have everything under control during the Grand Mufti's visit. Untoward incidents involving Arabs have stirred up considerable trouble in other places in the Empire in the past. The Administration has the King's African Rifles on standby, but they don't want to make a show of force unless it becomes necessary. The Arabs called Mombasa the Island of War before we came here. We don't want it to turn back into that."

Vera wished she might press her point, but she wanted peace between them even more. "I miss my father so much." The words slipped out of her. She saw immediately that he took it as a last-ditch appeal. A woman's form of insistence. She could take it back, she supposed. And she had merely told him the truth.

Justin bit his lip. She knew full well that the Administration of British East Africa moved men about, from the healthy, airy highlands to posts in malaria-ridden places like Mombasa and the shores of Lake Victoria and Lake Nyasa.

She was picking little bits off a crust of toast and dropping them onto her plate. When she looked up, her dark eyes were bright with unshed tears. She was not a girl who wept easily, intense as her feelings might be. She glanced into his eyes. "I am not weeping to get my way."

"I know that," he said gently, and reached out his hand and took hers.

Try as she might, she knew he would not relent. Justin's wanting to stay a policeman stemmed from more than his sense of duty. His fierce allegiance to his job was borne out of his sense of justice. His desire to find the truth.

She had to admit that he did his work very well, served justice better than most English policemen. The Justin she had seen during his investigation of her uncle's murder had proved to her that he was the man she wanted above all others. The way he had set his jaw and refused to yield to the district commissioner's demand for a quick, but unjust solution. He had pressed ahead, coming back often to her father's Mission. She had watched for him, cresting the hill on his stallion, with his askari lieutenant on a pony. How many times had she seen him, striding across the compound with that serious, determined expression, trying so hard to defend the falsely accused Kikuyu medicine man. His goodness had shone out of him in those sad, sad days. Their love had blossomed against that terrible backdrop.

She reached across the table and touched his arm, his strong arm that enfolded her. "You feel you must, don't you?"

"Do you want to go to the Mission and stay with your father while I take care of my duty?"

She took in her breath in shock. "Never." She could not imagine having to spend a whole day, much less months at a time so far from his embrace. "Perhaps we can entice Father to—"

At that moment, Miriam came out on the veranda. "A messenger boy brought this, Bwana," she said, and handed Justin a telegram. She curtsied and quickly returned inside amid the clatter of the bracelets on her wrists and ankles.

He opened the orange envelope. "It's from your father. But it's addressed to me."

Her breath stopped. It was bad news. If not, he would have written an ordinary letter and addressed it to her. Her hands gripped the arms of her chair. "Read it!"

The thin paper crinkled as he unfolded it and read aloud: *"Robert Morley needs help in a police matter. Stop. Please give assis-*

tance. Stop. Letter to follow. Stop." He gave her a quizzical look. "Who is Robert Morley?"

She let out an exasperated sigh. "A Methodist missionary," she said. "Very dramatic, but he and Father have been quite close. They worked together in the Anti-Slavery Society."

"Do you have any idea what this might be about?"

Vera shook her head.

Whatever it was, Justin was happy to have a favor for her father as yet another excuse for Assistant District Superintendent Tolliver to report for duty.

While Justin and Vera Tolliver were reading the telegram concerning the Reverend Robert Morley, Morley and his sister, Katharine, were also at the breakfast table, at the Methodist Mission. Katharine had announced her intention to walk to the native vegetable market next to the floating bridge between Nyali and the island of Mombasa.

Robert moved from the table to his little desk in the corner, took some coins from a drawer, and handed them to her for her shopping. "I will go straight over to the town by ferry," Morley said. "I have business to conduct with the Mission Society."

Katharine tied the coins into the corner of her handkerchief and thrust them deep into the pocket of her skirt. She sensed he was not telling her the truth, but she could never make such an accusation. Robert was a holy man. She could never question his goodness.

He did not seem to notice her momentary silence. Katharine pursed her lips. "I hope you are not going to go to Majidi. I do not trust him. He will hurt you."

"I assure you that I am not going to him. I have the law and the Lord on my side in the matter of his slave. It would be useless to appeal to him again. I have something entirely different to take care of." He lifted his eyebrows and gave her an arch stare, as if he were challenging her to question him further.

She looked down at the bare wooden floor, knowing he would take it as an act of submission, but also knowing that the action hid her doubts. There had been a time when nothing he did ever raised her suspicions.

When she looked up, he was smiling approvingly. "Take Joseph with you to the market, and keep him busy while I am gone. We don't want him wandering off into danger."

Katharine smiled back at him by way of assent. She fetched her favorite hat from the sideboard, the blue one that Robert did not entirely approve of. "I will keep Joseph in my sight."

They parted company at their front door, he making for the ferry to Mombasa and she to find Joseph among the Mission boys.

Joseph was not there. The others said he was still asleep. She was impatient to get her marketing over with before the hottest part of the day, so rather than wait, she instructed them to keep Joseph with them until she returned. She set off on the path toward the market, which took her through the dense forest of mangroves that grew in the salty swampland along the coast. Three-quarters of the way there, she stopped in shock. In the dim light of the early sun filtering through the foliage, the body of Joseph Gautura blocked her way.

Katharine gasped. Joseph's throat had been slashed. The flesh of his legs had been disturbed by an animal. She turned away, lost her breakfast at the foot of a thick tree trunk, and then she ran, stumbling over roots and vines, back to the Mission, wanting no one but her brother.

But of course he had already left. Frantic, she returned to the Mission boys. She found them sitting on the packed earth between the thatched roundel huts, eating a thick pap from wooden bowls with their long, graceful fingers. They leapt to their feet as she approached.

"Joseph has been—" She stopped, not willing to say the word *murdered*. "I found his body on the path." The inner vision of it turned her stomach again.

They stared at her in disbelief, frozen like four brown statues.

"He is dead."

They looked at the ground then, much as she often lowered her eyes before Robert.

"What do you know about this?"

They sputtered and spoke all at once, fell silent, and at last one confessed that they had known Joseph was missing but had been afraid to make trouble for him by telling her the truth. She sent them, one to find her brother at the Mission Society; one to look for him in the souk—in case he *had* been fibbing about where he was going; and one—with a spear—to guard Joseph's body and keep the animals off it. She dispatched the last man to the police station next to the market near the bridge to fetch the police.

She could not settle her mind. Niggling suspicions and fears nagged her. Could Robert be guilty of any part in this? She recalled his argument with Majidi in this room just yesterday. Robert's angry voice sounded in her mind, threatening Majidi— *Over my dead body.* Sometimes she hated that loud, certain way her brother expressed his opinions. Majidi's voice had been hardly above a cold whisper when he returned the threat. *Yours or his.* Robert would never have hurt Joseph. But what if he had now gone to the souk, where Majidi—surrounded by men loyal to him—could destroy Robert. Her thoughts swam with possibilities, each uglier than the last.

She was still pacing when one of the boys returned an hour later and told her the police had arrived at the body and taken over the situation.

Half an hour later, the boys she had sent after her brother returned, having failed to find him. She resumed her pacing. She uttered the name that had been ringing in her mind the whole while: "Majidi." He must be the one who had slain poor Joseph. She wished with all her heart to see the trader punished with the swift justice of an angel's sword. She tried to pray for Robert's safety, but she could not. All she could think about was that she wanted that disgusting slave owner Majidi dead.

CHAPTER 3

At nearly that same moment, in the bar of the Mombasa Club, Justin Tolliver was downing a large glass of quinine water only weakly flavored with gin. He shuddered a bit at its sour taste. Unlike some of his fellow British pioneers, Tolliver was not one to overdo alcohol so early in the day, but the hot, sticky climate of the coast made Mombasa one of the Protectorate's worst breeding grounds for mosquitoes, and quinine was a European's only defense. At any rate, his glass did not contain enough of the hard stuff to drown his disappointment.

He had come to the club looking for healthful exercise, but the members apparently played energetic sports only very occasionally. Too much foul heat during daylight and too many insects in the early and late hours, they claimed. When he asked the members how a chap was to stay fit, they looked away, as if his question was foolish and they were too polite to tell him so.

He understood full well what they were about. These were, he was certain, mostly officials in the Protectorate Administration who had come here from service in India and brought with them the ironclad pomposity of the Raj. European men chose their social companions based on rank and salary, a hierarchy more rigid than the Hindu caste system. On this, his first visit, he had not introduced himself as a policeman. But the European community in British East Africa was so small and closely knit, so fond of gossip that everyone seemed to know everything about everyone. In Nairobi, the members had wanted him for their club teams and so they had tolerated the second son of an earl who had had the stupidity to become a policeman. His prowess at sport had overruled their snobbery. If the men here in Mombasa did not take cricket and polo seriously, they would have no reason to want his company. And who were these tin gods? The sons of shopkeepers at best. Their self-satisfaction made him sick.

He put down his empty glass with a thump and said good-bye to the only person who had given him the time of day, a portly man with a drooping mustache—the one who had spoken to Tolliver and Vera on the ship, during the ceremony welcoming the Grand Mufti. Carl Hastings was his name. He had gone home to London for a respite from the heat and was now back here complaining bitterly about the climate. Evidently, he made a living hunting ivory.

Tolliver exited the club, telling himself without any real conviction that he had more reason to act the snob than the king's arrogant administrators in this backwater. By ordinary standards he was their superior in grace, education, and birth. Yet he was more open-minded than any of them. Why should he care for their opinions merely because they had worked their way up a tedious bureaucratic ladder and were now paid a higher salary than he?

He strode back in the direction of Ras Serani Point and the beach cottage. Since he had to pass near police headquarters on the way, he decided to take a moment to present himself to his district superintendent. D.S. Hugh Egerton was the son of a secretary in the Foreign Office and might have better manners than those toffee-nosed dolts at the club. But perhaps not. Egerton had after all moved here recently from service in Bombay.

The Idol of Mombasa

Though the walk to headquarters was less than half a mile, it meant leaving the open area around the club and entering the narrow streets typical of the town, where the damp heat pressed in. Growing ever more uncomfortable, Justin wondered if the men at the club might be correct. Mombasa was showing itself as not the sort of place where a man could exercise out of doors. A too-palpable reason to regret accepting this post. The playing fields had always been where he felt most at home, where he excelled for what he could do and not for who his father was, where he did not have to worry about committing social faux pas. The rules were clear and reasonable and he could be impressive and the hero of the day. And even if he failed to help his team to victory, there would always be another match and another opportunity.

He emerged into a quaint square, where the sea breezes blew away his nostalgia for the cricket pitch. The smell of the salt air called to mind his father's history books and his own boyhood dreams of adventure. He imagined that this place now smelled much the same as it had to da Gama aboard the Portuguese carrack *São Gabriel* when the great explorer entered Mombasa harbor, the first European to come to this place. This was a reason to be here. This had been a place of adventure for centuries. Whatever else Mombasa was, this was the sort of place that, as a child, he had always longed to be.

The look of the police headquarters further lifted his spirits. It seemed to have been built to impress, and it did. While the structures all around it were ramshackle wood-and-iron affairs, some with only palm thatch for roofs, the police unit was headquartered in a whitewashed stucco edifice with four two-story Ionic columns across the front and a red tile roof. Compared to the Greek temples he and Vera had visited during their honeymoon in Sicily, it was less than splendid, but in this landscape, its classic air lent importance to the service the police force rendered to the nation. Regardless of what those twits in the club might think, Tolliver knew they would shout for help from him and his fellow officers whenever they felt themselves in the slightest danger.

As soon as he entered the high-ceilinged lobby, he heard a man's words booming from the balcony above. In a theater, it might have passed for the voice of God. "I have studied the Koran," the voice was saying. "I know whereof I speak." The tone was preachy and juicy, and Tolliver could picture drops of spittle flying out of the speaker's mouth along with the words. He was glad he was not in the path of either. A more modulated male voice responded, but Tolliver could not make out what it said.

Tolliver inquired of a Sikh clerk at the reception desk and then mounted the steps toward District Superintendent Egerton's office. The sonorous voice had resumed its argument, more insistent than before, which hardly seemed possible. The noise came from the D.S.'s open office door. "You have not been listening," the speaker bellowed. "The Koran allows them to keep slaves if they are taken *in war*. Joseph Gautura had been enslaved to Majidi since he was nine years old. How could a child that age have been taken in war? Now that he has run away, it is our duty as Englishmen to see that he is left in peace."

Tolliver paused before approaching the office while the speaker—shouter, more like—went on. "If you do not heed my advice, I shall report this to the Anti-Slavery Society in London. They will speak to our friends in Parliament, and then we shall see how quickly you listen."

"I assure you," the modulated voice, which must have been Egerton's, said, "we will look into the matter. As I said at the beginning of this conversation, Mr. Morley, with the Grand Mufti's visit under way, we must be careful not to stir up trouble among the Arab traders."

Tolliver stopped twirling his hat and stood up straight. The booming voice belonged to Robert Morley, Vera's father's friend—the very person the Reverend McIntosh had asked Justin to help.

He stepped forward and knocked on the dark wood doorjamb. A large, unkempt man, who must have been Morley, swiveled in his chair and frowned disapprovingly at Tolliver, as if he were a rude and suspicious intruder. District Superintendent

Egerton stood up with a faint expression of relief, clearly hoping to escape Morley's raucous arguments.

The two men could not have been more different. Morley had an egg-shaped head on an egg-shaped body. Thinning hair, sweaty, dark, and ungroomed, stuck to his temples. His mismatched light linen jacket and trousers were rumpled, his white shirt collar wrinkled, his black bow tie askew. Egerton, on the other hand, was slender and spiffy in a white twill tropical uniform. His carefully brushed black hair showed the slightest bit of gray at the sideburns. His thin black mustache could have been drawn on his upper lip with a well-sharpened pencil. His neat eyebrows knit in a questioning glance at the intruder.

Tolliver took two steps forward and extended his hand to his superior officer. "I am A.D.S. Justin Tolliver, sir. I was passing nearby and thought I would stop by and introduce myself. I am sorry to have interrupted."

Egerton shook Justin's hand. "I am delighted to meet you, Mr. Tolliver, delighted. Mr. Morley and I were just finishing our meeting."

Morley heaved himself out of his chair. He seemed on the verge of objecting, but then he studied Justin and smiled broadly. "Why, you are Clarence McIntosh's new son-in-law, are you not?" He pumped Justin's hand and left it damp. "I am Robert Morley, the man your father-in-law wrote to you about. You are going to help me get justice for a runaway slave." It was a confident statement, not a plea for reassurance. Morley turned to Egerton. "This young officer is a family member of a zealous antislavery cleric. And he has promised to support my point of view."

The cordiality in Egerton's eyes vanished, replaced by disappointment and annoyance.

Morley's took Tolliver's hand again in his moist grasp. "Capital. Capital," he said. He smirked at Egerton. "Now we shall see what happens." He chuckled and made his gleeful way down the stairs, his heavy tread causing them to creak and squeal.

Egerton's expression changed from quite annoyed to something more neutral. He indicated the chair that Morley had just vacated. "We will worry about the reverend later. Can I offer you a cup of tea?" Without waiting for a response, he called for the hall boy and ordered two cups.

Rather than taking the position of power behind his desk, he pulled his chair around to sit next to Tolliver, and pointed to a manila folder on the credenza under the window. "I have read the file of your service in Nairobi, Tolliver," he said. His voice was nearly cordial. "I daresay you will want to have your sergeant— Zibalo, is that his name?"

"Libazo," Tolliver said, immensely surprised that Egerton seemed to have read not only his file, but also his mind. "Yes, sir, I very much think that he could—"

Egerton cut him off with a wave. "All taken care of. Sent a telegram as soon as I got your response that you were accepting this assignment. Already received a reply. He will arrive on the down train tomorrow morning."

"Thank you, sir. It is precisely what I would have requested. Awfully good of you to think of it."

"Nothing of the sort," Egerton said, continuing to warm. "Very happy to have you with us." They watched the boy deliver the tea.

When they had taken a few sips, Egerton got down to business. "You are not supposed to be on the duty roster until Monday, but I hope you will take up your post tomorrow. I don't want to cause you trouble with the little lady, but we need you right away. If you start tomorrow, you can be here when Libazo reports for duty. The force will be on parade tomorrow. It will be a good time to introduce you to the troops."

"Certainly, sir." Tolliver recognized Egerton's mention of "the little lady" for what it was: a challenge to see if Tolliver was in charge of his own wife. He was very glad Vera was not here. She would not like being called a little lady. And she would object to how quickly he had offered up the last two days of their honeymoon.

Egerton left no time for second thoughts. "Now as to this business with the runaway slave. I want you to understand that it is not the sort of thing we can pursue just now." Egerton spoke with calm certainty, seeming to have taken complete charge of the conversation. But Tolliver noticed that he had drawn his feet under his chair and braced them, as if getting ready to bolt—not the posture of a relaxed man.

Tolliver knew better than to challenge Egerton directly, but he need not give in without a question or two. "Vera's father asked me to help the Reverend Morley if I could, and my own principles would favor freeing any slave, but I made no representations to anyone. I am afraid what you heard from the missionary was merely an assumption."

Egerton stretched out his legs again. "I am glad of that. I don't think we are able to be at all helpful to him."

Tolliver blinked. He knew that slavery was outlawed on British territory, so he had expected the force to take the Reverend Morley's side against the Arab. "Sir," he said, hoping not to put the D.S. back on edge, "dealing with runaway slaves was not a part of my work in Nairobi. There are none up-country. I am afraid I am not clear on what exactly the law is on this point."

Egerton smiled at him. "No need to apologize about that," he said. "Most of our junior lads started out not knowing the finer points of the law. But law or no law, I am afraid this is an area that is not as black and white—so to speak—as the citizenry back in England imagine it to be. Here, we have many considerations to sort out."

Tolliver sipped his drink. "But British law does forbid slavery."

Egerton drained his cup and put it down with a thump. His feet were back under his chair and he had clenched his jaw. He took a deep breath, making no effort to hide his displeasure. "Yes, but as I just said, we are not in London. You understand, I think, that this part of the Protectorate has a status different from the rest of the country. Though most who live here are Africans, this coastal strip functions more like Zanzibar—as an Arab preserve. Our government came here with many goals. One was to stop the slave trade. And in many ways we have. No more trails of misery and corpse-strewn paths—not since the railroad went in anyway.

But we are also here to develop the economy of the Protectorate. And ..." His voice trailed off. He looked out the window, as if seeking a proper explanation in the cloudless sky.

Tolliver looked into his now empty cup and waited through an uneasy silence.

Finally Egerton sighed and continued. "I have always supported England's role in the suppression of slavery. Taking the moral high ground on this subject is one of the reasons we can hold up our heads as supreme among nations, but—" He moved to the edge of his seat. Tolliver could see that Egerton himself was walking a tightrope. "Dash it all, man, like any other beast, slavery has a tail, and we are dealing with that tail here. You see, we have to keep peace with the Arabs to maintain our control, not only here and in Egypt on the ground, but also on the seas between here and India. The Arabs take any interference with their way of organizing their households as a personal insult. It is deuced difficult keeping the balance between our morals and what they see as their right."

"Is slavery, then, completely legal here, sir?" Tolliver had tried to keep out any note of disapproval, but he had not entirely succeeded.

Egerton's tone also took on an edge. "The treaty we made with the Sultan in 1897, after a great deal of tedious negotiation, declared that anyone born after 1890 is free, but those born before remain slaves. It is not what you might have wished for, Mr. Tolliver, but there it is. And this would be the worst possible moment to protest the arrangement." It was clear that the D.S. was trying his best to seem commanding, but his body had become completely tense and his ears had taken on a red tinge.

Egerton's discomfort was embarrassing Tolliver. The man seemed to have a conflict within himself. Perhaps his own beliefs warred with what his work required. Or it might be that he desperately needed to keep Tolliver on the force and feared that the moral choice might drive Tolliver to resign. Whichever it was, it would be best to mollify him. "Sir," Justin said, "I imagine you are saying that during the visit of the Grand Mufti, with all the accompanying rise in the sense of Arab pride, we cannot just now safely take up the Reverend Morley's cause."

Egerton collapsed back into his chair and let out a long breath. "Finally," he said, "a man who understands the line we have to walk. Khalid Majidi, the man whose slave has absconded to Morley's mission, has a great deal of influence. The last thing we want while the Grand Mufti is on the scene is to give him a reason to incite revolt. And suppose the Mufti turned the Egyptians against us. We have to think about the importance of Suez. Trouble there would not help anyone."

Tolliver found himself torn. It was unlikely that defending the rights of one slave here would close down the canal. That seemed a bit far-fetched. Still, there was no knowing what upsetting the Grand Mufti might cause. Serving on the force over the past year, he had learned how pragmatism was often the best policy in this young country. The somewhat-seasoned policeman in him saw the practicality of Egerton's attitude, despite the anti-slavery sentiments of his childhood. But he had been in love with Vera for all of the past year. She did not have to be here to tell him where Egerton's argument went wrong. In his mind, he could hear her declaring that slavery was slavery and right was right.

Egerton gave him a querying look but also held his peace.

Tolliver chose his next words carefully. In this case, wherever the road to justice led, it could not go through insubordination. "Well, sir, what exactly can we do about Majidi and his runaway slave?"

"I am trying to put across to you one essential point, Tolliver. To the Arab, slave-holding is not only legal, it has been the custom of his forefathers through the ages. No matter what we may think in our hearts, we absolutely must not aggravate the differences between us and the Mohammedans. No action is often the right action in such cases. So we will do precisely nothing."

"I understand," Tolliver said, though he did not entirely agree, and he feared the row that would ensue when Vera found out that her father's friend was pursuing a hopeless cause, at least for now.

At that same hour, returning from the market bearing the makings of a nice lunch for herself and Justin, Vera found an Englishwoman waiting for her. The lady had a confused air about her, half apologetic, half defiant. She looked to be about thirty-five, tall and skinny, wearing a long linen skirt, a loose-fitting jacket, and a white shirtwaist with a high collar, trimmed with a bit of lace. She had a rather old-maidish, dry look, except that her blue straw hat exactly matched her startlingly beautiful eyes.

Vera stopped at the door. The stern glance of her visitor made her feel as if she were intruding on the woman and not the other way 'round. "How do you do," she said. "I am Vera Mc—I mean Vera Tolliver."

The woman turned up the sides of her mouth—more a show of very large teeth than a smile. What was evidently meant to be a friendly expression somehow made her look even more pinched. Underneath her tenuous exterior of calm, something deeply troubled this woman. This was no simple social call. She put down her parasol, drew off her right glove, and held out her hand. Her fingertips were cold despite the heat of the day. "Mrs. Tolliver, I am Katharine Morley." She squeezed Vera's small hand so hard it hurt.

Nevertheless, Vera's smile was sincere. "How do you do, Miss Morley. I have met your brother several times when he visited my father at the Mission up at Athi River. It is a pleasure to meet you at last. Won't you come in?"

Katharine's smile was a tiny bit cheerier this time. She reached up, pulled out her hat pin, and took off her hat, revealing her hair, pulled back in a very tight bun of a lovely dark shade of ginger. "I wonder if I might sit down. I took a rickshaw from the Nyali Bridge to the top of your road, but I could walk faster than the poor boy could drag the contraption over the sandy path to your door. The heat is fierce at this hour, but I did not have a moment to lose." Her voice was low and determined and carried a heavy Midlands accent.

"I am sorry. Yes, certainly. Please come out to the veranda. The sea breeze will cool you. May I offer you something? A cup of tea?"

With the mention of tea Katharine's angular face visibly relaxed. Vera went in and asked Miriam to bring them tea and bread and butter. When she returned she found Katharine looking out toward the sea, taking in the lovely view—the charming cove and white sand, the coconut palms, the fishing nets and traps arrayed against the neatly thatched native huts. "This spot really is very pretty," Miss Morley said. "Robert told me it would be. I've been at the Nyali Mission for nearly eight years, and yet I've never come here."

Vera thought to invite her to come for a bathe, but she could not imagine Miss Katharine taking off her prim high-button shoes and cotton hose to sleep at night, much less to frolic in the sea.

At this moment, despite Katharine's gracious remark, her eyes were filled with distress. She looked across the table to Vera. Her thin lips disappeared completely when she pressed them together. She took a deep breath. "I am sorry to trouble you, a person I have never even met," she said. "I came running to you because I did not know what else to do. I cannot find my brother. He set off for the Mission Society office this morning, but when I went there to look for him, they said he had no appointment there today. I thought he might have gone to the souk, but he was not there either. I cannot tell where he is. I had hoped to find your husband at home. There has been a…a murder on the edge of the Mission grounds."

Vera listened in shock to Katharine Morley's description of the slain runaway slave and her conviction that his master had killed him rather than let him go free.

Katharine paused in her story when Miriam brought out the tea. She accepted the cup Vera handed her with pure desire in her eyes. "Oh, how I need my tea at this moment," she said, as if she had been offered medicine to relieve a sharp pain. She gulped it down in a less-than-ladylike way. "I know my brother appealed to your father about Joseph's fate, Mrs. Tolliver. Robert is so passionate about the fight against slavery. It is the one note that vibrates in his entire being. Do you think…" Her voice trembled on the last few words. She was fighting down the urge to weep.

Vera poured her another cup of tea. She drank it down and took in a ragged breath. "My brother…I am afraid for him… Majidi…"

Vera reached for her hand. "Do you think Mr. Morley is also in danger?" Vera's voicing of the possibility collapsed Katharine Morley's restraint. She pulled a lace-edged handkerchief from the sleeve of her shirtwaist and buried her face in it.

Vera scolded herself. Her mother had told her a thousand times not to blurt things out. She cast about in her mind for something, anything to comfort the poor woman. "I cannot believe your brother has come to harm in broad daylight," she said with as much conviction as she could muster, but not quite believing her own words.

Shaking her head, Katharine leapt up and jammed on her hat. Her expression showed a war between hope and despair. "I must go home," she said. "I must hurry. I can only hope I'll find him there. Please. Please," she begged. "Ask Captain Tolliver to look for him."

Vera was also on her feet, determined to repair the damage her ill-chosen words had done. "Please send me word the minute you find him. My husband will do all he can. I know he will. I promise you that. My family so values your brother. And you too. We value you too."

Katharine squeezed Vera's hands with her bony fingers and gave her a pleading glance. "Pray that he hasn't…that he… Please pray for him." And she was gone.

CHAPTER

4

As soon as he could politely tear himself away from Egerton, Tolliver hurried back to the cottage on the beach. He stripped off his uniform jumper and asked Vera to take a walk with him along the shore, claiming that he sorely needed the sea breeze to cool him off after the heat of the town. What he really wanted was to break the news to her gently that he would not be able to do much for her father's friend.

"Robert Morley—" Vera began as if she had read his mind, which sometimes she seemed all too able to do.

"Yes," he said. "I have seen him."

"Is he all right?"

"Yes, certainly. He is a bit overwrought about his own concerns. But he strikes me as that type—prone to becoming overly emotional."

"I think that tendency may run in his family," she said. "But come walk with me. It is so lovely and cool here, and I have something to tell you."

They left their shoes on the veranda and made their way along the damp sand between the mangroves to their left and the sea to their right.

Vera had a great deal she wanted to say, but she held back. She could tell that Justin also had something to get off his chest. She decided it would be politic to let him speak first. Better to catch him in an elevated mood before she brought up the question of finding the murderer of the runaway slave. But then, when he explained the disturbing rationale for the Protectorate's allowing the beast of slavery to have its tail here along the coast, she burst out against it.

"That's ridiculous! Ludicrous! Appalling!"

This was the Vera who got on his nerves. Sometimes, in situations like this, she seemed to have no ability whatsoever to modulate her own emotions. Or to see the other side of the question. He had no doubt that she would have behaved exactly the same way if Egerton had been present for this discussion.

He took a deep breath of sea air and held his temper. Bitter experience had taught him that strongly asserting his authority would not turn her into a compliantly proper British wife.

With effort, he held her hand gently and asked her sweetly, "Please hear me out."

"I am sorry," she said, after a pause. "I want to be a better wife. I really do. I hate it when I disappoint you."

He had always known how she would be. He knew other men would have rejected her because of this fire in her. He had not. He had married her despite it. In fact, no matter how he disliked it at this moment, he knew he had married her because of it.

She twined her fingers into his on her shoulder and held her tongue while he explained about the tail of slavery.

"So you see, my darling," he said at last. "Egerton is not going to let me do anything about Robert Morley's runaway slave. I am an assistant superintendent, dearest, with the emphasis on *assistant*. I do not choose my own assignments."

Her arm around his waist tensed. He expected another angry outburst, but she said nothing. He willed his own tension to dissipate.

"Morley will have to try and keep the slave with him until the concern over the Grand Mufti's visit blows over."

She stopped in her tracks. "You don't know?"

"Know what?"

"Katharine Morley was here," she said. "The slave Joseph Gautura has been murdered."

He looked down at her in disbelief. "Why did you not tell me immediately?"

"You said you had seen Robert Morley. I thought you knew."

"I did see him. Just about an hour ago," Justin said. He went back in his mind to the interview with Morley. He was absolutely certain that the missionary could not have then known that Joseph Gautura was dead. Nothing about his behavior would have made sense if he had been talking about a dead man.

Vera stopped and looked up at his face. "His sister was here at that time. She was quite alarmed as she couldn't find her brother. She had looked for him in the places where she expected him to be, at the Mission Society office, the souk."

"Well, evidently while she was looking for him in those places, he was at police headquarters with Egerton and me." It was the only plausible explanation.

"I can see," Vera said, "given what you have told me, that you will not be able to do much for Mr. Morley now, but there is one thing I would like you to do."

He steeled himself for an annoyance. But none came.

She gave him a serious, nearly pleading look. "Would you make sure that Robert Morley arrived safely at home?"

It seemed a trivial request. "I doubt anything could have happened to him, darling."

"That is precisely what I told his sister, but she seems a very nervous sort. She hurried back to the Mission to see if he had gone home. But I would feel better about the whole affair if you would make sure he is safe."

"Certainly. I will send one of the boys to check. But is this all you want me to do? I do not believe you are accepting the D.S.'s dictum so readily."

Vera put her arms around his neck, kissed his soft lips. "Don't worry, dearest. I am plucky, but I am not so foolish as to involve myself in something I know so little about."

He was not at all convinced. He did not trust the speed of her compliance. But he said nothing more.

Once the shadows had begun to lengthen and the day to cool, Vera and Justin Tolliver set out for MacDonald Terrace to have a look at the police-issue bungalow they would occupy during Justin's tour of duty. They met District Superintendent Egerton at police headquarters. "I'll accompany you. I am going that way," he said. "There is another confounded ceremony being conducted by the Grand Mufti. The inauguration of a new mosque at the top of the street. We had to burn down the old one last year, because of an outbreak of plague. It was a very touchy thing. At least the Sultan is paying for the party, not His Majesty's government. The Liwali will be holding forth." He then took great pains to explain that the Liwali was the official who made sure Britain paid over the tribute due to the Sultan of Zanzibar. "And takes whatever else he can get for himself into the bargain," Egerton added with a wrinkle of his elegant nose.

Tolliver listened politely to the discourse, though he and Vera already knew all that Egerton was telling them. Vera, despite her habitual forthrightness, managed to hold her tongue and avoid reminding the D.S. that she had been born in East Africa and most likely knew a great deal more about it than he, who had only lately arrived from service in India.

Leaving police headquarters, they crossed the road and started uphill. Vera found it hard to keep up with the strides of her tall companions, especially since she could not stop herself turning every once in a while to gaze with delight at the ever-widening vista of the sea or to pause and admire the exotic carvings on the lintel of a doorway, or the grace of a passing Somali woman.

The air carried an undercurrent of spice. Mombasa was more an Arab than an African city, the kind of place where one expected to see Aladdin walking along, carrying his lamp. It had been this way for eons. Egyptians, Phoenicians, even the Chinese had traded on this coast. But Vera had seen it change, during her mere twenty years, from a city dominated by Persians and Ottomans with Swahili servants to one with many Indian settlers and a minority of British newcomers mixed in.

Up in the highlands around Nairobi where she was born and had grown up, the English Administration allowed only Europeans to take land. Many Indians had been imported to build the railroad. Once it was completed, if they wanted to stay, they had little choice but to plunk down here in the port, which everyone said developed new aspects every month. To Vera, its exotic inhabitants and their ways had always made it strange. Until now, she had readily accepted her parents' judgment that it was a smelly and dirty place. But in the past two days, she had begun to see its glamor. It intrigued her. And this afternoon, she was seeing it at its most glittering.

The cobbled street around them was thronged with stately Arab gentlemen, each in a long white gown of spotless linen and sporting a bright-colored, close-fitting turban. Their leather sandals flapped against the stone paving with a rhythmic beat. For today's special occasion they wore waistcoats and over them, open robes of splendid brocade. They looked more like displays of luxurious fabric than like serious members of the town's elite. One slender man passing by, almost as tall as Justin, was resplendent in midnight-blue silk embroidered with silver and gold. Vera wished she had had a dress of such cloth to wear to the Christmas ball at Castle Howard in Yorkshire last month. None of Lord and Lady Carlisle's guests would have intimidated her in the least had she been arrayed in the likes of that.

"These chaps must all be going to the ceremony," Egerton said. "The district commissioner has asked me to be there to show the colors. I don't see what I can do other than smile. The whole speech will be in Arabic, I imagine. Won't understand a word of what they're saying, will I?"

Justin smiled broadly. "It's hard to believe any of them make any sense out of it," he said. "It goes by so quickly. They wiggle their tongues more in a few sentences than an Englishman would in a month."

Egerton laughed.

"I think I will try to learn to speak some Arabic while I am here," Vera said. She hated it when her countrymen made out any language but their own to be gibberish.

They both looked at her as if she had announced her intention to become the next Grand Mufti.

Egerton harrumphed. He drew a small bunch of keys out of his pocket and pointed across the road to a tiny bungalow. It was a charmless one-story box of stucco, whitewashed, with mud-brown trim around the windows and a typical corrugated-iron roof that would make the interior oven-like. It sat behind a sagging white trellis fence overgrown with tangled vines. A couple of tall coconut palms rose just behind it. A narrow flagstone path led to a little porch and the front door. The garden was covered in weeds. "That's it, I'm afraid." He handed the keys to Justin and looked at Vera, as if he were afraid she would burst into tears at the sight of the bedraggled yard. The building was not fit to house the groundskeepers at Tilbury Grange, Justin's family's estate, which they had just visited in Yorkshire. At her granny's mansion in Glasgow, they would have used it as garden shed.

She saw the apprehension in Egerton's eyes and smiled it away. "It has potential," she said. "It will be lovely once I have put some effort into it. Making it so will give me something to do." Of course she did not reveal that before taking on anything else, she would have to complete her family's obligation to Robert and Katharine Morley.

Egerton breathed an audible sigh of relief. He was a bachelor. It tickled Vera to imagine him so intimidated by the possible displeasure of a young woman who barely came up to his chin.

He turned to Justin. "I am very happy to have you with us, Tolliver. In times like these, England expects that every man will do his duty."

At that moment, a police sergeant in a turban came running up the hill. "District Superintendent, sir," he said. "You must come quickly. We have arrested a man who was carrying a knife, sir."

"Every man jack in this city is carrying a knife and most have swords as well," Egerton said.

"Yes, sir, but this man was heard to say that he wanted to use his knife on the Grand Mufti."

Vera looked at Justin. As she expected, he was immediately on the alert, looking at Egerton, ready to leap into action. "Shall I come with you, sir?" he asked.

"No." Egerton gestured at the crowd of resplendent Arabs mounting the hill. "You follow that lot and keep close to the Grand Mufti. I'll see to this blighter making threats."

Vera took the keys from a crestfallen Justin. Clearly he would have preferred to go after the miscreant. Egerton was already jogging down the hill with the Sikh sergeant.

"I must," Justin said, an apology in his glance.

"Go ahead. Please be careful." She watched him in his white uniform, head and shoulders above most of the men in brocade who swarmed up toward the mosque.

Vera let herself in and looked over the gloomy bungalow where she and Justin were meant to live for the next year. She convinced herself that the garden at least could be made beautiful. And besides, she couldn't worry about this now, with Robert and Katharine Morley's troubles weighing on her mind. Rather than bother now about this sad excuse for a home, before sundown she took a rickshaw back to the lovely beach cottage on Ras Serani Point.

When he returned home later that night, Justin brought Vera good news. He had sent one of the askaris to Morley's mission. The man had found the reverend safely at home. This made for the loving night Justin had desired.

The next morning Vera was full of plans for making the cottage a comfortable home and arranging the lovely things they had brought back from Scotland and Yorkshire. She rhapsodized about having her piano and his cello and being able to play duets as they so often had at his parents' home and on board the ship.

After she explained her plans to Justin, they left the cottage together and parted company at the intersection of Vasco da Gama Road and the Ndia Kuu. Vera was on her way to find workers to help them move. She hoped also to find skilled men who could freshen the paint on the bungalow and start in on rescuing the garden from weedy oblivion.

For his part, intent on being at the station to greet Kwai Libazo, Justin marched off along the gravel road to the railway terminal, grateful that the down train arrived early in the morning, making this walk invigorating, rather than what it would be in a couple of hours: a sticky trek through damp heat that seemed to want to kill a chap.

The way to the station was thronged with white-robed Arabs, Swahilis, Goans—every description of man who inhabited the town. Some sported a red fez, others a turban, each carrying something to ship on the train once it started its journey back toward Lake Victoria. Carts were piled high with cartons that purported to contain sewing machines, lighting fixtures wired for electricity, carpenters' tools, and, according to the label on one, the very latest in women's fashion hats. A mule-drawn cart was laden with about a dozen brand-new bicycles, and an elegant Somali man in a silk vest and sash pushed along a perambulator full of small bundles wrapped in brown paper. Coming in the other direction were three native women naked to the waist carrying water jugs on their heads and jangling along with a clatter of bracelets audible even in this din. Mombasa was an intriguing paradox. Some of its women were half naked; others were so completely covered that not even their eyes were visible.

Justin wove through the crowd; the platform was no less crowded than the road had been, but he was tall enough to see over the crush of people and parcels. As soon as the train arrived and the compartment doors opened, he spotted Libazo descending from the third-class car. The two men moved toward each other as swiftly as the throng allowed. Tolliver accepted his lieutenant's salute and, contrary to the practice of European policemen with their askaris, shook Libazo by the hand.

From the very beginning of Tolliver's service on the police force just over a year ago, he had worked side by side with this brave and canny half-Maasai, half-Kikuyu. In a sense, Libazo had saved Tolliver's life during an incident in a bar in Nairobi. In all their work together, Libazo had proved intelligent as an investigator as well as swift in physical action. They had developed such a rapport that Tolliver could not imagine doing his work efficiently and effectively without Libazo at his right hand.

They were very alike in stature, both tall, with broad shoulders and strong physiques, though Kwai Libazo was more lithe than sturdy. In coloration they could not have been more different. Tolliver was blond, blue-eyed, with a pale, rosy complexion that his own sister had envied aloud to a maddening degree. Libazo was mahogany brown; his head, under his red fez, was shaved as both his Maasai and his Kikuyu ancestors had shaved theirs since the Iron Age. Libazo was, as ever, spiffy and tidy, his black puttees perfectly wound on his legs, his khaki twill uniform clean and looking neatly pressed though he had been on the train for nearly twenty-four hours.

Libazo saluted a second time. "Sergeant Kwai Libazo reporting for duty, sir," he said, with an emphasis on his rank and a twinkle in his eye: he had not lost the pleasure of presenting himself with a title he had never hoped to achieve. He had earned it, and Tolliver was proud of having helped him secure it.

Libazo shouldered a rucksack that must have held all his worldly possessions.

"You'll get settled in your barracks before evening," Tolliver said. "For now we must go off to the gymkhana. A contingent of native policemen will be on parade to welcome me to Mombasa."

"And to welcome me too, Bwana?"

"I doubt you will be joking for long, Sergeant," Tolliver said in feigned stern voice. "Mombasa is not the young town we had in Nairobi. It has been here long enough to become truly decadent."

By the afternoon, that remark would prove to have been more accurate than he could have imagined.

For now, they made their way directly to the parade ground in an open area on the outskirts of the city, near the campground of the 4th King's African Rifles.

The policemen of the city's contingent were lined up in perfectly straight rows—members of several different tribes, all looking very smart in uniform, a sight better than the ragtag getups one saw in the more remote areas up-country. Quite a few sported navy-blue turbans, indicating that they were Sikhs from India, who were prized for their bravery, loyalty, and intelligence. Tolliver glanced at Kwai's reaction to them. As usual, for all Libazo's expression changed, he might have been made of stone.

It occurred to Tolliver that many of the constables, imported from India to build the Protectorate's police rank and file quickly and efficiently, would look down upon his preferred lieutenant. True, the boys from the Raj had the advantage of knowing the laws, which had also been imported from the Indian Colonial Code, but he would always choose Libazo, who had proven himself on a personal level. The bothersome thing was that the Indians would very likely snub Kwai as they did all Africans. And the Africans had their own bitter rivalries, which the British Administration encouraged, saying that they must not be allowed to get too chummy, a code Tolliver knew was based on the possibility that one day the Administration might have to use one tribe against another. There was a time when Tolliver might have agreed with that approach, but a year in love with Vera had persuaded him that it might be better for all concerned if the tribal people were encouraged toward teamwork rather than enmity.

For today, at least, the askari corps showed nothing of the underlying strife. They stood at attention, saluted crisply, and marched in precise formation. Libazo took his place with the ranks of sergeants in the second row—taller than most of the others.

Egerton introduced A.D.S. Tolliver to the gathering and walked with him as they inspected the troop. Once Egerton had dismissed the men, he and Tolliver rode together in a trolley back to headquarters. Tolliver took the opportunity to question the D.S. on what his first official assignment would be. "I imagine, sir, that you will want me to delve immediately into that threat to the Grand Mufti."

"Not at all, I'm afraid," Egerton answered. "District Commissioner Hobson-Jones insists that I handle that personally."

Disappointed, Tolliver thought to press the point. He wanted to play a role, though more out of curiosity and for the challenge to his skills than any desire to protect the Egyptian clergyman. But he did not yet know Egerton well enough to pressure him. "Yes, sir," he said instead. "I can imagine why."

"I will be taking that threatening blackguard before the magistrate straightaway. I will need you to come to the courthouse as well. It seems someone has stolen the cash box from the fines collector. Talk to the desk sergeant at headquarters. He knows the basics of that investigation so far."

As best he could, Tolliver hid his pique at being offered such a petty assignment, but he could not stop his jaw from clenching.

Until Kwai arrived that morning, he had known the city only from descriptions given by fellow tribesmen over the years. His first impression of his fellow askaris was not positive. As they dispersed on the parade ground, if they spoke to him at all, they did so with an attitude of superiority. Many, of course, were Hindus and Sikhs, who always thought themselves better than any black man. His African comrades might have skin a similar color to Kwai's, but here at the coast they were almost all Somalis, Akamba, and Wanyamwezis, each quite snobbish in his own way. The English treated all the African tribesmen as if they were interchangeable, but there had been fierce rivalries in this country long, long before the British or even the Arabs arrived. In Kwai's own birthplace near Nairobi, the Kikuyu and the Maasai had been bitter enemies for hundreds of years. And he was half from one tribe and half from the other, trusted by neither and, if he admitted it to himself, trusting neither. How then could he trust the people in this place or expect them to trust him?

The only person in the town that he had faith in, aside from himself, was the only person he knew—A.D.S. Tolliver.

Just now, Kwai was following Tolliver through crowded, narrow streets to the law court building. Unlike the broad streets of Nairobi, where you could turn an oxcart around, these felt far too cramped and close. "Are we going to prosecute a criminal, sir?" he asked of Tolliver.

Tolliver allowed himself the faintest smile at Libazo's use of *we*. Askaris ordinarily acted as if they were pieces of equipment, since that was the way their officers used them, but Libazo had reason to think of himself as a cohort, not only because of the way he had performed his duties in Nairobi, but also because of the way Tolliver acted toward him. Tolliver was happy to treat Libazo like the man he was. Truth be told, except for Vera herself, the native policeman was the closest thing to a true friend Tolliver had in British East Africa.

"No, Sergeant," Tolliver answered. "Strange as it may seem, someone has stolen the cashier's box from the courthouse."

Libazo gasped. He could not imagine a thief so bold.

"It's insane, I know," Tolliver said. "Evidently, there has been a rash of burglaries in the town. There is hardly a European household that has not been broken into."

They had investigated many thefts in Nairobi. There, Libazo understood many things about who in the town would be likely suspects. Here, he had no idea. Other pedestrians along this stone-paved street were as foreign to him as white people had been in the up-country. More foreign, actually, since these people seemed completely exotic, while in the highlands everything was familiar. He had grown up at a time when an increasing number of white settlers were arriving every year. He could not remember when he saw his first Englishman. The British missionaries had been in Africa, he was sure, from the time he was born. Here in the port city, he saw varieties of people he had not imagined existed: some with dark skin and light eyes, some as dark as he, but with perfectly straight hair, wearing rich garments and jewels on their fingers.

"This is very grand, isn't it?" Tolliver was speaking of the court building, not of the robes of the men walking up the steps in front of them.

"Yes, sir."

Unlike most of the other structures they had passed this morning, this one did not look as if it were so old it might fall down. It sat isolated on a lawn, newly built completely of stone with a red tile roof.

As they were mounting the long staircase to the entrance, Tolliver stopped. "Something tells me," he said, "that you should wait here. If you see anyone run out the door, follow him. When you catch him, wrestle him to the ground and sit on him until I reach you."

"Do you think the thief is still inside?" The building was huge, larger than Government House in Nairobi, until now the largest Libazo had ever seen. There must be many places inside where a man could hide, but it seemed unlikely to Libazo that a man who had stolen money from the judges would stay in the courthouse with his booty.

Libazo saluted and took up a post at the top of the steps. Tolliver went under the arched gallery, grasped the polished brass handle, and disappeared inside the heavy door of carved mango wood.

Libazo stood stock-still as he had been trained to do while on guard duty, not seeming to notice the people who came and went. They were from every group who inhabited the port, and Libazo took note of everything about them. He did not know words to describe the things that the Arab men wore, of cloth that looked like flowering hillsides after the long rains. He had seen people so decked out only in books—in pictures of olden-days kings and queens of England. He thought it very strange that men so arrayed entered the court with daggers in their sashes. In Nairobi, weapons were never allowed in the court building.

From his vantage point atop the long flight of stairs, he looked out over the street in front of the building. The first thing he had noticed about Mombasa was still the strangest of all: the way it smelled. Up near Nairobi, where he had lived all of his twenty-five years, there were many smells—stewing meat and pumpkin, the crops, smoke from the cook fires, the dung of the animals, and nowadays the sooty smell of the train engine. What he loved most there were the scents of the herbs of the forest, the trees, the earthy smell of the land after the rains. Just recalling them made him long to be back where his nose was at home. Here the air was redolent with strange, often unpleasant cooking spices, the rotten odor of too many people in too much heat, and the salt-laden breezes that he wished would wash away all the stinks. He wanted to know what the sea would smell like if he were alone with it.

Despite the strangeness of the place, he was glad to be back again with A.D.S. Tolliver, doing the work that had become the most important thing in his life. He had not had his own place in the world until he became a policeman. He had been rejected by both his mother's and his father's tribes. Tolliver's sense of justice was the first thing he had found that captured his heart. He had always been an outsider, a man who had no purpose on earth until he learned, working with Bwana Tolliver, to find and bring to justice men who did bad things. No Maasai who killed a lion with a spear could have been prouder than Kwai had been the first time he saved a person's life by stopping a man who wanted to kill.

A loud shout from inside the building stopped his reverie. All at once, the door swung open and through it burst two men. Kwai reached out and grabbed the first one. The second, who wore the same long white linen *kanzu* as nearly every male in the city, knocked into them both and sent them sprawling on the steps. Kwai hung on to the shirt of the man he had grasped, who twisted and shouted, kicked and swore. The other man, who wore a round orange cap, jumped down the last five steps in one leap and ran off.

"Not him!" Tolliver shouted as he came through the door. "The other one. With the orange cap. After him, man. He is going toward the bazaar."

Libazo leapt up and, leaving his original captive behind, sailed off the steps and took after the escapee, whom he could see only intermittently ahead of him. One glance over his shoulder told him that Tolliver was not bothering to keep up.

The man Libazo pursued dashed between a hurtling trolley and a donkey cart. Kwai vaulted over a fruit seller's stand, upsetting a display of melons, nearly lost his footing by stepping on one, and followed his quarry through the entrance to the bazaar.

He could see over the heads of most of the people blocking the aisle in front of him. The orange cap was turning to the right. Kwai pushed through while shouting, "Stop that running man!" He had no idea if the people thronging the aisle understood English or had any respect at all for a black policeman.

When Kwai turned the corner, he saw that the man he had been pursuing must have entered what was a narrow cul-de-sac that dead-ended about twenty feet from him, deep enough for only one shop on each side. There was no sign of any man.

Standing before a gaudy display of fabrics in front of the shop on the right was a beautiful girl wrapped in red cloth and smiling enchantingly. Her head was not shaved, like a Kikuyu or Maasai girl's; instead her hair was plaited into tiny braids, wound with red cords.

Kwai slid to a halt on his government-issue sandals and demanded to know if she had seen the man who had just come around the corner at a run. Kwai spoke as best he could in Swahili, a language he had barely any occasion to practice in the highlands.

She was taller than any of the Kikuyu girls he had dallied with. As tall as the stoic, aloof Maasai girls, who had never appealed to him. This girl's warm smile spread and brightened her lovely eyes. "You are a policeman, but I have never seen you before." She said it as if it made him the most interesting man she had ever met.

"I am a sergeant of the British East African Police," he said wishing but unable to make his voice appropriately stern. The girls he had lain with were often quite naked when he first saw them, as tribal women usually were. Their lack of clothing was nothing to remark upon. They covered themselves around English people, but not when they were alone with their own. This girl's torso and legs were completely wrapped in cloth, and her head was draped with a filmy shawl that exactly matched the fabric wound around her body. Covered, she attracted him the more *because* she was clothed. This was a shock to him.

She giggled, but she did not seem silly. There was a dignity about her, an ease and confidence he had never seen in a girl so young.

He wanted nothing more than to talk to her, to find any excuse to keep looking at her. But he had a culprit to find. He stiffened his back. "I demand to know if you saw a man."

Her smile faded, and she looked right into his eyes. What he saw in hers was both a glimmer of fear and a plea, as if she were asking him to take her meaning, though she had not spoken. Her glance flickered in the direction of the bookshop to her left.

He understood. Someone was watching them. She wanted to help him, but without giving herself away. "I shall have to search both shops, since you refuse to help me," he said in a voice loud enough to be heard by whomever she feared. "I will start with this bookseller." He turned in the direction of the store her eyes had indicated. As soon as he did, he realized that in his effort to protect her from anyone knowing she had helped him, he had also very likely warned the person inside the shop that he was about to enter.

He grasped the handle, and when the door swung open a bell tinkled. He found himself face-to-face with a dour-looking, paunchy man who had a long black beard and wore tiny spectacles. He was nearly a foot shorter and twenty years older than the man Kwai had chased through the streets. Kwai looked about. There were leather-bound books occupying every possible square inch of the small shop. The place smelled of dust and body odor. A heavy brown drapery covered a doorway that led to the back.

"Is there anyone here besides you?" Kwai demanded.

The man looked at him, puzzled and confused. "I do not understand you."

Kwai realized that he had spoken badly in his rusty Swahili. He repeated what he had said slowly and then added, "I am looking for a man. The man who came in here just now."

"There is no man," the bookseller said.

Kwai drew near and towered over him. The smell of sweat was not coming from the bookseller. He pushed aside the brown drape. A woman completely swathed in blue, her face veiled, only her eyes showing, squatted on a low chair in a corner.

She turned away and looked down at the floor. She might have fooled Kwai, except for the stink that could have come only from a man who had been running through the hot streets; the dirty foot in a man's sandal that stuck out from the hem of "her" garment; and the orange cap just visible under the chair.

Kwai grabbed the man's arm, dragged him up, and pulled away the veil. He wrestled the stinking offender in women's garb through the door into the corridor. The bookseller was shouting in a language Kwai had never heard before.

The girl in red was gone. But as soon as Kwai emerged with his prisoner, Tolliver rounded the corner, closely followed by a Sikh in a uniform identical to Kwai's.

"Excellent man!" Tolliver said to Kwai.

"Is this the one who stole the cash box from the courthouse?" Kwai asked. "He was not carrying anything when I chased him to this place."

"No," Tolliver answered. "He was there because Sergeant Abrik Singh here and D.S. Egerton were bringing him up on charges. He has made a threat against the Grand Mufti. He escaped while waiting for the magistrate to charge him."

Kwai explained where and how he had found the man.

"Sergeant," Tolliver said to Singh, "take him into custody. Libazo and I will bring in the shopkeeper." He turned to Kwai. "I'll go inside and apprehend the other one. I don't know what he has to do with the case, but he was harboring a would-be assassin. You keep guard here." He strode into the shop, where the paunchy bookseller was jiggling a string of beads and looking decidedly overwhelmed.

While the formidable Abrik Singh fixed handcuffs on the prisoner, Kwai held the man by the shoulders. He nodded in the direction of the fabric store. "What do you know about that place?" he asked Singh.

Abrik's black eyes sparkled, and he smiled broadly. "That," he said, "is the most famous brothel in Mombasa."

Justin Tolliver waited while the bookseller locked up his shop. Then he and Kwai Libazo marched the Arab to Fort Jesus, which held the prison. The man mumbled in Arabic and nervously fingered a circlet of beads the entire way, but answered Justin's questions neither in English nor in Swahili.

"This is a sensitive situation," Tolliver told Libazo. He knew Egerton had to be the one to bring the thug who made the threat to justice. The bookseller was obviously an accomplice. "Lock him up for the time being while I confer with the D.S. on exactly how he wants to handle this."

But before Tolliver reached Egerton's office in police head-quarters, he was accosted on the stairs by Robert Morley. The missionary trumpeted a joyous greeting at Tolliver as soon as he spotted him. "My boy, my boy. You are the very man I have been waiting to see. A chap in a turban told me that you were making an arrest in the bazaar. I wanted to thank you for taking that assassin into custody."

Tolliver blinked, shocked that Morley knew so much about the arrest he had just made. "The bookseller? His nephew?" he asked in disbelief. "What do you know about him?"

"Bookseller? I know nothing of a bookseller." Morley seemed no less confused than Tolliver. "He sells ivory. And people, I warrant."

"Who?"

"Majidi!" Morley was indignant now and louder than ever. "Majidi. He has killed Joseph. Surely you have heard that Joseph Gautura was murdered at the edge of the Mission grounds. Majidi had threatened to do just that, right to my face. And now he has made good on that threat. Men from the police force came and took away the body."

"That's not my investigation to pursue," Tolliver said, his heart sinking. A wave of annoyance quickly followed by a wave of guilt stopped him from saying more. He had promised Vera's father nothing, but he did not want to disappoint that kind man, damn it. Clarence McIntosh had suffered enough losses over the past year. Justin had decided to stay in Mombasa. It was the right thing for him to be doing now. But he was also aware that by settling here for the next year, he was depriving his father-in-law—who was warmer and kinder to him than his own father had ever been—of the company of the daughter he loved. For what solace it would give, he wanted with all his heart to fulfill the Reverend McIntosh's wishes. But, much as he ached at having to admit it, a threat against the Grand Mufti had to take precedence at this moment.

Morley took advantage of the silence to bellow, "'Thus says the Lord: Do justice and righteousness, and deliver from the hand of the oppressor him who has been robbed.' Jeremiah 22:3. 'When justice is done, it is a joy to the righteous but terror to evildoers.' Proverbs 21:15."

Before the missionary was able to catch his breath to go on, D.S. Egerton appeared at the top of the steps. "What in God's name is all this noise about? A chap can't think."

"Nothing! Nothing in *God's* name! God evidently has nothing to do with this place." Morley had not lowered his voice one decibel. "I came here to demand justice. You must arrest that murderer Majidi."

Egerton's expression hardened. "Mr. Morley, sir. I will thank you to lower your voice. You may be the Lord's servant, but have a care you don't destroy our hearing."

Morley sputtered. "We said we would not try to convert the Mohammedans. But that does not mean they can be a law unto themselves."

Tolliver put a hand on his shoulder, as if he were the older and wiser of the two. He spoke sotto voce, hoping to encourage Morley to do the same. "We cannot start a holy war over this, sir. Please try to understand that the Protectorate is just that—a Protectorate." He lowered his voice even more. "We are here by the leave of the Sultan of Zanzibar. Surely you can see that means we must tread a fine line, especially while the Grand Mufti is on the scene."

Morley sighed deeply and seemed to collect himself. He was clearly still distressed, but he finally found the sense to lower his voice. "That has nothing to do with protecting God's innocents from those who would buy and sell them." His eyes took on a defeated cast, but that did not stop him from stomping down the stairs while muttering, "Oh, yes, I have heard it all before. We have the Germans to our south who are encroaching on our rights. We have to keep the Sultan on our side. All that rubbish that has nothing to do with what is happening here and now." When he reached the bottom he looked up at Tolliver and Egerton above him on the steps. His expression was defiant. "It is clear to me that I will get no support from the police. But I will not accept this situation. I shall just have to take matters into my own hands." He looked for all the world as if he would burst into tears, but he merely jammed on his hat and swept through the door to the street.

Egerton shrugged a gesture of disbelief at Morley's stubbornness. "I expect he is going to cause trouble for you with your father-in-law."

Tolliver mounted the few steps between them. "I hope that is all he does."

"Well, in the meanwhile, we have much more pressing matters to deal with. From the look of satisfaction on your face when you arrived, I take it you have caught that rascal with the cash box."

Tolliver kept a triumphant smile at bay and told Egerton about capturing the escapee and arresting the bookseller.

"Excellent," Egerton said with relief. "I will take over with them. You will need to see to two other matters. The Arabs are complaining about the English lads getting into their cups and staging raucous downhill trolley races. They are disturbing the peace at the palace where the Grand Mufti is staying. And on top of that, the Liwali feels that we must, especially at this moment, blot out the disgrace of those Somali girls prostituting themselves in the bazaar. We are going to have to arrest them."

Tolliver could not help but stare in disbelief. The man could not be serious. "I am sorry, sir, but these matters seem petty to me. With the threat to the Grand Mufti, shouldn't we be making sure there are no others planning the same? I know I can be helpful there." He bit back an urge to point out that Egerton had let his prisoner escape, and Tolliver had recaptured him.

Egerton shook his head. "That's as may be, Tolliver, but these other issues also deserve our attention. They have to do with our esteemed visitor's comfort. The noise should be easy enough to take care of for the next few weeks. Post some askaris at the top of the hill and enforce some sort of speed limit on the trolleys. And the scandal of those Somali girls is not a minor thing. They were raised as Mohammedans. What they are doing in the bazaar is not at all a minor thing from the Grand Mufti's viewpoint. I have known girls like them to be beheaded by their own fathers in Persia and Egypt. We have to show we can control matters here to the Sultan's liking."

"I see," Tolliver said evenly, and not able to resist, added, "In the meanwhile, who will interrogate the bookseller and the man who escaped the courthouse this morning?"

"I will," Egerton said with perfect finality.

In the dark of the following midnight a tall Englishman with a drooping mustache and a self-important air entered the bazaar.

Anyone of any race or creed who might have noticed him would have assumed that he was going to have himself serviced by the girls in the silk shop opposite the bookseller's. But Carl Hastings did not make his way to the rear of the market. Instead, after a quick glance around, he rapped two slow beats and three quick beats on the door of Majidi, the ivory trader. He paused ten seconds and repeated the signal. Behind its windows, the shop was dark, but the door swung open immediately. After Hastings entered, it closed without a sound.

Not until Majidi parted the heavy drapery that led to the back did Hastings find enough light to follow his host.

The rear office was lit only by a small paraffin lamp that sat on Majidi's safe on the floor in the corner. The dim atmosphere suited Hastings, who was determined not to show his apprehension. Any show of weakness would doom his efforts with Majidi.

The Arab took a seat behind a large, elaborately carved ebony desk piled high with ledgers. Without asking, he poured two glasses of whiskey and handed one to Hastings.

They sipped their drinks in silence for a few moments, each waiting for the other to offer an opening gambit.

Hastings weakened first. "I hear the slave is dead." He might have said more or asked questions, but he had to tread carefully. The more Majidi thought he knew, the more chips he would have to play in this game.

Majidi grunted but was not otherwise forthcoming.

Hastings held his peace until he had emptied his glass, after which he could not stand the silence. "The missionary is raising a great noise."

With his habitual precise hand movements, Majidi reached for the crystal decanter and recharged their drinks. His long fingernails made little clicking noises against the glass, which along with the almost feminine delicacy of the Arab's gestures always disgusted Hastings. As did his perfect confidence when he spoke. "The British will pay him no heed. They know I have a lot of allies. If I want to stir up trouble for them all I have to do is complain that they are trying to impose their law here, even when it goes against the Shari'a."

Hastings squirmed in his chair. The depth and breadth of Majidi's power was not a comfort to him. What the trader held over Hastings was far too dangerous. If their activities were discovered, an Arab could wriggle out of what hung over them both, but Hastings could not, and Majidi knew it. As an Englishman Hastings was liable to rot in jail forever if their crime were discovered.

Hastings squeezed his glass with both hands and leaned forward. "I think, under the circumstances, that I need to leave off hunting for the time being." He was whispering, though he did not know why.

"I think the opposite," Majidi said. "A trip to the hinterlands to hunt ivory could be very helpful to us at this time, and the distraction of the Grand Mufti's visit is the right circumstance for our venture to continue."

"How will we proceed without Joseph?"

"I have a substitute on his way from Zanzibar. And I have a buyer ready."

Hastings drained his glass and rose. The whiskey had not warmed or comforted him. "Very well, then, I will get ready to hunt. Our terms will be the same?"

"I had thought to be more generous with you," Majidi said. "Sixty-forty instead of seventy-thirty."

The concession surprised and puzzled Hastings. The Arab was not one to give if he did not have to.

"You are surprised at my generosity," Majidi said. "Do not be. You are my best procurer. Without you, my latest expedition did not meet my buyers' needs. You know as well as I that since you British came into the territory, it has been nearly impossible for anyone but a Brit to make any headway. Your countrymen issue ivory permits only to their own kind. All the elephant hunters are Europeans now. You are the one I know well enough to trust. I want to deal with you."

Hastings heard the message beneath Majidi's words. He wanted to work with Hastings because he could not as easily control anyone else he might bring into his business. And the canny trader knew better than to squeeze a man too hard. The extra ten percent would relieve Hastings of some of his money troubles, but it was not enough to free him completely. The Arab was a clever bastard, but a bastard nonetheless.

As Majidi rose, Hastings shook his hand to seal the deal. "When does your new majordomo arrive?"

"He is on his way by dhow. If the winds are good, he should be here in two days."

"I had better get busy with the planning then. I will come tomorrow with a list of what I will require by way of men and supplies."

Later, in his room at the club, Hastings's fingers froze while undoing his shirt buttons. A chill flashed on the skin of his back. That canny old thief expected him to be grateful for the extra ten percent. But he never gave a gift without expecting something in return. What price would he extract? And what danger would it bring?

CHAPTER

6

The following morning, Tolliver and Vera awoke amid half-unpacked cartons. At breakfast, Vera talked of her plan to get her garden project under way as if there were nothing else on her mind. Katharine Morley had told her of an Englishman who had had a somewhat troubled past, but was an excellent gardener. Vera said she would seek him out and then go to the market just across the bridge from Robert Morley's mission, where, evidently, the best plants were on offer. She went on about hibiscus flowers, jasmine vines, and how fast a poinciana might grow in this climate. She felt vaguely guilty to be purposely misleading Justin about her intentions. She knew he would be burned up if he found her out. But what did he expect her to do? In public, he expressed admiration for her spunk whenever other British people raised their eyebrows at something she blurted out. But then in private, gently, with his arms around her, he admonished her to try to act more conventional. If he could have it both ways, why couldn't she?

So as not to make herself a complete liar, Vera did go to the Public Garden in Treasury Square and she spoke briefly to

Frederick Dingle, who readily admitted problems in his past with alcohol and passing bad checks. He told her he had had even become a Mohammedan at one point to try to lose his drinking habit, but that it had not helped. He was, even now, serving a prison sentence and was let out only during the day so that he could keep the Public Gardens and do whatever other landscaping work he could find. Every day at dusk he had to return to his cell. This was the story she had heard, along with universal admiration for the work he did. To be convinced of his gardening abilities, Vera needed only to look about at the beauty of the tropical flowers display and to hear Dingle wax poetic about passionflowers and how attractive and useful were Cape tree tomatoes. He certainly seemed every bit the master gardener Katharine had said he was. And his demeanor was that of a timid but amiable man, certainly not that of a hardened criminal.

Vera made an appointment with him to begin work at the bungalow the following morning. Done! She had set her conscience to rest about what she had told Justin she would be doing. Now for a rickshaw to the mainland bridge and on to the mission.

When she arrived, she found the Reverend Morley much as he had always been on his visits with her father—focused only on the rightness of his own opinions about slavery. She agreed with him there, but he repeated himself to an irksome degree. She had always wished she could adopt her father's patience and feel admiration for his fellow missionary. But did he have to boom out his points as if he were speaking before Parliament?

She did her best to hear out him and his sister on the subject of Joseph Gautura's death and the part Majidi must have played in it. One message came through clearly: he would never let the matter drop until the murderer had been apprehended. And Vera was glad of that. Justin, she was sure, would disagree, focused as he was on investigating possible other threats to the Grand Mufti. He had spoken last evening of little else. If anyone was going to help the Morleys as her father had asked, it would have to be her.

The Idol of Mombasa

By the time she left the mission, she had convinced herself that her father would want her to do anything she could to help his friend. A niggling doubt, though, deep in her conscience, told her that her father would want nothing of the sort, especially if it meant bringing herself in contact with the likes of Majidi. She shooed the feeling away as if it were a harmless lizard in the garden and, upon leaving the Mission, made her way immediately toward Mr. Majidi's place of business in the souk.

The Arab quarter of Mombasa had always fascinated her. The narrow streets were flanked with ancient houses whose front doors of thick wood were carved with geometric patterns and studded with brass nail heads the size of shillings. Balconies on the second stories overhung the street, some separated overhead by no more than a few feet. When she and her brother, Otis, were twelve and six, walking here with their parents, they had imagined an adventure tale where a hero leapt across the space to escape pursuing pirates.

Embedded in the cobblestones were tracks along which, every few minutes, Swahili men propelled privately owned trolley cars and fought for right of way with a melee of traders, shoppers, and servants. The shouts for precedence raised a dreadful din. The trolley boys usually won.

Khalid Majidi's place of business was, as Katharine Morley had described it, very easy to find—just inside the wide entrance to the covered market, beyond a stall that displayed a rainbow of beautifully embroidered silk shoes and directly across from a large concern that sold dried fruits, nuts, and spices.

Vera paused in the aisle, unsure of how to approach the man whom Robert Morley so despised and whom she was sure was a murderer. She told herself she was perfectly safe. Even if Majidi had done away with his former slave, he did not know Vera from Eve and would have no cause to harm her. Her plan was to tell him she was looking for furnishings for her new home and to pretend he might supply her, but when she arrived at his shop window, she saw it contained only ornate marble boxes and vases inlaid with silver and ivory for which she had no use and which looked frightfully expensive. Perhaps she could ask him about carpets. Sooner or later, all Europeans came to the bazaar looking for carpets.

She paused in front of the bins of dried fruits and nuts across from Majidi's door. The fruit seller's boy, a handsome young Arab in the ubiquitous long white *kanzu* and a white skullcap, approached Vera. His thick lashes would have been the envy of any girl of any race that Vera had ever known. He put his hands together in front of his face and bowed. "Lady, would you like to buy some of our delicious dried apricots? Would you, lady? They are the best in the souk." He called her "lady" in English, but otherwise he spoke in Swahili, the lingua franca of this polyglot city. Vera's command of the language was halting since she had spoken mostly Kikuyu and English in Nairobi and environs. She decided to practice her Swahili by speaking to the boy for a few minutes before she tackled a conversation with the ivory dealer.

Seeing her interest, the boy took a wide pewter spoon and deftly scooped up a single dried apricot and offered it to her. She drew nearer and took it. It was sweet and tangy and delicious.

"Good, yes, lady?" The boy smiled. His teeth were as perfect as his eyes and his hair. He was about fifteen. Nearly the age her brother was now. Vera's heart wobbled. It was so painful to think that Otis, wherever he was, had had a birthday since she last saw him, his first away from her. He had run away in the aftermath of their uncle's murder, thinking that he was taking the blame. She was sure he did not know what had transpired after he left. No more than she knew where he had gone. And her father and Justin had said it was best to leave those matters alone. Her heart ached to see him, to know how he was getting on. And she feared she never would.

She could not suppress the pain inside, but she forced herself to turn to the boy and smile. She asked for a small amount of apricots and some currants, which she would make into scones to surprise Justin at their first tea in the bungalow. Then she pointed across the corridor to Majidi's sign. "Does that shop sell carpets?" she asked the boy as he was spooning her purchases onto squares of tan paper and twisting up the ends.

His soft eyes turned angry. "The man who owns that shop is not a good person." His voice was suddenly a harsh whisper.

Vera leaned toward him and whispered too. "Why do you say he is not a good person?"

The boy glanced over his shoulder toward a blue-black curtain that separated the display of fruits and nuts from the back of the stall. He leaned closer. "He does not obey the teachings of the holy Koran."

"Taimur," a man's deep voice called sharply from behind the curtain. He spoke then in Arabic, which Vera did not understand at all. But it was clear from the tone and the frightened look on the boy's face that he was taking a scolding. Before the man finished speaking, he emerged from behind the curtain. He was short and slight, hardly taller than Vera, dressed in the same blue-black as the curtain, had a long black-and-gray beard, and eyes as hard as the boy's were soft. He went on berating the boy for so long that Vera wished she could run away. Instead, she took out her change purse and pointed to her purchases.

"My grandson and I have just been to hear the Grand Mufti speak about how a truly devout man must act in worshipping the true god," the old man said to Vera in Swahili. "My grandson has taken an important lesson today in true devotion to Allah. You are hearing the result of how moved he has been by the Grand Mufti's words." He took the packets and weighed them. The grandfather asked the boy a question in Arabic and then gave her the price of fifty *pices*.

"He seems a very nice boy," Vera said. She glanced over her shoulder at Majidi's shop. "I was asking him about the man who owns that shop."

"We are Shi'a," the grandfather said. He wrinkled his nose at the door across the aisle as if he smelled corruption emanating from it. "He is a Sunni." From his expression, he might have said, *We are human beings. He is a reptile.*

"I am afraid I don't know the difference."

The old man scowled. "Think of it as like the rift between the Papists and the Protestants in your own country," he said. "We consider him as the English consider the Papists. Hateful."

It surprised Vera that the old man knew of such religious conflict so far from his own country. "I see," she said, and then wondered whether the Swahili words she had used had actually meant not only that she understood, but that she also agreed. Flustered and wanting to stop the conversation, she counted out her coins and took her small purchases.

Before she reached Majidi's door, it opened with the tinkling of a bell and then swung with such force that it nearly hit her. From behind it emerged the bluff gentleman who had been on the ship with her and Justin. He was jamming his sun helmet on his head. Obviously, he was in high dudgeon about something. She was sure he mumbled, "Bastard," under his breath. Then he noticed her, coughed, and lifted his hat in a quick salute. She was about to ask him if he knew Majidi, but now thought better of it. "How do you do, sir," she said instead. She held out her hand. "My name is Vera Tolliver," she said. "We spoke aboard ship, but I did not have the pleasure of really making your acquaintance."

"Carl Hastings," he said, and gave her hand a perfunctory shake. "I saw your husband at the Mombasa Club. He's a policeman." He uttered the last few words with the usual English upper-class disdain for the men who provided the peace and security in which they lived.

"That's right," Vera said, with pride and a hint of rebellion. "I am sure all of the king's subjects are grateful to have men like him here, providing law and order."

Hastings gave her one of those shocked looks the English put on whenever she had the temerity to express an opinion that contradicted their own. He blinked three times, coughed again, and then pointed his thumb over his shoulder at Majidi's door. "You don't have business with this blighter, do you?"

"He is an acquaintance of a friend of my family's," she said, hovering near the truth, not actually lying. "I thought he might be able to advise me on the best place to buy carpets." A truth of sorts, since—though far from her real purpose—it was what she had meant to ask of him.

"I wouldn't ask Majidi about carpets. He'll only send you to a relative who will cheat you." He made a show of patting his breast pockets. "Sorry," Hastings said. "Must go back into the shop. Forgotten something. Best carpet man is Mahmoud." He pointed around the corner. "All the way at the back and to the left. Make him take the rugs out into the sunlight before you buy them. But once you select a good one, he will give you a good price. You will have to jew him down, of course."

"Thank you for the advice." She turned away, pretending to follow his instructions. But she glanced back and watched while he opened Majidi's shop door and went back inside. She turned the corner, intending to wait a few minutes and double back once she had heard Hastings leave, but then she saw a familiar face that made her grin from ear to ear.

"Sergeant Libazo," she said, certain that using his rank would please him.

He bent his arm at his waist and bowed. "Miss McIn—Mrs. Tolliver. How happy I am to see you."

She stood on tiptoes and looked over his shoulder, thinking she would see Justin.

"A.D.S. Tolliver is not here. I was actually here on a personal errand. We are going to be on duty nearby in a few minutes, over-seeing a crowd attending a speech by the Egyptian visitor. We have to make sure that nothing untoward happens, you know."

"Yes, Mr. Tolliver has told me all about that."

"On my way to the Baraza Hall, I took the opportunity to stop here to see a friend," Libazo said. His eyes took on the look Justin's might have when he was about to blush. But of course Kwai's mahogany skin did not turn red.

Vera did not have the nerve to ask him if this friend was a girl.

"I must go," Libazo said. "Or I will be missed."

"Good-bye, then. We will see each other often, I hope," Vera said. She was about to go back 'round the corner to Majidi's shop when she saw Katharine Morley coming toward her.

Libazo slipped away.

"Mrs. Tolliver," Katharine Morley said in surprise, as if she hadn't known that Vera was coming to the bazaar.

Vera was about to report to Katharine that she had not yet spoken to Majidi, when the muezzin began to sing out the call to prayer from the minaret of the mosque adjacent to the souk. At once, the place fell silent. Many of the men in the nearby stalls disappeared behind their curtains. Some rolled prayer rugs right in the aisles, knelt, and faced Mecca. The Hindu shoe seller and the man who sold pots and pans disappeared into the backs of their shops. The two women had suddenly become conspicuous. Vera felt it somehow sacrilegious to continue their conversation. She pulled Katharine into a nearby corner, out of sight of the men at prayer.

"I followed Robert here," Katharine said in too loud a voice.

Vera put her index finger to her lips and pulled Katharine farther into the corner.

"Sorry," Katharine whispered, "of course, we don't want to be accused of blasphemy."

"I thought you and the Reverend Morley were going to let me find out more about Majidi." Vera did her best to keep her voice even, but it miffed her that Katharine might be seen with her, which would spoil her hope to approach Majidi anonymously. How would she be able to get anything out of him if he knew she was in league with the missionaries?

Katharine closed her eyes and shook her head. "I am keeping my part of that promise, but I am afraid Robert will not. He has been acting very strange in the past few days. Away from home more than he ever was. Always letting his emotions run away with him. I wanted to make sure he would not do anything foolish, so I followed him when he went out. His trail led me here."

"I did not see him," Vera said. She wondered if Katharine always spied on her brother, but of course she could not ask that.

"He entered from the side. You know what a rabbit warren of twists and turns this place is. I lost him in the crowd, so I was making for Majidi's shop when I saw you."

"He did not come this way," Vera said. "I have been here near Majidi's shop for some time, and I have not seen him."

"What did you find out about Majidi?"

"Nothing as yet." As soon as she answered Vera realized that she did know two things she had not known before—that the trader did business with Carl Hastings and that the boy and his grandfather in the shop across the way intensely disliked him. But these things did not have any bearing on his relationship with Robert Morley.

The praying men were beginning to move about again, but Vera could not approach Majidi now, with Katharine in tow. She would have to come back later, though she despised the delay. She was more curious, and more determined than ever to find out about Majidi. "Why don't we just go to the club and have tea? Ladies are allowed in the tearoom during the day."

As before, the mention of tea brought a light of desire to Katharine's lovely blue eyes. Conspiratorial talk about how they would get information from Majidi occupied their walk to the club, but once they'd arrived, Katharine began to inquire about how Vera's father was faring alone these days, a subject that grieved Vera. She was sure her father felt lonely, and she felt guilty that she was not there to keep him company.

CHAPTER

7

While Vera and Katharine Morley lingered over tea at the club, Kwai Libazo stood guard at the front entrance of the Baraza Hall. On the other side of the broad double door was a Somali policeman whose rank was only corporal, but still, though he obeyed Libazo's orders, he assumed an air of superiority that clearly said rank mattered less to him than his race's assumed precedence over the darker-skinned tribesmen from the interior. It was a circumstance that nearly elicited an audible sigh from Kwai. In the few days he had been here on the coast, he had developed an intense dislike for Somali men. But he kept his feelings to himself.

That morning, in a quiet corner of the souk, he had had only a few minutes to introduce himself to the first Somali woman he had ever spoken to: Aurala Sagal. My, she was lovely. He was moved by everything about her. The warmth of her smile. Her pretty teeth. Her voice, low and soft, but sweet. Her eyes that gazed at him and made him feel important. The way she moistened her lips with her tongue. Even though he could not see her body, he knew that he wanted it. She was the most beautiful girl he had ever seen, in her silky wrap that was the color of a tamarind blossom and matched the little shoes on her delicate feet.

He did not want to think about the fact that she sold her love for money. He just wanted to think about her.

He paid attention to his work now, scanning the crowd of men streaming into the hall to hear the Egyptian priest, alert to any trouble. He had to be ready to respond to any disturbance, but he could not help recalling Aurala's soft, lilting voice that sounded as if she were going to break into laughter at any moment.

"You are not Swahili," she had said to him, the merriment leaving her eyes for a few seconds. He hoped that did not lessen him in her eyes. All the tribes of Africa seemed to look down on all the others.

"No, I am from up-country," he said.

When her eyes scanned his body, she seemed to be deciding whether she wanted him. Everything he knew about the Somali people's beliefs told him that no girl of theirs was supposed to be so brazen. "You do not look to be Kikuyu or Luo," she said as if she could not make up her mind if she liked him.

"No," was all he answered. His background and his feelings about it were not what he wanted to talk about. "You are Somali." He made it a statement. Only Somali girls were tall and graceful, dressed like this—in Arab fashion—and had such exotic hair dressings. She might not behave like a girl of her tribe, but people did not always follow their customs, especially if they lived in cities instead of villages. This was true even of the English.

She smiled with her mouth but not with her large, glistening eyes. "I am from there, yes. And you? Tell me."

"My mother is Kikuyu. My father was Maasai."

She reached out and touched the sleeve of his uniform. Her demeanor had turned serious. "Then you are like me. Not fit to belong where you ought to belong."

He had wanted to say that perhaps they belonged together. But he did not. He did not think that a man said such things to a girl who did what she did.

"I think I will see you again," she said after a silence.

"I think so too." He did not want her to read his thoughts, but it seemed she could, and he could not hide them from her.

"Smile," she said, and when he did, she giggled. "I knew your smile would be beautiful."

Kwai was reveling in his memory of her beauty as she tripped away from him, but then a sudden hustle and bustle inside the Baraza Hall dispelled his reverie.

The noise came from just behind the door. Kwai slid his rifle off his shoulder, at the ready. At that moment, A.D.S. Tolliver emerged, followed by an Englishman with a photographic camera and the important Egyptian priest, who always dressed in black with a towering white hat. He was as tall as Kwai and the captain, even without that hat. Soon the photographer was making a great show of setting up his machine and arranging the Grand Mufti with some other people—one was an old man in a dark blue *kanzu*. He had a long salt-and-pepper beard. Beside him walked a boy in white whose eyes and eyelashes put Kwai in mind of Aurala Sagal's.

Tolliver came and stood next to Kwai. "Evidently," he said, "the boy has been chosen to go to Cairo to study with the Mohammedan teachers there. It is to be a great honor for his family. They are going to put this picture in the paper." It was surprising that the captain spoke such things to Kwai Libazo. None of the English officers in the police force did so. Kwai knew, also, that he was the only one on the force, black or white, to whom Tolliver spoke in such a forthcoming way. He felt pleased with himself because of that. And because of the way the girl Aurala had looked at him.

That afternoon, taking a rest from her gardening, Vera sat down with the newspaper and was amused to see on the front page a photo of the Father Christmas Grand Mufti with the boy who had sold her dried apricots. She was leafing through the news trying to persuade herself to take an interest in the doings in the city that would be her home for the coming months when she noticed that, down the hill from her veranda, the white flag had gone up at the post office. It signaled to the town that the mail was ready for distribution. Though it was the hottest part of the day, she decided to walk the quarter-mile to fetch the post. Perhaps there would be a letter from her father.

She was not disappointed. As soon as she arrived back at home, she put aside three other envelopes—letters for Justin from his mother and his sister and one from her granny in Glasgow—and read her father's news. He said nothing of how much he missed her. But she knew he did.

She wanted to answer him immediately, but she needed to cool off first. She went to her room and, after sponging herself, could not bear the thought of re-donning the typical Englishwoman's twill ensemble, which was supposed to protect her from the sun. She had no intention of going out again in this afternoon, when even her lightest frock would smother her. European women in Africa had given up their corsets. How many decades would it be, she wondered, before they adopted the mode of African dress, more comfortable in this climate, especially here at sea level, where the air made her feel as if she were floating on a raft in a pot of soup. Even without stockings and in bare feet, she wished for the comfort of a simple Kikuyu *shuka*, just a light cotton cloth tied at the shoulder, the likes of which she had sometimes borrowed from her tribal playmates when her mother was not watching.

There was no one in the house. The gardener had gone off to eat and nap, so she need not worry who would see her. She went to her bedroom cupboard and found the blue-green filmy silk harem pants she had bought on a whim in the bazaar. She pulled them on. They were as light as sea foam. She tied an oblong piece of matching silk around her bare chest and put on over it a cunning little embroidered and beaded vest of bright yellow. She regarded herself in the mirror and laughed. If she had had another scarf to tie around her head and to use as a veil she might have passed for an Arab girl. Her hair and eyes were that dark. As it was, she looked as if she were on her way to a costume ball, not that any proper Scottish girl would ever be seen in public in this getup. But she was so much more comfortable than she would have been in her ordinary clothes.

She sat down at her desk in an alcove of her bedroom to answer her father's letter. A thought of her mother brought her a wave of embarrassment over her relative dishabille. Her mother would never have done anything this frivolous.

Grief soon drove away any thoughts of unseemly attire. Her mother had been dead for less than a year and in the intervening months Vera's thoughts had often turned to her, to how little love she had felt from her mother until nearly the time of her death, to the confusion and terrible sense of loss she had felt after her mother was gone. Now, as a young wife in Africa, she thought often about her mother, who within just a few months of coming here had given birth in what was then a completely wild country, without another white woman nearby for company. Her mother had borne her under such circumstances, with the help only of tribal women with whom she did not share even a language and to whom she could not relate as friends. What courage that must have taken! A terrible regret washed over Vera, that she and her mother had never been close. And now there was no way to rectify that loss.

She glanced down at the writing paper on the table in front of her. What would she say to her father? His letter was full of reasons why Justin must help Robert Morley to keep Joseph Gautura free. Papa was busy with his converts and the harvest on his coffee plantation outside of Nairobi, where no newspaper would bother to report the death of a runaway slave in Mombasa.

Her father had come to Africa to bring the natives to Christ but—in his mind anyway—his real purpose had been to save the Africans from slavery by making them Christians. White Christians, he had thought, would not have the heart to buy and sell African Christians like so many bales of cotton or sides of beef. He had been so heartened when it had seemed that Britain had stamped out slavery worldwide. She could not bring herself to tell him that his pleas to free Joseph Gautura were too late.

She preferred to write him a chatty letter, pretending she had not received his that lay on the desk in front of her. She picked up her pen and wrote:

> *Dearest Papa,*
> *You will be happy to know that Justin and I are now ensconced here in a simple but comfortable bungalow. I wanted Justin to buy his way out of the army so he might leave the police force, but he is determined to do his bit for King and Country for a little while longer...*

She put down her pen. How bland was her description of what had transpired between her and Justin in their bedroom at his father's estate. It was the same argument they had had before and since. The only one they ever had, really. The one she could not give up, though she could not find a reason to convince him, perhaps because she herself was not sure of the reason. She only knew in her bones that he must not.

That chilly day in Yorkshire, Justin had stood the whole while, staring out the window at the snow-covered terrace. The marble statues on their ornate pedestals had looked like men frozen in place. And that was what Justin had been—unyielding, unwilling to speak the heated words she was sure were in his heart. No more alive, no more warm than the stone men silhouetted against the dark, distant pines, he spoke only in whispers, through clenched teeth. While she could not control her temper.

"Why? Just explain to me why you won't leave the police force and free us from having to live where they tell us, and me from having to be without you while you do your duty day and night?"

"Lower your voice, Vera."

"Why should I? If you can be so cold to me, why can I not be heated with you?"

"This sort of thing is just not appropriate," he had said as if he were quoting the local ordinances to a criminal.

She had opened her mouth and closed it over again, humiliation and guilt warring with anger and despair within her. She had promised herself that she would not misbehave while they were under his parents' roof, that she would never give his family the slightest reason to disapprove of her. She was the right wife for him. And he was the right husband for her, whatever they might think of her lack of breeding, of her grandfather having been in trade. She wanted to punch him in his stiff back. But all she could do was bite her lip till it bled and burst into tears. She had turned away and gone into the dressing room, to not let him see her weep, to not allow him to imagine that she would use tears to change his mind.

He was gone when she returned to their bedroom.

As today, she had tried that afternoon to write the truth to her father. But she could not. Her father loved Justin as he loved the son who had run away. It would be too wrong to sully her father's affections for him. Her father needed to think her completely happy. That meant never revealing to him the chink in the armor of her and Justin's mutual love—the difference between who they were and who they liked to imagine each other to be. That rift only disappeared when they were together in bed, or out in the wilderness, where what other people might think did not matter.

She picked up her pen and wrote:

Oh, Father, you know that I would rather be with you. Won't you consider coming to us for a nice extended visit? I so long to have you near.

The loneliness she described wrung her heart. Somehow putting it in writing made it more intense. She loved Justin; she wanted her life to be with him. But he had a place in the Protectorate—his work as a policeman, his teammates and supporters in sport. She was an outsider among the settlers. She had immediately been attracted to him when they met, but she had thought that she—a missionary's daughter—would never have a chance with a young nobleman, especially one as handsome and dashing as he.

After he joined the police force, he had often asked her to dance at parties at the Nairobi Club. Still, she had tried to resist an attachment to him, imagining it would only break her heart. But by that time it was too late. She was in love with him. And then his investigation into her uncle's murder had thrown them into close company. In those difficult times, they had both revealed their love. It had seemed then that being Justin's wife was all she wanted and that if she could be with him, nothing else would trouble her. Now she knew that was not entirely true. He was hers and she his. Everything about their love was wonderful. But life did not stop at loving.

She picked up her pen and held it over the paper again, trying to force herself to write less than she felt. She was isolated here. She might be mistaken for an Arab girl in this getup, but she was not one. She could look for friends among the administrative set here in Mombasa, but in attitudes she would certainly never be British enough to satisfy them. Loneliness was crushing her.

She crumpled the paper she had been writing on and dropped it into the basket beside the desk. She would not write to her father until she had good news to tell him about Joseph Gautura's murderer being brought to justice.

Right now she would change into her proper clothing and without hesitation go and find out something about Majidi that would help bring him to justice. She might not belong to any group in Mombasa, but she would do whatever she could to fulfill her father's wish.

A noise from the front of the house interrupted her thinking. She started for the door, but then looked down at her silly costume. She could not bring herself, dressed like this, to go and investigate who it was. Within seconds, she heard Justin's footsteps, and he came through the bedroom door.

One look at her and he laughed.

"You're usually the one who blushes," Vera said, "but I would now if I had your complexion. I—"

He held up his hand. "Just stand there a moment," he said. Then he began to unbutton his uniform jacket.

"It was so hot that I—"

Again his raised hand stopped her words. He continued to disrobe, in silence, never taking his eyes off her. He did not let her speak until he was down to his bare skin at which point she did not want to say anything, just to let him take her in his arms.

At that moment, but for Justin's delightful distraction of her, Vera would have been making for the bazaar, which as it happened was the goal of almost everyone she knew in Mombasa.

Seething with anger, Carl Hastings was on his way to give Khalid Majidi a piece of his mind. The English hunter had met with Majidi's new majordomo, an arrogant black eunuch from Zanzibar named Ismail Al Dimu, who had the audacity to tell Hastings that he was overruling his new arrangements with Majidi. The bloody towelhead had demanded a twenty percent cut for himself, to be taken out of Hastings's share of the value of what they shipped. This meant that Hastings would now be reduced to only twenty percent for himself, when until now, he had been getting thirty. What was more, Majidi had only just promised him the forty. It would not do. It just would not do for a bastard without balls to make such demands. Hastings charged along the thronged street, sweating as much from his boiling temper as from the torrid air.

Not many paces behind him, a no-less-sweaty Robert Morley beat the same path. His purpose earlier that day had been foiled by the sight of his sister nearby. He could not allow her to know his secret. There had been nothing for it but to abandon his goal. Now, having assured himself that she was taking her customary siesta, Morley had returned with even greater determination.

Katharine Morley, however, had also learned her lesson that morning. Fond as she was of her bright blue hat, the one vain indulgence she had ever allowed herself, she left it behind. It was far too recognizable. She followed after her brother, wearing a sun helmet of the sort so ubiquitous in tropical English settlements as to make her invisible. Thus it was easy for her to follow Robert discreetly, close enough not to lose sight of him as he entered the bazaar.

Katharine seethed with indignation. She had devoted her life to supporting her brother's work. She had come to this point with perfect faith in his righteousness. Like her parents, she had always considered Robert's Mission work the most important on earth. For the first time in her life, today, the rock of her faith in him felt unsteady under her feet. He was keeping something from her. What could he have to hide but some betrayal of all they believed in and had worked for? She had never imagined that he would do such a thing. But for weeks now, since Joseph Gautura had run away from his master, Robert had been acting very suspiciously. It was quite possible that he meant to harm— she could not let herself think the words *to murder*—Majidi.

Though her distrust felt like an act of betrayal, how else but by spying on Robert could she put to rest her doubts about the purity of his intentions? And what if he was contemplating a terrible sin? She must stop him before he reached the brink of perdition. She must.

Just then, a tall African policeman sped past her. Though she was distracted for only a second, when she looked back, Robert was gone.

❀ ❀ ❀

Kwai Libazo took no notice at all of the tall English lady with the bright blue eyes. He knew no English people in Mombasa other than A.D.S. and Mrs. Tolliver. Kwai's quarry was the only person in the town that he cared to know better—Aurala Sagal. He had two hours' respite before he would have to take up evening guard duty at the police station at the entrance to Ndia Kuu. He wanted to make love to her, but not as part of a transaction involving money. He had no idea how much such a service might cost. Or whether an African man would be welcome as a customer. He worried a great deal about these questions. He was certain, though, that he wanted to be near her and that the more they knew about each other, the better things would become between them.

Without taking any notice of who was walking in the same street, he rushed past first Katharine, and then her brother, and finally an Englishman with a drooping mustache who was mumbling obscenities under his breath like a man who belonged in a hospital for the insane.

When Kwai arrived at the silk shop, he noticed that the bookshop across the way was shuttered. It satisfied him deeply that the man he had chased down and the bookseller who had harbored him were in jail.

Unlike the first two times he had come to this part of the bazaar, Kwai did not find Aurala Sagal standing in front of the silk shop. A wave of upset washed over him. Was she inside making sex with another man?

Kwai had been on raids of the brothels in the Indian market in Nairobi. Whenever he and his fellow askaris entered those places, they would cause a panic among the lowlifes hanging about. This place might be the same. But the women who worked in houses of ill repute in Nairobi were tribal girls who, as A.D.S. Tolliver described them, "had gone wrong." None of them seemed to him remotely like the lovely, graceful girl whose company he sought. He paused only momentarily. He could not resist her. He went in.

As soon as he did, he heard a gasp and a flurry of activity coming from the back. There were bolts of silk, one below another, suspended from chains attached by hooks to the ceiling. The bright display of cloth hung down at different lengths and screened what was behind it. Within a few seconds Aurala herself emerged. She was dressed as usual, but today in a golden color.

"Sergeant Libazo," she said. Her eyes smiled at him, but her voice was too loud. She was not only speaking a greeting to him but also a message to someone behind the curtain of cloth.

Kwai Libazo had been raised in the tribal way, without the European romantic fantasies that seemed to have entered his heart in the past twenty-four hours. It took half a minute for Sergeant Libazo the askari to win out over Kwai Libazo the lover. He took a deep breath and moved swiftly and silently behind the fabric screen.

The rear portion of the shop stretched back for about ten yards. There was a narrow aisle at its center that led to a door at the rear. On either side of the aisle were walls of various colored draperies that seemed to delineate three rooms on each side. Kwai had no idea whether the door at the back might lead to the street or to another room.

The space in which he stood held a large table to his left. Sitting at it were a Swahili boy of about nine and a woman who looked quite like Aurala but about five or six years older and dressed, not in the colors of the sunset, but all in black—like a woman in mourning. They both gave Libazo shocked and then frightened looks, glancing at what lay on the table before them— an unsheathed Arab dagger. It had a deadly-looking curved blade. The handle was silver inlaid with ivory and had embedded in it an emerald the size of Libazo's thumbnail.

He looked from one of them to the other. He saw fear in Aurala's eyes and defiance in her sister's as they glanced at the knife and back at him. "Why is it that you did not want me to see that thing?" Kwai demanded of Aurala, pointing at the dagger. He knew very well that up in Nairobi the brothels at the rear of Victoria Street were places where thieves stored and sold their stolen goods, but those were squalid places, not at all like this, which resembled the inside of a silken tent.

When no one answered, he took the child by the elbow and stood him up just roughly enough to frighten the boy further. He wore only dirty khaki shorts that might once have belonged to a household servant, but now were ragged and missing a button on the fly.

"I found it. I swear I did not steal it. It was in the mangrove forest. Just lying there. I picked it up. I only picked it up. I go there and look for things to eat. I found this. I—"

Libazo patted the air in front of him. "Be quiet," he said sternly, though he pitied the poor filthy child. "Why did you bring it here? If you found it, why did you not bring it to the police so we could locate its proper owner?"

The boy looked up at the woman in black seated next to him. "The child is starving," she said with a weary air, as if she had had this exact conversation many times before.

"What is your name, please?"

"I am Leylo Sagal," she said. She had Aurala's beauty of face and form, but she did not glow with it. She seemed beaten down, powerless. Her dark eyes were lifeless.

Aurala stepped forward. "She is my older sister."

"I thought so," Kwai said, though he did not know why he bothered to tell them. He turned back to the boy. "And you, boy. What is your name?"

The urchin folded his arms across his chest and raised his head, staring Kwai in the eye and pursing his lips. He was a brave little scamp, refusing to answer a policeman.

"His name is Haki," Leylo Sagal said. She stood up and faced Kwai squarely. She was even taller than her sister, nearly eye to eye with Libazo. "Many people believe that all establishments like ours also serve to buy and sell stolen goods. The people who told him to bring the thing here thought we were one of those, but we are not. It is the Indian-run establishments that do that. He did not know this. He thought he could get money from us for this *janbia*." She pointed to the dagger.

"What were you advising him to do when I arrived then?" Kwai suddenly saw that he had been assuming Aurala was as good as she was lovely.

Suppose she was a thief as well as a prostitute. Perhaps wanting her was making him a stupid policeman.

"I believe the boy is telling the truth, that he found the dagger," Leylo said. "If he had stolen it, he would have taken the sheath as well. It would have far more jewels than the hilt— certainly the more valuable of the two parts."

"I looked for it," the boy said sullenly.

"And?" Kwai spoke sharply, pretending he felt no sympathy for the waif.

"The mangroves are very thick there. You can't move around. You can't. Only because I am small and skinny, I can go inside the swamp. It was early in the morning. The sun was still coming from the ocean. It was the sun that showed me the shiny thing. I almost got stuck trying to find the rest of it. I didn't find it." The boy spoke as if he were afraid of being scolded for not doing his chores.

Kwai believed his story. "What are you going to do now, Haki?" Kwai leaned over and picked up the knife.

"Go to jail." The boy looked into Kwai's eyes as if daring him to make his fear come true.

Kwai forced himself not to smile. "No, you will not go to jail. But I will take this dagger to the police station. I will look into the record to see if anyone has reported it stolen or lost. If someone claims to have lost it, nothing at all will happen to you. The police will give it back to the owner, and I will ask the owner to give you a gift as a reward for finding it. If it was stolen, that will be another matter. You may be accused."

Haki showed no fear of being charged with theft. "And if no one says he has lost it? If it has been there for many years, dropped there by some pirate?"

Aurala Sagal smiled. "That cannot be. If it had been in the swamp for a long time, it would be very tarnished, black as all silver turns when it has not been polished for a long time. It is too clean to have been in the sea for a long time."

"I wiped it off on my pants," the boy said.

"That would not have been enough to make silver shine," Aurala answered.

This impressed Kwai. She was better at figuring out such things than many who called themselves policemen.

"If no one claims it in a period of time, it will be yours to do with whatever you want," Kwai said.

"How long?" the boy demanded.

"I do not know the law about this," Kwai answered. "It may be half a year."

Haki pouted. "What am I supposed to eat while I wait?"

"Whatever you have eaten until now," Leylo Sagal answered in a tone of resignation.

Kwai took the boy's hand. "No," he said. "You will come with me and take a bath. You will earn decent clothing and food by polishing my brass buttons and cleaning my shoes. And you will steal nothing. If you do not do exactly as I say, you will find yourself crawling through the swamp again looking for something to eat. If I have reason not to trust you, you will never get back this knife. Even if no one claims it. Is that clear?"

"Yes," the boy answered, fighting but failing to keep the defiance in his eyes.

"Good," Kwai said. "That way I will not have to take you up-country to the Athi Plain where I come from and feed you to the lions."

At that moment, Aurala Sagal gave Kwai Libazo the smile he wanted from her. One that said she liked him in a way that had nothing to do with wanting him to give her money in return for her love, which made him want her more than ever.

8

Later that afternoon, in the Tollivers' bungalow bedroom, Vera's exotic costume was still strewn on the floor. Justin was delighting in the softness and warmth of her skin and the satisfaction he felt in being married to a girl who wanted to make love to him as much as he wanted her. Vera's hunger for him was born of love, as much the giving of herself as the taking of pleasure from him. If a genie came into the room at this moment and offered him a wish, he would not be able to think of anything more he wanted than to be with her, like this. He hated the wretched idea of having to get up and go back to the station and deal with all the complexities of enforcing the law in this city. He had been clear about how to do his work in Nairobi: taking in European drunks who were out of control, solving burglaries against and by every variety of resident, arresting vandals smashing other people's possessions in fits of temper. Here nothing was clearly right or wrong. He wanted to do his job well, but—

A loud knock at the front door dispelled any notion that he might take a nap before returning to his duties. In a few seconds,

Miriam was in the hall outside the bedroom calling out, "It is your sergeant, Bwana. He says it is very urgent."

"Minute," he called, hearing a huskiness in his own voice.

Vera opened her arms and let go of him.

He kissed her naked shoulder and leapt up, pulling on his clothing with all possible speed.

"You are perfect," Vera said.

"We are perfect." He leaned over and without stopping his fingers from buttoning his shirt, kissed her mouth. "I have to go, dearest love," he said, grateful that the emergency, whatever it was, had not arisen earlier. He tied his tie, smiling a bit smugly, he thought, over how happy he was about what had arisen the moment he laid eyes on Vera in that harem outfit.

"I will be back as soon as I can," he said.

He found Kwai in the front garden, fairly dancing with excitement. The askari saluted and stood at attention. His shirt was damp. Obviously he had run all the way in this heat. "Sir," he said urgently, "they told me you had come home briefly." He paused to take a breath. "Sir, it is very bad, sir. It may upset the Grand Mufti."

"Out with it, Libazo."

"You must come to the bazaar forthwith. It is the ivory dealer. Majidi. He has been found dead on the floor of his store."

"Good God," Tolliver exclaimed. He started for the Arab quarter at a dead run.

Vera, having pulled on a robe and crept out to listen to the news, slumped against the wall on the other side of the door. She did not want to believe what was screaming in her brain—that the person who most despised Majidi, enough to kill him, was Robert Morley. It seemed impossible that her father's friend would commit such a sin. He was fiery in his antislavery sentiments, but everything else she had seen of him showed him to be a rather prissy man. She could imagine him shrinking from the sight of a mouse much more easily than wielding a murder weapon. Yet it was undeniable that he might have. What would her father say then?

A.D.S. Tolliver jogged down the hill toward the bazaar, but soon slowed his pace. The afternoon sun was sinking over the mainland.

"Who is guarding the body?" he asked Libazo. If the policeman on duty had a brain in his head, they would not need to move so quickly through this soupy air.

"Sergeant Singh."

Tolliver slowed his pace. Singh could be trusted to treat the murder scene properly.

They commandeered a canvas-roofed trolley at the corner of Kimathi Road and careened down the hill toward the fish market at breakneck speed. Once they reached the waterfront, however, they had no choice but to thread through the sweat-stinking crowd that thronged the narrow streets toward the bazaar.

As they moved, Libazo told Tolliver all he knew, which was not much. He had been at the souk himself and noticed nothing untoward, but almost as soon as he got back to the station next to the fort, a boy had come running at double time from the market shouting about bloody murder. The Goan lieutenant on duty had sent Singh with four constables to Majidi's shop and sent Kwai to fetch Tolliver.

Tolliver suppressed a niggling thought that had fallen into his mind almost immediately, one he abhorred. His best suspect was Vera's dear father's friend, the missionary Robert Morley.

When they entered the bazaar, the scene of the murder was easy to find and almost impossible to get to. The aisle was jammed with men clad in bright brocades. The cheeriness of the colors belied the mood of the crowd. The onlookers were all talking at once in angry voices, and ignoring the two policemen who fairly towered over them and commanded them, "Make way," in English and Swahili. No one moved.

Tolliver and Libazo had to elbow their way through to the shop door where two constables held the boisterous gawkers at bay. Inside, two more askaris were standing at attention before the curtain that led to the back. One of them moved to part it, revealing Sergeant Singh squatted on his haunches, examining the body that lay on the floor. The heavy air of the space reeked with the sweetish smell of blood.

Singh rose and revealed the victim's head. "He has been bashed," the Indian said.

"Move back, please," Tolliver ordered. "Have you touched anything?"

"No, sir. Absolutely nothing."

Khalid Majidi lay on the floor on his left side, his torso and legs on the carpet, his head resting on bare tiles. His face in profile looked undisturbed, but there was a horrid gash, deep and gruesome, in the crown of his skull. His legs were drawn up. A pool of blood surrounded his head and some of it had soaked into the brocade of his jacket and the edge of the carpet. There was a large black marble box on the floor near the corpse. It was inlaid with ivory and silver and bloodied on one corner. The top was ajar, and there were coins scattered on the carpet next to it. The most surprising thing about the scene was the open safe before which the body lay. Inside were piles of rupee notes and several folded documents. The bottom shelf held what looked to be quite a number of British banknotes. Tolliver leaned over so that he could see the contents better. There were seven thick stacks of English money, each tied up with string. The one nearest the front had a five-pound bill on top, which alone amounted to what Tolliver earned in a week. If the rest of the money in the stack were the same denomination, that one bundle would contain more than all the king's administrators in this city earned in a year.

"The safe was open like this when you entered here?" Tolliver asked, without turning around.

"Yes, sir, just as you see it," Singh answered.

That fact was astonishing. Why would the murderer have left all this cash? Clearly the motive was not robbery. A glance around the shop confirmed that. Another fortune in silver and ivory items was stored on these shelves and in the front room. Even if the murderer did not want to risk disposing of stolen goods, there was enough here in cash to tempt all but the saintliest conscience.

Tolliver straightened up and turned to face his men. "Who found the body?"

"An English lady," Singh said.

"Where is she? I want to question her."

"We don't know, sir. She sent a boy from a nearby stall to fetch us. By the time we got here, she was gone."

"Do we know her name?"

"No, sir. As I said, she was—"

Tolliver stopped Singh's words with a wave and bit back a curse. He glanced at Libazo and saw his own disappointment reflected in Kwai's downcast expression. "Surely you kept the boy nearby so we can question him," Tolliver said to Singh.

Singh glanced from Tolliver to Libazo and back again. "As I said, sir, his family has the stall next to this shop, where the women buy their shoes."

"Libazo, go and find the lad and bring him into the front. I need to find out exactly what he saw, but I don't want to subject a youngster to this horror."

Kwai saluted and left.

Tolliver took out his handkerchief and with it picked up the elaborately decorated black marble cask. More coins spilled out as he did, some rolling away under the furniture. The box was extremely heavy. Even for him, with his large hand and arm strong from swinging a tennis racket and a polo mallet, it was impossible to lift the box with one hand. It had undoubtedly been used to make that gash in the ivory trader's skull.

Tolliver placed the box on top of a stack of ledgers piled on a chair. There was an empty space in the corner of the desk just big enough to hold the cask. "Have we called for a squad to take away the body?" he asked Abrik Singh.

"They should be here very soon."

Tolliver went to the front room. It was atypical of places of business in the souk. Ordinarily, every inch of space would be jammed helter-skelter with goods for sale. This one was lined with glass-fronted vitrines, each held closed with a small brass lock. They contained obviously precious objects—smaller than, but otherwise much like the ones in the back room—casks, vases, small jewelry boxes, all of black marble decorated with inlays of silver and ivory. The workmanship was superb. A waist-high counter stood facing the door. Its top was also inlaid, with a floral pattern of many colors of stone—like the ones Justin had seen in the galleries of Florence. But all the rich objects on the shelves were covered with a fine layer of dust. No one had picked them up to examine them recently. Tolliver had begun to suspect that none of the cash in the safe came from selling the objects before him.

Kwai soon returned with a frightened-looking boy of about twelve—a chubby Indian lad with a nervous smile that showed a broken front tooth. Two askaris quickly followed, carrying a stretcher. Tolliver bid the boy to sit on a stool in the corner, and blocked his view while they carried out the corpse, which they had, at any rate, covered with a black cloth. "Shall I go with them to the clinic in the fort, sir?" Libazo asked.

Tolliver wondered how his sergeant already knew the procedure, since Libazo had been in town less time than he had, and he had not known it. "No," he said. "You stay here with me. Sergeant Singh, you go with them. And take the box that I left on the chair in the back."

Singh started to part the curtain.

"Oh," Tolliver said to him, "and don't touch the box with your bare hands. Do you have a handkerchief?"

"No, I do not."

"Here take mine. And tell the doctor we want to take the fingerprints of the corpse. Then take the box to Inspector Patrick. Tell him I will speak to him about it in the morning."

When Singh escorted the corpse out into the corridor, the crowd outside the shop windows grew even more raucous, but soon dispersed as it became clear that the dramatics were over.

Tolliver sent Libazo into the back room to search around for anything that might tell them something about who had killed the ivory dealer.

He then turned to the boy—who stared with wary eyes and worried his broken tooth with the tip of his tongue. His skin was the color of coffee with milk. "Tell me," Tolliver said, trying his best to adopt a threatening tone, "about the English lady you say sent you for the police."

The boy looked at the floor and spoke in a whisper. "Her skin was very white and she wore a hat like the ones all the English ladies wear."

"What about her clothes?"

"She wore tan clothes, like the ones the English ladies wear."

"Was she tall? Was she fat?" Tolliver was becoming exceedingly impatient. It was always this way across races. Witnesses often remembered telling details about the appearance of members of their own group, but almost no distinguishing characteristics of someone very unlike them.

"She was taller than my mother, but not as tall as the Somali women. Her skin was very white. She did not have any bracelets." Since native and Arab women sported so many, this must have seemed to the boy to be the most unusual part of the lady's attire.

Tolliver had to give up before he exploded, which would not have been helpful. His approach of frightening the child into giving up information had backfired. He had made the boy too intimidated to think clearly. He moderated his tone. "You may go, but I want you to think hard. And to watch for her. If you see the lady again, ask her name. A policeman will come back tomorrow to ask you if you have remembered anything more or if you have seen her again." He smiled at the lad and gave him a rupee coin.

The boy's eyes looked up in disbelief.

"Try to remember her more clearly."

"I will, Mr. Police," he said, and sped away.

While Tolliver was questioning the Indian boy, Kwai Libazo gave the back room of the shop a thorough going-over. He began with the floor, which except for the bloody part was cleaner than the floors of most places he had searched in his two years as a policeman. Only a bit of dust. The assailant had not dropped any clues. There was a pair of threadbare slippers under the desk. They were small to be a man's. They were smaller than a Maasai woman's feet, but Kwai imagined they had belonged to Majidi. He had not noticed if the corpse had worn shoes. He felt a wave of disappointment in himself. A.D.S. Tolliver was always warning him that he must observe every detail if he was to make a good policeman. But he had not looked at the dead man's feet. Only at the nasty gash in his head.

He scanned the shelves of goods, looking behind the larger objects, opening all the richly decorated boxes, and turning over the vases. But he did not touch the contents of the safe. He was sure Tolliver would prefer to do that himself.

He started in on the drawers of the desk and in the first one, the top left, he spied an object that caused him to catch his breath. He picked it up and examined it carefully. It was the sheath of an Arab dagger. Without its knife! Silver and curved as were the sheaths of all the *janbias*. But this one was familiar to Kwai. It was set with a large emerald that in design and cut matched exactly the large emerald embedded in the hilt of the knife that young Haki had found in the mangrove swamp! The realization sent a chill over Kwai's scalp and down his spine. He took the sheath into the front of the shop where Tolliver was inspecting the display cases.

"Sir," Libazo said. "I have found something of great interest." He held out the sheath for Tolliver to see and explained how the dagger that almost certainly went with it had come to be in the police station near the ramparts of Fort Jesus. He expected to receive one of Tolliver's looks of approval and pride, but instead he got a frown.

"You've touched it with your bare hands." The tone of dismay in Tolliver's voice troubled and puzzled Libazo. Touching evidence had never been a problem in Nairobi. But Kwai had seen Tolliver pick up the murder weapon today with a handkerchief, and he had advised Abrik Singh to do the same. Singh had known what that meant. Kwai did not want to be the only one who did not know what this meant. Without really understanding the significance of it, he did his best to defend himself. "I don't have a handkerchief."

"Do you know then, about fingerprints?" Tolliver looked surprised.

After a second's hesitation, Kwai gave in and admitted ignorance. Once Tolliver explained what fingerprints were and what they could do, Kwai was glad he had not pretended to understand. He could never have imagined the truth of them. In fact, he looked down at his own fingertips and wondered that they could be so completely different from someone else's. It seemed more magic than real.

"Here," Tolliver said, taking a sheet of brown wrapping paper from under Majidi's sales counter. "Put the sheath here. We will take it to Inspector Patrick for analysis. You will have to give him your fingerprints, so they can be distinguished from any others on the object."

It was well past sundown when they locked up the shop. Tolliver had taken the money from the safe and left two armed constables to guard the shop's remaining contents. The bazaar was relatively quiet, except for the food shops. The town must have been abuzz with gossip, given the murder of a powerful man, but wherever those words were being spoken, it was not here. Not in public.

Tolliver also took the sheath. "Right now, we have to deliver the cash to Mr. Smallwood at the Treasury." He took out his watch. "We will have to rush to get to him before he locks up for the night.

Once the money was in the Treasury safe, Tolliver bid Libazo good night. "Meet me tomorrow morning first thing at police headquarters—on the top floor, at the door that says *Inspector C. W. Patrick*."

After eating his evening meal at the barracks, Kwai Libazo toyed with the idea of going to find Aurala Sagal, but he could not bring himself to chance finding her with another man. As he lay in his bunk, the only thing that distracted him, even momentarily, from thoughts of her was this new thing he had learned about: fingerprints. Good as his eyes were, he could not see anything particularly special about his fingertips. Still, he gazed at his hands in wonderment when he thought that the patterns on them were his and his alone and would distinguish him from every other person in the world.

CHAPTER

9

The next morning, Kwai arrived at Inspector Patrick's room a few minutes before A.D.S. Tolliver. The office seemed to Kwai to be too small to house a whole department. It was about half the size of a railway carriage. The walls on two sides were lined with cabinets with narrow drawers. A few of them carried white labels with the letters of the alphabet written on them in black. *A–C* and so on. At the far end, in front of the window opposite the door, stood a table that was painted white on the top.

"Good morning, Inspector Patrick, sir," Kwai said. He saluted and then stood at attention, wondering whether Inspector Patrick would, like most officers, treat him as if he were an idiot. He had learned on joining the force to turn himself into a statue, showing not the least emotion.

After a cursory glance in Kwai's direction, the inspector held up one finger and continued to pour some kind of powder into a small bowl. Libazo was reminded of the powders that the tribal medicine men kept in pottery containers in their huts and used for their magic. This studious-looking Englishman must be their kind of witch doctor.

Inspector Patrick was a slight man of medium height, wearing not the typical police uniform, but a tan linen suit and starched collar. His bald head shone in the bright light coming through the window. His eyes were pale blue, and his light brown mustache was bushy and thick, as if it were trying to make up for the lack of hair on his head.

When Inspector Patrick had finished what he was doing, he looked enquiringly at Kwai and said only, "Well?"

"I have touched a piece of evidence, sir."

Patrick scowled as if he had caught Kwai pissing in public. "Come here, boy. Show me your identification card."

When Kwai obliged, he took a white slip of paper from a box on the table. On it, he wrote *Sergeant Kwai Libazo*, and copied *23972*, Kwai's askari number, which was printed on Kwai's identification card. He then took out a flat tin box with a wet-looking black cloth inside. "Give me your right hand." He took Kwai's fingers and one by one placed them on the black pad and then pressed them on the paper. Kwai saw very clearly the swirls and lines that A.D.S. Tolliver had described. But seeing them did not make the idea of solving a crime by reading them any less wondrous. In fact, it made it even more intriguing.

Tolliver soon arrived and gave Patrick the sheath that Libazo had found in Majidi's desk drawer. "Have you fingerprinted the corpse?" he asked.

"Not yet," Patrick answered. "Dr. Sutton stayed late examining the victim. He was not in yet when I arrived this morning. It won't be long, I imagine, before he calls me over there. You can wait here if you like."

"I have to meet D.S. Egerton," Tolliver said. "Sergeant, you go and get the dagger that the boy found. I imagine it is still locked in the evidence storage at the citadel station."

"Yes, sir."

"Bring it here. Make sure you wrap it in a cloth before you touch it again. Then wait here for Inspector Patrick's report. I will need to have that straightaway."

"Yes, sir." Kwai left immediately and sped to the station, where he instructed the Goan lieutenant to hold a cloth over his hand when he picked up the dagger. The officer gave Libazo a warning glance, as if what he had said was a personal insult, as if he had implied that the officer's hands were not clean. Libazo tried to explain about fingerprints, but the man told him to shut up. He then made a great fuss about getting Kwai to sign a receipt for the item. He said the words *valuable* and *large emerald* over and over, as if he were warning Kwai not to steal the dagger that would not have been in the evidence drawer in the first place if Kwai had not turned it in.

When Kwai returned to the Fingerprint Department, Inspector Patrick was peering at the murder weapon through a magnifying glass, which he put down as soon as the new evidence arrived.

He drew on white cotton gloves, unwrapped the dagger, and, holding it gingerly, brought the two parts of the *janbia* together. It was clear that they belonged to each other. He then separated the pieces, brushed the dagger's blade and handle with his magic dust, and looked at the dagger through the glass. Then he examined the card with Kwai Libazo's fingerprints on it, and looked back at the sheath again. Over and over.

Once he took off the gloves and put the glass aside, he spent a long time writing his report on the police form. From time to time, he went back and reexamined the sheath and the dagger and then returned to writing.

Kwai stood immobile against the wall, as he had been taught to do, and listened to the pen scratching out Inspector Patrick's words. But all the while, he wished he could take up the glass and peer at the marks on the card and the ones on the dagger and the sheath. He wanted to learn how to read these signs. He thought if he could learn to do that, he would be more powerful than the medicine men of the tribes, who drew their authority from knowing things that other people did not. The medicine men's knowledge did not seem to make them happy men. Most of the ones he had known were very quiet at best, and often cranky. Kwai was certain, though, that if he could learn to read fingerprints, it would bring him joy. The inspector confirmed this by smiling broadly when he looked up from his report.

An askari Kwai did not know knocked and entered. "I have come from the doctor, Inspector, sir," he said. "You can come now and take the fingerprints of the corpse. The doctor requests that you bring the murder weapon to him so that he can confirm that it killed the dead man."

Kwai looked at his fingertips again, still stained a bit by the ink. He knew it could not be true, but something in him vividly imagined that a person's fingerprints would disappear when he died.

Inspector Patrick folded his report and made Libazo extremely happy by not sealing it in an envelope before handing it over. "Take this to Egerton and Tolliver," he said. "Tell them it is preliminary and that I am going to the morgue to take Majidi's prints."

Libazo took the report and saluted. He waited while Patrick placed work tools in a wooden tray, and then put the murder weapon on top of them. Kwai held the door and let the inspector exit first. He followed until the senior man reached the bottom of the stairs. Kwai then climbed to a deserted corner of the top floor and unfolded the report. The inspector's handwriting was very clear and easy to read:

Mombasa, the Protectorate of British East Africa
On the morning of Tuesday, 30 January 1912, Inspector
C. W. Patrick performed fingerprint analysis of
evidence concerning an investigation into the murder
of Khalid Majidi, late of this city.
Conclusions are as follows:

1. The alleged murder weapon, a very large and heavy
black marble box richly inlaid with silver and ivory,

with blood encrusted on one corner—showing prints of only two individuals, at this point identity unknown. One set is suspected to be those of the deceased as the box was in his possession. The other set is assumed to be the prints of the murderer.

2. Sheath of Arabic dagger, recovered from the deceased's place of business in the Mombasa bazaar— fingerprints clearly matching one of the sets on the alleged murder weapon, also likely to be those of the deceased. Also clear fingerprints of Constable #23972, an ignorant askari who mishandled the evidence when it was discovered.

Kwai bristled at the judgment against him. How could he have known what to do and what not to do if no one had ever told him? The British gave themselves excuses when they did wrong things, but they never imagined any explanation but stupidity for people like him. He suppressed a sigh and went on reading the last entry.

3. Blade of matching Arabic dagger, taken to the Fingerprint Department from the police station near Fort Jesus, only clear prints are those of aforesaid Constable #23972 and small prints that appear to be those of a child.

Kwai refolded the report and sped around to the front of the second floor and D.S. Egerton's office, smarting at the thought of having to deliver a report that made him out to be a dolt.

When Tolliver reported to Egerton's office that morning, he expected that the only topic of discussion would be the murder of Khalid Majidi, but Egerton first took up the threat against the Grand Mufti and the role of the bookseller and the other man, the one Kwai had chased into the souk. He had turned out to be the shop owner's nephew.

"I questioned them myself," Egerton said, "with Sergeant Singh as interpreter. The old man told us nothing. It took some effort, but the nephew, in the end, told all." The D.S.'s voice took on a cold edge that disturbed Tolliver. He could imagine what had been contained in "some effort." He did not want to think the D.S. was one of those men who would brutalize an accused to get a confession. He knew those methods were widely employed, but he did not believe they ever produced the truth. He imagined that beatings only caused men to say whatever they thought their assailants wanted to hear.

Egerton went on; his tone had turned ironic. "It seems, for all that the bookseller sits all day in a shop full of religious tracts, according to his nephew, he actually makes his money from the infamous brothel across the way. They were afraid it would be shut down because of the G.M.'s constant religious harangues about stamping out debauchery—the need for greater devotion to the Koran and all that sort of rot."

"Such sermons might be a good thing," Tolliver put in, "if they make the Arabs better behaved. Surely good Mohammedans adhere to the Ten Commandments."

"Not necessarily, old chap," Egerton said. "It seems the G.M.'s idea, when it comes to the whores in the silk shop, is that they should be returned to their fathers to be dealt with. They are Somali girls, you know, and were raised as Muslim women. You know what their male relations are likely to do to them for prostituting themselves."

Tolliver shuddered. He had heard stories when he was in the army about girls who had been found with men. Beheadings! "Surely the bookseller and his nephew did not think they should assassinate the Grand Mufti to stop him preaching."

"Who can tell," Egerton said, less as a question than as a statement of the uselessness of trying to understand such a foreign culture.

"What will the bookseller and his nephew be charged with?"

"I would like to say corrupting the morals of minors. Evidently, according to Singh, most of the girls are only thirteen when they are taken into that place." He threw up his hands. "I can't imagine how we are to handle this without getting the whole town up in arms. They will riot if we try to give British law precedence. They say a girl is of age when she is only twelve. That's to be married off by their male relatives. But still. We can't debate the point now. Our first aim is to keep the G.M. safe and happy and to ensure his support of Britain when he goes home to Cairo. So we jail the bookseller, or the sin-seller, whichever he is, for making a threat. That will keep him on ice until the G.M. goes home."

Egerton seemed satisfied with that solution. Tolliver was considering challenging him on the question of whose laws they were supposed to be enforcing, when Kwai Libazo knocked on the door and entered carrying Patrick's report.

Once both officers had read it, Tolliver spoke first and to Libazo. "Have you the vaguest idea where to find the young scamp who found the knife?"

"Yes, sir. I know exactly where he is."

Egerton looked surprised, but Tolliver knew Libazo was far more capable than Patrick's report made him out to be. "Permission, sir, to go and interrogate the youngster while we wait for further results on the fingerprinting."

"Granted," Egerton said. "In the meanwhile, I will report to District Commissioner Hobson-Jones that we have assured ourselves that the bookseller and his nephew were working alone. If the Commissioner gets grief from the Liwali, it will find its way here." He gave Tolliver a piercing look. "If you take my meaning."

Tolliver took the words for the warning he knew them to be. If a head had to roll, it would be his.

Vera made her way to the Mission by hiring a rickshaw to take her to the floating Nyali Bridge and then walking across, trying to enjoy the sea breeze and to ignore the fact that the wobbly structure seemed to be threatening to pitch her into the drink with every step.

Safe on the mainland end, she fretted instead that she might find neither Robert nor Katharine Morley at home. She had decided to take them by surprise rather than give any warning that she was coming. Absurd as it was that Mr. Morley might be suspected of murder, she wanted to catch any whiff of any guilt when she announced Majidi had been murdered. Her father did not have friends who killed people.

Still, Robert Morley needed to establish an alibi. She fervently hoped he would have a good one. But he must have it ready and tell it calmly. Not fly off the handle, as he was so prone to do.

The path to the Mission through dense vegetation gave her another worry. Upland, one never walked unarmed in wild places where deadly animals could be lurking. She picked up her pace, her glance flitting from side to side, watching for snakes as she went. When she reached the Mission clearing, she was relieved to hear the familiar hymn "Praise God from Whom All Blessings Flow," played on a pedal organ and sung at the top of Katharine's rather nasal voice. Vera understood that nearly all Mission women learned to play hymns so they could provide music for services. She wondered if they all took out their frustrations by playing them over and over again at top volume whenever their nerves were overwrought. She had heard her mother do the same. With her mother, it would have been "Onward, Christian Soldiers" and played with more grandeur and sung with a better sense of pitch than Katharine Morley now exhibited.

Vera moved toward the music and found Katharine in the chapel, a picturesque building—stone halfway up and then open on three sides, with a red tile roof. A profusion of magenta bougainvillea climbed up the sides and hung across the entrance.

Vera took up singing the hymn as she neared. She and Katharine finished it in harmony and then went to the veranda of the house, which was shaded by a lovely mango tree. Katharine ordered tea from the houseboy. They said nothing till it arrived. Katharine looked away, as if she wanted to avoid talking. Vera tried to find the right words to open a conversation, but could not. Everything she thought to say was too shocking. Or not shocking enough. A dog of indeterminate breed came to the step and looked at them but then went to the tree trunk and lay down to scratch its fleas.

Once the boy had delivered the tea tray and withdrawn, Vera forced out the news, choosing her words carefully. "I have something dreadful to tell you."

But Katharine interrupted with a wave of her strong, skinny hand. She lowered her head and kept her voice unusually quiet. "Majidi has been murdered. I know. I was the one who reported it to the police."

Vera gulped. It took her a moment to be able to ask a coherent question. What had Katharine been doing so close to Majidi's shop at the time he was murdered? Had she seen her brother there? "How did that come to be?"

Katharine downed the last of her tea and refilled her cup. She cradled it in both her hands. "You remember what I told you when we met in the bazaar yesterday morning. Well, I was foiled trying to trail Robert then. When I found him gone again in the afternoon, I went straight to Majidi's shop, hoping to get there before Robert did something..."

"Wait a minute," Vera said. "Do you mean you were afraid that—" She couldn't say it—that Katharine suspected her brother was out to kill Majidi, might have actually done it. She stifled that thought. "I came here to warn him," Vera said instead. "I am afraid that the police will...That they will want to question him."

Katharine glanced around, evidently afraid Robert would overhear, but then she gave Vera a determined stare. "I want to question him myself," she whispered through clenched teeth. She finished her second cup of tea and poured herself a third.

"Did you see him at Majidi's shop?"

"When I arrived there, I saw through the glass in the door that the showroom was empty. It was very quiet. I thought the shop might be closed, though there was no sign to that effect on the door. I tried the door. It opened. A bell tinkled. I waited for Majidi to come out. Nothing happened. I called out, but still nothing."

Vera took a sip but her tea had gone cold. She bit her lip. She wanted to urge Katharine on, but she was afraid of what she might learn. Was Katharine not the benign, sisterly person that Robert had always made her out to be in his visits to her father? She seemed almost to want to find him guilty.

"I could not stop myself," Katharine said after a few more sips. "I went snooping to the back and pushed aside the curtain." She looked away as if pained anew by the sight she recollected. She sighed and shook it off. "I must say that it was not as bad as seeing poor Joseph Gautura. That was truly horrible. But Majidi looked..." Her voice trailed off.

"So you went to the police with the news." Vera said it as if she knew it to be true.

"I did not," she said, as if such an action would have been absurd. "I told the boy at the shoe seller's stall to run to the police station near Fort Jesus. And I came directly home, hoping to find Robert here."

Vera could not help asking, "Was he?"

Katharine's eyes betrayed determination and fear. Her pale lashes blinked. "Please never tell this to another soul, Mrs. Tolliver."

Vera nodded her assent. "Call me Vera, please," she said.

"I have never questioned my brother's goodness, but—" The tears overflowed. She drew a handkerchief out of the sleeve of the linen shirtwaist and dabbed her eyes. "Oh, what's the use?" she cried. "I am not sure I know my brother as well as I imagined I did."

Vera waited a second for her to go on. When she did not speak, Vera reassured her: "I came here to try to protect Mr.

Morley, Katharine. My husband has told me that he was very—that he was overwrought after the murder of Joseph Gautura."

"Oh, Vera. You must stop them thinking that Robert killed Majidi. You must." She reached out and grasped Vera's left hand with her right. Her grip was urgent, powerful.

"Where is the Reverend Morley now?" Vera feared the answer.

"That's just it," Katharine said in desperation. "I have no idea."

Tolliver followed the boy and Libazo down a narrow path near the shore of the mainland, across the harbor from Mombasa island. Monkeys chattered overhead, and butterflies flitted around flowering vines that hung from the trees. The air smelled salty with a dank undercurrent of rotting vegetation. A bird cooed somewhere to his left, but he could not see more than a few feet into the dense thicket. The overwhelming beauty of the place did not dispel an air of danger.

"The boy doesn't look like the dirty urchin you described him to be," Tolliver said to Libazo.

"I forced him to take a bath and bought him some decent shorts and a shirt," Libazo said.

"You did so with your own money?" Tolliver blurted out. Libazo had little enough, and Tolliver knew he sent most of what he earned to his mother.

Libazo took no offense. "Yes, sir."

"I see," Tolliver said. And he did. Libazo had taken pity on the child. His sergeant was far more emotional a man than he ever demonstrated on the surface. Kwai had done what Tolliver would have done under the circumstances. And preferred to understate it, as Tolliver would also have done.

"Is he staying somewhere I should know about?" Tolliver asked, suppressing a smile. It was against regulations for askaris to have visitors of any sort in the barracks. And Tolliver knew that Libazo had no friends in the town who would harbor the child for him.

"No, sir, but during the day he does hang about the police lines, polishing shoes and buttons and running errands to earn a few rupees."

Tolliver purposely did not ask where the boy slept. What would be the difference if the men made the orphan a pallet in some corner?

"The boy will behave, sir," Libazo said. "I am seeing to that." He had raised his voice enough to be sure the child heard.

Tolliver winked at Libazo, and then wondered if a police officer of the Protectorate had ever before exchanged such a signal with an askari.

The boy suddenly ducked into the rank, nearly impene-trable undergrowth beside the path. He disappeared under some hanging vines and then emerged on a large mangrove limb that was practically horizontal. A person larger than he would have found it impossible to go where he had gone. "Here is where I found the dagger, sirs. Right here. But the water was up. It goes up and down, you know."

"With the tide." Tolliver had noticed it when he and Vera were staying on the beach. The tides were nothing like they were up in Yorkshire, where they could reach fifteen feet. Here on the equator they were far less dramatic but, depending on the phase of the moon, they did rise and fall a few inches, which could make a difference in these swampy areas. "Why did you go in there?" he called to the boy. He was having serious doubts that the waif had come upon the dagger by accident in such an inac-cessible place.

"Coconuts," the boy called back. He threw out his tiny chest and spoke in a tone that said Tolliver did not grasp a most obvious fact of life. There were indeed palms that stuck above the other vegetation all along this coast. Tolliver had never before thought of them as a source of food.

He looked about him. What was an item as valuable as that dagger doing in a deserted spot like this? He turned to Libazo.

"How sure are we that the child is telling us the truth? Could he not have stolen the dagger from Majidi?"

"I believe he is telling the truth," Libazo said. "It is true that wild boys like him might steal, but it would be very difficult for him to get near enough to an important trader to do so. He described this place to me before we even knew whose *janbia* it was."

"Makes sense," Tolliver said. "But there is nothing around here. Why would Majidi have had any reason to be in an out-of-the-way place like this?"

The boy had come back to the path and stood close beside Libazo. "The holy English people are near here," he said. He pointed through the dense vegetation with his tawny finger.

"Show me," Tolliver said. His skin chilled with the realization that this could be the very path on which the runaway slave was murdered. If Majidi had done it, he might have used his dagger. But then why would he have tossed it into the thicket? It was too costly a thing to throw away.

Tolliver followed the lad along the path. He knew few details of the slave's death, but he did know that the missionary's sister had found the body. She would know if he had been killed with a knife.

"I remember something else, sir," Libazo said. "When I found the boy with the dagger..." His voice trailed off as if there were some guilt attached to the incident.

"Out with it," Tolliver ordered.

"Well, a person there said that if the boy had stolen it, he would have taken the sheath as well." He paused. "Is it not true, sir, that the boy would have taken both? Certainly, the price for both parts would be much more than the price for one."

Libazo's tone made Tolliver curious. "Where exactly did you discover the child in the first place?"

"In the brothel in the souk, sir." If anything, the timbre of Libazo's voice had deepened.

Tolliver was contemplating what could be the meaning of that when they emerged from the path into a clearing that held the Mission grounds, which seemed strangely hidden here. He was about to ask if there was no road between here and the harbor when he was shocked by the sight of his wife sitting on the veranda of the house with another woman, one with flaming red hair. He strode across the patchy lawn to them. He wanted to be angry. But he did not want to cause a scene.

Vera leapt to her feet as soon as she saw him.

"My dear," he said as he approached her, keeping his tone as even as he could. "What are you doing here? I did not expect to see you."

"Nor I you," she said. Her gaze was level.

Tolliver swallowed an exclamation. Dash it, she was hiding something.

Vera indicated her companion. "Katharine, this is my husband, Assistant District Superintendent Justin Tolliver. Justin, dearest, this is Katharine Morley, the sister of my father's dear friend, Robert Morley."

He reached out and briefly clasped the lady's bony hand. "Actually, it was you I came to see, Miss Morley," he said.

He was about to ask her to describe the dead slave's body when Vera said, "Oh, you are here because it was Katharine who first discovered Mr. Majidi's body."

The missionary's sister gasped. Vera's fingers went to her mouth. She looked at Katharine in bewilderment. "Oh, I am sorry," she said. "I thought—I did not know you hadn't—"

But Vera's realization came too late. She had blurted out something that Katharine Morley had wanted to keep from the police.

Justin kept his expression as neutral as he could. "I'm afraid, Miss Morley, that I will have to ask you to come to police head-quarters so that I can get a full report from you."

Vera gave Justin a look she might have reserved for a husband who had just betrayed her. He stifled any reaction to her shock.

He turned back to Katharine Morley. "And is your brother here? I will have to speak to him also."

She held up her head in a way that made her look defiant. "He is from home," she said. "I am sure he is on the Lord's business." From the way she gripped her fists at her waist, though, and the stiffness of her stance, she looked like a woman trying to convince herself.

CHAPTER

10

Once back in Mombasa, Tolliver sat down to interview Katharine Morley about how she came to be in Majidi's shop. She put on a great show of being outraged at any suspicion of her brother, but she failed to disguise the underlying desperation in her voice. She insisted her brother had gone to counsel Majidi to confess to murdering Joseph Gautura. Tolliver did not remark on how patently ridiculous that sounded. Nor did he remind her that she had tripped over all of Mombasa's available corpses in the past three days.

Despite her behavior, Tolliver had trouble imagining that slitting the throat of a runaway slave and bashing an Arab to death were the work of this prudish maiden lady. It seemed clear that she was trying to cover up for her brother.

Tolliver had her sign her statement and reminded her that he needed to see her brother first thing the following morning. He sent her off and went to talk over what he knew with Egerton.

He hated to say it, but Vera's father's faith in his fellow clergyman seemed to have been misplaced. At least that was what the evidence seemed to indicate.

The D.S. had no trouble suspecting that the missionary was a murderous lunatic and that his sister could be his accessory. "I was afraid you would think it impossible that Morley did it, what with his being a missionary chap like your father-in-law. If you ask me, he's half mad."

Tolliver remained silent and let Egerton warm to his subject. "The way the man rants and sputters, it's almost comical. You know what the strong African air can do to people's minds. The poor bloke has been here with little company but his sister's since '04. His mind could very well have turned, given how long he has lived in this heat. His sister's too. Have you seen her?" He did not wait for Tolliver to answer. "The very picture of an eccentric English old maid. I wouldn't be surprised if she goaded him into it. It happens, you know, brother and sister, mother and daughter. A couple of potential loonies living together isolated like that. Half the market towns in England have a pair like them living in some deserted farm on the outskirts."

By the time Tolliver left the D.S.'s office, he had heard Egerton repeat his theory so often he was himself on the verge of believing that Morley and his sister were in it together, that they suffered from some common delirium that made them think they could be the instruments of the Lord's vengeance by killing the slave and claiming Majidi had done it. All very far-fetched, but Tolliver had actually seen some queer behavior among English people, even up in the highlands where the air was not so maddeningly humid.

Much as Tolliver wanted to resist the appalling idea that an Englishman of the cloth and his sister had murdered both Joseph Gautura and Khalid Majidi—and done it in the name of stamping out slavery—he had to admit that the missionary's behavior had never seemed that of an entirely sane man.

And when he had arrived at the Morleys' home, Vera had been sitting on the veranda sipping tea with the man's sister. It would have been natural for her to visit a friend of her family's, but why had she not told him that was what she intended to do?

He refused to consider that his wife might know anything that she had not told him. He would not dignify such an idea by asking her about it. It was patently absurd that she might know one of them to be guilty and not tell him. On the other hand, if she thought them innocent and they were not, she just might insert herself into the investigation in such a way as to queer his chances of discovering exactly what they were up to. Oh, dear lord, he thought, let that not be so.

The sun was going down as he climbed the sandy street up to the bungalow. When he turned, as had become his habit, to look at the sea before going in, there were purple clouds on the horizon and the waves of the ocean glowed with an eerie phosphorescence.

After supper, he and Vera passed the evening playing music. Ordinarily, playing together—he on his cello, she at the piano—brought them closer. But that evening, instead of uniting in their emotions, they played at cross-purposes, unable to synchronize their rhythm—she rushing ahead when he wanted their pace to caress a particularly beautiful passage. When they gave it up as a bad job, Justin did not ask the questions or state the suspicions in his mind, and Vera did not offer explanations or opinions that might have dispelled his worries about her father's friends and what she might know about them.

For her part, Vera wanted to warm the chill between them, but she feared attempting it. It would only bring them back to the same argument they always had—he saying she was too emotional and she saying he was too English. That evening, neither of them had the courage to try to part the curtain that seemed to have fallen between them.

The two slept fitfully. In the wee hours they were both awake, and each knew the other was also. At any previous time, that sleeplessness would have led to a beautiful interlude and ended in happy kisses. As it was, both felt that their love had taken a turn away from its sweet perfection. And both worried that the distrust that had arisen between them could do permanent damage.

❀ ❀ ❀

Early the following morning, when Tolliver arrived at headquarters, he sent an askari to remind Morley that he was expected to come and give a statement.

He then took over a small, vacant office and told the Indian constable at the front desk to direct the Reverend Morley to him as soon as he arrived. He made some notes on the blank sheets before him on the desk, formulating theories about the deaths in this case. No inquiry at all had been made into the death of the slave Joseph Gautura. There were good reasons for that, not the least of which was that His Majesty's government had bigger fish to fry. Justin had agreed with the D.S. about which was the lesser evil: letting that "little" murder go unattended, or getting the Arabs into an uproar during a politically delicate time. Still his conscience niggled at him. The British government ought to stand for justice for *all* under its control. Certainly they had to assert authority. Otherwise, their humanitarian efforts would go nowhere. But what right did the British have to claim the moral high ground if they gave justice only to the powerful?

He had evidence in the fingerprints that Majidi had killed the slave with his dagger. Only his were on the sheath. He must have used the knife on Gautura and then thrown it into the swamp. Or more likely, given its value, had accidentally dropped it on the path in the dark, only to have some animal carry it off. Baboons were prone to picking up bright things. If one had, on finding he could not eat it, he might have flung it away. But then Tolliver immediately thought it was possible that Morley or his sister had stolen the knife. But how, without its sheath? And why would they have tossed it in the swamp? No, there was no way to connect either one of them with the dagger.

And now there was another murder. One that could not be ignored. If it turned out that the missionary had killed the slave owner, there would be hell to pay all around. The Grand Mufti would likely raise a holy ruckus with his fellow Muslims.

A great deal was riding on Tolliver's investigation—including, he thought sadly, Clarence McIntosh's goodwill. And Vera's along with it.

He had found Vera at the Mission the day before. How far might she go to help her father's friend? Tolliver's thoughts froze on that suspicious idea. It was unthinkable. But he could not banish it. To rile him more, he heard the rotund missionary's heavy tread on the stair.

Tolliver did his best to greet the man cordially. He asked him if he would like a cup of tea. Morley, in an obvious huff, refused the tea and sat down so hard that Tolliver feared he would crack the chair.

"I know your superiors think me loud and uncouth," he said without any other greeting. "I care not how you judge me. England, of all the nations of the world, has taken the field against the abominations of slavery. It is only by seemingly rude expressions of concern that the public of Great Britain have come this far in the fight."

It sounded like a rehearsed speech to Tolliver. He gave one in response. "I am well aware that Englishmen have spent blood and a king's ransom in treasure to stamp out slavery, Reverend Morley. But we are here to speak of something entirely different."

The missionary pressed his lips together and glared at the papers on the desk as if they already contained his death warrant.

"I have asked you here," Tolliver said in his most mannerly and formal fashion, "to clear up some of the details in our inquiry into the murders of the runaway slave Joseph Gautura and the ivory trader Khalid Majidi."

Morley still said nothing—merely glanced into Tolliver's eyes and then folded his hands over his protruding belly and sat in glum anticipation, as if he were waiting for a funeral to begin. His pouting lips had a faintly revolting feminine shape.

"I wonder, sir, if you would care to begin by telling me what you know about the death of Khalid Majidi."

Morley raised his eyebrows. "You have ordered me to come here. I am here. It is up to you to ask me a direct question."

All right, thought Tolliver, I didn't expect you were going to make this easy for me. Nor will I make it easy on you. "I have reason to believe that your sister Katharine may be the murderer."

Morley gasped, just as Tolliver had hoped he would. The man could not have been more shocked if a mortar round had hit the room. He opened and closed his mouth several times. Tolliver waited a few beats and then followed up. "I must ask you your sister's whereabouts during the night when Gautura was killed and also on the afternoon when Majidi was murdered."

Tolliver then sat very still and waited, letting the silence make the man uneasy, watching him fidget and sigh until the tension force him to speak. When he did, he was loud and indignant. "You are mad to think my sister capable of murder. This is insanity. I shall report you for having lost your mind, young man." He began to rise from his chair.

"Please sit down, Mr. Morley," Tolliver said firmly. "I assure you that any complaint you might make to my superiors will go entirely unheeded." Given Morley's experience of being ignored by the authorities, Tolliver was counting on his statement to further rile the missionary.

The older man's mouth resumed its imitation of a fish in a bowl. He half rose out of his chair again and then sat back down, defeated at last.

"Very well," Tolliver said, claiming victory. "Why don't you just tell me what you know? If I am entirely in the wrong, can you prove me so?" When Morley did not fuss any further, Tolliver pressed his question. "Kindly tell me where your sister was on the night Joseph Gautura was killed."

"In her bedroom fast asleep." The missionary had taken on a distinctly sanctimonious air.

"You know that for a fact?"

"Yes, of course. It is where she has been every single midnight of her life." Morley was obviously still shaken, but he was trying very hard to get the upper hand.

Tolliver put him back on edge. "You saw her there yourself? Entered her bedroom and made sure of her whereabouts?"

"How dare…how *dare* you?" The missionary was out of his chair in a second, sputtering with outrage as if Tolliver had out-and-out accused him of incest.

Tolliver did not try to calm him. Riled up was how he wanted the man. The more emotionally distraught he became the more he would reveal. "I see," Justin said, uncapped his pen, and pretended to make a note. "So you assume that she was in her bed though you did not actually see her there? You were, I take it, in your own bed that night?"

Morley's hard, dark little eyes flickered away from Tolliver's stare—a good indication that he was about to hide the truth. "Where else would I be?" He settled back into the chair, feigning calm.

"Where indeed? And yesterday? You were in the bazaar yesterday, were you not?" Tolliver did not know this for certain, but he said it as if he had seen Morley there with his own eyes. "You were there when your sister went to Majidi's shop?"

"I was not with her, no." He spoke quietly now, as if he understood that, on some level, he had no choice but to acquiesce.

Tolliver waited. He did not believe that Katharine Morley had killed Gautura or Majidi. But he was about to get what he really wanted out of this conversation: the truth about Robert Morley's whereabouts at the times of the murders.

"I cannot vouch for where my sister was."

"Why is that, sir?"

Morley slumped against the back of his chair. "I suppose I have to tell you where I was."

"That would be best."

"I cannot believe that my sister killed either of those men."

"Your telling the truth will be the quickest way of dispelling any suspicion of her."

Morley looked longingly at the window, as if he wanted to turn into a bird and fly out of it. Then he stared up into the corner of the room. "I have—" He paused and glanced into Tolliver's eyes for a moment. "Can we keep this between us? I would not wish my sister to learn this."

Tolliver folded his hands on the desk in front of him. "As long as it is not evidence needed to convict a criminal, I will keep your confidence," he said.

The defeated clergyman looked back into the corner. "I have—ah—formed an attachment to a—to a native woman." He looked into Tolliver's eyes, begging for understanding.

Tolliver was not sure how successfully he hid his sympathy for the man. The chances of an Englishman finding a suitable spouse this far from home were next to nil. Morley was not an attractive man, but that did not mean that he lacked a man's appetites and desires. "So you were visiting that lady?"

Tears welled up in the reverend's eyes. "You are right to call her a lady, for so she is." He sniffled and drew out a handkerchief. Tolliver waited while Morley regained control. "She is about to have a child." Once those words were out, he lost all control of himself.

Tolliver stood and walked to the window, giving the missionary time to recover himself. Whatever else he was learning, he was becoming convinced that Robert Morley was not the murderer. Not of Joseph Gautura and not of Majidi. It did not seem that a missionary who could perform such an act would be so filled with remorse for having got a native woman with child. Tolliver hoped that his belief was wholly the result of a good detective's instincts and not wishful thinking on his part.

Morley blew his nose and then spoke. "I do not think it at all possible that my sister had anything to do with those killings. Do you have any proof that she had? Tell me she had not."

Tolliver retook his seat. The missionary looked wary, as if he feared that Tolliver might say yes: more evidence that he most likely had not committed the acts himself. "I do not believe so, sir. But you must see how critical it is for me to find the murderer and bring him to justice. An important Arab has been murdered at a very sensitive moment. The whole community here might explode in violence if we do not give them satisfaction in this matter. We are here to show that British justice is true justice."

"Dear God! What can I do?"

A knock at the door interrupted. Morley's mouth clamped shut.

"Come," Tolliver called.

Libazo came in and handed over Patrick's latest report. Tolliver scanned it. "Not conclusive, but certainly allows us to draw conclusions," he said to no one in particular.

Robert Morley stood up and took a deep breath. "Do you know about Joseph Gautura's kinsman Juba Osi?"

Tolliver, distracted by the report in his hand, had to ask the missionary to repeat what he had said.

"Joseph Gautura has…had a kinsman living here in Mombasa. An ex-slave named Juba Osi. Isn't it possible he will know something that will lead you to the real murderer?"

Tolliver capped his pen and laid it on the papers on the desk. "Thank you for the information about Juba Osi. I will continue my investigation," he told Morley. "For the time being, you may go."

Morley looked up at Libazo, who might have been part of the woodwork for all he reacted. The missionary coughed and said, "You will not speak to Mrs. Tolliver of—"

Tolliver held up his hand. "For now, what you have just told me need not be revealed to anyone," he said.

Tolliver followed Morley into the hallway. For the first time since they had met, he saw the reverend descend the stairs and leave the building without a single angry word.

He picked up Patrick's report and turned to Libazo. "Please send a couple of constables to find this Juba Osi right away. I am going to bring this report to D.S. Egerton in person."

When Tolliver reported the scientific evidence in the case to the district superintendent, he found Egerton's response almost dismissive. "You believe then that the fingerprints tell you something important even though Patrick says they are not conclusive?"

ANNAMARIA ALFIERI

"Yes, sir, at least insofar as they corroborate that Majidi killed the slave. His and Libazo's were the only fingerprints on the sheath found in his drawer. He must have put it there. Only Libazo's and the boy's were on the dagger itself. It is true that the boy said he wiped off the handle before he took the dagger to the brothel." He held up the report. "Dr. Sutton says Gautura's throat was very likely slit with just such an instrument. I suppose there could have been a third person who used the dagger after it was taken from the sheath, but it seems highly unlikely that anyone would have carried a knife that sharp all that distance to the Mission without its sheath. Taken all together, I think we can safely conclude that in actuality it was Majidi who used his dagger to slit the throat of his runaway slave. Having done that, he threw the knife into the swamp or lost it along the way, but took the sheath back and kept it for the precious stones that were in it. It's the only scenario that explains all the facts."

Tolliver thought he had made the case very convincingly. He therefore could not understand why the D.S. continued to frown.

As if he had read the question in Tolliver's mind, Egerton explained: "Are you sure you are not trying to take the side of your father-in-law's friend?"

The implication of prejudice miffed Tolliver, but he held his temper and spoke respectfully. "No, sir. I mean, I am sure, sir. My conclusion has nothing to do with my family's position. The facts point only to Majidi as the murderer of the slave."

"It could not have been the boy? Could he not have stolen the dagger without the sheath, wrapped it up, and carried it to the spot and..." His voice trailed off.

Tolliver held his tongue. Egerton had not seen how skinny and small the child was, even for a nine-year-old, but evidently he understood that it was absurd to think a youngster could have reached up and slit the throat of a tall, fit adult.

"Your sergeant found the boy trying to sell the dagger. What was one of our askaris doing in that brothel in first place? Some of these native policemen are not much more than criminals themselves, in my experience. We have caught them at all sorts of mischief. And worse."

Tolliver wanted to turn his body to stone as the only way to hide his outrage. How could Egerton accuse Kwai of—of he did not know what. Libazo was twice the policeman those Indian imports that Egerton considered the backbone of the force were.

Tolliver swallowed hard. "Perhaps, sir, we should put aside my theory about the slave's death for the time being and concentrate on finding out who killed Majidi. Perhaps when we know that, we will have a definitive answer to the other question."

When Egerton made no reply, Tolliver went on. "That marble cask is definitely the weapon used to kill Majidi. According to Patrick, there are two sets of prints on it. Most are Majidi's own. The placement of the others is consistent with someone picking it up and holding it in such a way as to bash in Majidi's head. There is only one curious thing about the prints."

Egerton's curiosity was piqued. "Which is?"

"Patrick is not sure they are a man's fingerprints."

"A woman's?" Egerton looked stunned at first, but then said, "I suppose it could be. Those Arab women are so ill-treated. One of them might have sought revenge."

Relieved that Egerton had not immediately leapt to suspecting Katharine Morley, Tolliver emphasized the dubious nature of the evidence. "As I said, Patrick is not sure. They *could* be a woman's, but they are much more likely to be a man's, depending on the man. One whose fingers are much smaller than the typical Englishman's. The greatest percentage of murders, by far, are committed by men, especially the violent murders. And this one was exceptionally so."

Egerton stood up. Tolliver had no choice but to do the same. "Very well," Egerton said. "You will have to pursue all possibilities. For now, I have another assignment for you. I have heard from the G.M. that he wants to say something about the murder of Majidi. I want you to go and take his statement." He picked up a pen and took a slip of paper from a leather tray on his desk and wrote something on it. "Here is the address where he is staying.

It's the Liwali's house. It's at the harbor end of da Gama Road, just past the African Hotel."

Tolliver reached for the paper.

Egerton held it back. "And while you are there you will not say anything to anyone about Majidi having murdered the blackie. Do you understand?"

"Of course I won't, sir." It galled him that Egerton thought he needed to be reminded of such a thing.

"Not a word," Egerton said. "You will only stir up trouble with your theories. I will not have trouble."

"No, sir. You will not."

Egerton gave Tolliver a rather arch look but said, "Get on with it then," and handed over the address.

Tolliver read it, stuffed it into his breast pocket, and made a smart about-face. He had barely taken a step down the stairs when the question hit him. Why was Egerton sending him to take the Grand Mufti's statement? If it was so important and delicate a matter, why wasn't the district superintendent going himself?

CHAPTER

11

On the pretext of beginning his search for Juba Osi, Kwai Libazo went to the bazaar, but once he was there, he made straight for the silk shop and Aurala Sagal. He found her actually cutting a length of fabric off a bolt and selling it to a Somali man in a white *kanzu* and a white embroidered hat very like the orange one the bookshop owner's nephew had worn when he escaped from the court building.

When the customer had taken his change and his package and left, Aurala turned her beautiful eyes on Kwai. "So, Sergeant Libazo, you have come back to visit me." This time she did not say his name very loudly as if to warn someone behind the curtain. She seemed to be speaking just to him.

He had tried to plan what he would say to her. He wanted to tell her she was beautiful. But he did not want her to think he was just saying that because he wanted to make sex with her. He had changed his planned speech with every step he had taken on the way. There was no way to politely ask what he really wanted to know—how she felt about what she did for money, so he spoke of something else. "I have to find an man named Juba Osi." The words fell from his lips. They made him feel stupid. She made him feel stupid. He had not ever thought he would have accepted feeling stupid. Until now.

"Do you think he could be here?"

"Not here, but perhaps someone in the souk can tell me where to search."

"Do you know what work he does?"

"I know nothing about him except that he is a kinsman of Joseph Gautura, the one who was a household slave of Majidi."

At the mention of Majidi's name, a look of terror passed through her eyes. They darted to her left and right. She turned and looked at the bookseller's shop behind her. The door was still locked. There was a sign on the door in Arabic that Kwai could not read.

Libazo pointed to it. "That man—" he started to say.

"Let us not talk of all these men," she said. She put her finger to his lips.

Her touch overwhelmed his thoughts. He could not talk of anything. He did not care about anything but her. He took her hand in both of his and kissed it.

She brought her lips close to his ear and whispered, "Do not speak here. Can you come inside with me?"

He should not do so, and he knew it. He wanted her, but not in the way of men who came to a place like this. He wanted to walk down the street with her, to find her at the end of every day.

She whispered to him again. As she leaned toward him, he caught the scent of her hair, which smelled like a fruit he had never tasted. "I want to tell you something about the dead man, but it is dangerous for me to be seen speaking it to you here."

He looked around. No one was near enough or taking any notice of them. Still, she was frightened of people unseen. He followed her into the silk shop, refusing even to think of the other name that men used to describe the place.

The Liwali's residence was in an ancient Arab building near the customs godowns on Vasco da Gama Road, across from a sadly neglected ancient cemetery. Its entrance was more attractive than the others along the narrow street, but not ostentatious. The front door was of teak carved with a cunning basket-weave pattern that was matched by the design chiseled into the stone lintel above it. Typical of buildings thereabouts, a balcony on the second floor overhung the entrance and gave the added benefit of a patch of shade for the arriving visitor. There was an old covered well across the way. Its base was a square of marble carved with vines and flowers, giving an air of ancient grace to everything around it.

As Tolliver approached, the Liwali's door opened before he had a chance to pull the cord for the bell. After the modest look of the façade, the elegant attire of the man who greeted him and the rich décor of the entry hall surprised him. The doorkeeper was tall and slender and sported a black beard, trimmed to a perfect point. It seemed as if all the Arab servants in Mombasa were appointed for their good looks. This one was dressed in loose white trousers and a golden silk jacket that came down to his knees; it was trimmed with silver braid and matched his fez. The inevitable dagger was tucked into his sash. He bowed and asked the blessings of Allah on Tolliver, who removed his sun helmet, bowed in turn, gave his name, and stated his business.

"Be pleased to follow me," the man said in English. He led Tolliver into a hallway and through to a lush interior garden that smelled of orange blossoms. A carved stone fountain in the center gave it a moist and musical atmosphere. It felt ten degrees cooler here than out in the road.

Down another hallway, they entered a small room exquisitely tiled in floral and geometric patterns in subtle colors. There was a frieze just below its domed ceiling with writing in Arabic that went right around the room.

The man in gold indicated a settee of ebony, upholstered in horsehair nearly as black as the wood. "Be pleased to sit and wait," he said, before exiting through a carved sandalwood door. Tolliver was pleased to sit and wait and admire the decoration and contemplate the fact that nothing one saw from the street prepared one for the size, the opulence, the elegance of this palace.

He was barely over being awestruck when the door opened and the Liwali himself invited him into the next room—a large salon with pure white walls, furnished with heavy, intricately carved ebony furniture like the settee Tolliver had just left, but here upholstered in red and gold. A matching carpet covered the center of the tile floor.

The ever-courtly Grand Mufti occupied an armchair at the opposite end of the room, which was twice as long as it was wide. Like all his fellow Orientals, he wore his headgear indoors—the same conical hat he had sported on his arrival. It sat on his head like a crown. He spoke in a language Tolliver did not understand.

The Liwali invited Tolliver to sit and explained that the Grand Mufti did not speak English but had important things to tell the British police about the death of Khalid Majidi.

Tolliver wondered then if he could trust the Liwali to properly report what he and the Grand Mufti were saying. Since he had no choice but to comply, he felt he must have a record of what was said in English. "Do you mind if I take notes?" he asked.

"Not at all," the Liwali said. He snapped his fingers and signaled to an attendant standing with his arms crossed next to the door. The servant placed a small table in front of Tolliver, who opened the dispatch case he had been carrying and took out paper and pen.

At once, a rush of words issued from the Grand Mufti. He looked at Tolliver while he spoke. He was a light-skinned man. As the little girl on the ship had said, his features were very like those in a drawing of Father Christmas, but his expression was not at all jolly. More worried and fatigued than any Santa Claus. Tolliver imagined that the long sermons he had been giving and all the events in his honor—morning, noon, and night—had exhausted the man.

The Liwali sat near Tolliver. He was a stout man, handsome, with a gray beard, but no mustache. His most impressive feature was the brightness of his green eyes, flecked with gold, which contrasted with his dark skin. Their effect was enhanced by the green and gold of his coat, his sash, and the cloth wrapped around his head. His jewel-encrusted sword clanked against the chair as he sat down. "The Grand Mufti wants to assure the British Administration that he is aware of their care during his visit. He very much appreciates the King of England's desire that his visit to Mombasa be a peaceful one. These are concerns that he much welcomes."

Tolliver wondered again why some official higher up than he had not come to this meeting. From the drift of the discourse, these were words that should have been spoken to the provincial commissioner, if not to the high commissioner himself. "His Majesty's government is taking every care to ensure the Grand Mufti's safety and comfort," Tolliver said, feeling like a fraud of a diplomat and wishing he had been left to his duties as a minor police official.

The Liwali responded without translating Tolliver's message. "The Grand Mufti understands this. It is why he is speaking to the officer in charge of the investigation into the death of Khalid Majidi. He wants to tell you there is no danger at all of being any trouble because of Majidi's death."

This statement stunned Tolliver. Now he was certain that he was the wrong person to be representing his country at this meeting. Not knowing what would be a proper response, he wrote down a close approximation of Liwali's exact words, including the rather quaint English. Then he said, "I will report this to my superiors." He started to recap his pen.

The Liwali patted the air between them in a gesture he must have meant to be comforting. It did not quell Tolliver's misgivings. "The Grand Mufti wants tell His Majesty's government," the Liwali went on, "that Khalid Majidi was not a true follower of the Holy Prophet. He was not a good man. It is not necessary for the British police to find his murderer."

Another stunning thing for these people to be saying. Tolliver was sure Egerton had had no idea of the gravity of the subject these men had meant to discuss. If the D.S. had had any inkling of the delicacy of the situation, he was insane not to have sent a diplomat.

Tolliver looked at the G.M., who seemed to be following the conversation. Was he feigning an inability to speak English? He said something to the Liwali, who answered in whatever language they were using. After a brief exchange, the Liwali turned back to Tolliver. "The Grand Mufti believes it is appropriate for me to report to you that Majidi has broken British law. He did this in such a bad way, you should erase any need to investigate his murder."

Tolliver nearly blurted his misgivings about why they were telling this to a person as unimportant as he. "In what way has Majidi broken the law?" he asked instead.

"Majidi was guilty of some grave acts."

Tolliver found the answer vague and said so as politely as he could.

The Liwali gave him a knowing look but offered only another cryptic answer. "His business dealings were unseemly."

Tolliver wanted to be polite, but he needed a clear statement. "Please, sir," he said. "It would be best to be blunt."

The Liwali raised his eyebrows and looked into Tolliver's eyes. "Very well then. To put it bluntly, Majidi trafficked in whores."

The askari who came to Vera with a message found her in the garden, covered in dirt, working with Frederick Dingle to rescue some Cape moonflower plants that the garden workers were about to pull up as weeds. The note the native policeman handed her was from Justin inviting her to dine with him at the club. *There is a ladies' dinner tonight*, it said, *and we have something special to celebrate. Meet me in front of the tramway office at six.*

She barely had time to bathe, scrub the mud from under her fingernails, and get into an appropriate frock. She donned Justin's favorite—a silk dress of ivory, pale green, and dusty rose in a flower print. And the sweet strand of graduated pearls he had bought for her in Rome. She wondered if the *something special to celebrate* would be a way for him to make it up with her. He had been angry that she had gone to the Mission. He had sensed immediately that she was involving herself in something he thought she must stay clear of. They ought to have talked it through, had it out, she thought, not for the first time. But he never would. And whenever she insisted, it turned into an all-out row with his saying, *Why must you always insist on talking and talking. It just brings on a spat and bad feelings.*

So she had not insisted on discussing the matter. Instead, their instruments had argued their way through the Schubert, and they had gone to bed without a proper good night. Now he was expecting her to go on as if nothing had happened.

And she would.

She hired a public trolley at the end of MacDonald Terrace and arrived less than ten minutes late.

The terrace of the club overlooked the sea and English Point on the mainland. It was crowded with the usual group—members of the British government, prosperous men in trade and their wives, settlers either on their way up-country or here in the port ready to embark for England and home leave.

The cool sea breezes raised the spirits of the crowd almost as much as the gin and quinine water they took for "medicinal purposes." Justin and Vera carried their drinks to the balustrade overlooking the ocean. Red clouds, reflecting the setting sun, hung over the horizon. From the citadel flew the Sultan of Zanzibar's scarlet ensign, a reminder to the denizens of the Europeans-only club that they were there by leave of an Arab potentate.

Justin pointed to it and described for Vera his visit that afternoon to the Liwali's palace. "It is truly elegant, dearest, everything bright and beautifully arranged. Lovely colors. I am certain there is not an Englishman's residence in the entire Protectorate to equal it. I wish you could have seen it."

She smiled up at him. How could she not forgive him his Englishness? But she could tease him. "Perhaps I *will* learn to speak Arabic. Then the Liwali can invite me to tea, and I can see for myself," she said with a impish grin.

He caressed her cheek. "If any woman can do that," he said, "I am sure it would be you."

She took his hand and squeezed it. "Now tell me about this wonderful surprise we are celebrating."

"Let's take a table in the dining room, and I'll order some champagne."

"Champagne! Delighted, I'm sure." She threaded her arm through his as they made their slow way through the knot of drinkers at the bar and found a quiet table in a corner.

When the wine was poured, Justin lifted his glass. "I raise a toast to a stroke of good fortune, You are married to a wealthy man, my dear. I have received a reward of five hundred pounds."

She was too astonished to drink. It would take him two years working as an A.D.S. to earn as much. "Whatever for?"

"Capturing murderers."

Her jaw dropped. "Majidi's?"

"No, no. These were men I arrested in Nairobi, last year. They were shooting up the bar in the Masonic Hotel. After they had served six months in da Gama's great pile of rocks next door, we shipped them back to Johannesburg, where—it turned out—there was a price on their heads. The reward and a commendation arrived here with today's dispatches."

She clinked glasses with him. "My hero," she said, with a giggle. "Does this mean I can increase my spending on plants for the garden?"

"Yes, but no more than fifteen shillings," he said, his eyes laughing. "It is Crown property we occupy there. If His Majesty wants it to be beautiful, he can do it with his own money."

Vera asked what the Grand Mufti was like and what he had had to say.

"I do want to talk to you about it," Justin said, suddenly more serious. "I have not yet reported it to Egerton and..." He leaned across toward her and dropped his voice to a whisper. "I am not at all sure I want to tell him the whole story."

She found this at once thrilling and frightening. "Tell it to me."

He paused while the waiter put down their food. The roast beef smelled delicious. He tucked in and for a few moments their talk was postponed.

A large group of German men had taken a long table nearby. Like many of their ilk, they kept to themselves and spoke their own language. Soon their hearty conversation obscured what Justin and Vera were saying to each other from any others in the room. "There was something very odd about it," Justin said. "The Grand Mufti and the Liwali told me there will be no Arab outrage over the murder of Majidi. That he was not as highly thought of in their community as we British thought. That we need not bother to investigate his death. He owned the brothel in the souk. They seem happy that someone did away with him. But I do not think that they were telling me the whole story of his crimes. They seemed to be keeping back more than they said."

"It would not be the first time that your instincts were right in such a way."

"I knew you would understand. I have the strongest suspicion that the whole thing was staged just to call off the dogs. And that I am the dog. When I was with them, I kept wondering why they wanted to tell this to me and not to someone higher up. Now I am convinced that not only the Liwali, but Egerton as well would prefer that I drop the whole question."

"If I know you, you won't." She wished as much as believed it to be true. Her Justin would insist that justice be served. And like hers, his curiosity would beg to be satisfied. She thought to tell him something that he might not know. "Do you remember that man with the drooping mustache from the ship?"

"Yes. I met him shortly afterward at the club one afternoon. Hastings is his name."

"Yes, that is he. He had dealings with Majidi." She knew she was putting herself in the way of Justin's disapproval, but it was too important not to tell him what she knew and how she knew it.

"How do you know this?" His voice was edged with accusation, as she had known it would be.

She looked away and lowered her voice. "After Joseph Gautura's death, I went to see if I could pry information from Majidi. Hastings was there." Justin looked as if he were about to forget his Englishness and shout at her in public. She bit her lip and bore Justin's shocked and scolding expression. "I knew you would not approve." She took in a quick breath. Before he had a chance to say anything, she held up her palms. "Darling, please do not look so hateful. I never saw Majidi." She paused to let it sink in. "Really. I never entered his shop. But I think what I learned may be important. I encountered Hastings as I approached the door. He came out muttering under his breath. He cursed Majidi."

"My dearest darling," Justin said in that patient, restrained tone that she tried to accept as a dutiful wife should. She could only resent it. She bit on her bottom lip and with effort heard him out. "You know how much I admire your pluck," he went on, "but you are not just some adventurous girl now. You are my wife. You must not—"

She reached for his hand to stop his condescension. It silenced him, but she read his thoughts in his eyes. He loved her for her spirit, but...He admired her pluck, *but*...There was always that *but*... How could he expect her to be both of the people he wanted her to be?

In the end, he patted her hand and smiled more or less forgivingly. "Hastings is likely to be here somewhere at this hour. Would you excuse me for a moment? I'll try to speak to him. Signal the waiter and order me the trifle for pudding. I'll be back in a moment."

It pleased her that, at the very least, given a choice between haranguing her and accepting her information, he was off now to find Hastings.

The waiter was just bringing the sweets when Justin returned, looking quite triumphant. "I found Hastings. He is coming to meet with me in the morning," he said.

Her pleasure faded. She wanted him to credit her for having given him a critical piece of information. She wanted to be his heroine as much as he wanted to be her hero. But this world was not made that way. Lady Vera, wife of an Earl's son, was supposed to take her happiness from her husband's accomplishments and be glad that he loved her. She was proud to be his wife. She wanted that to be enough. She wished it could be. *I'll get used to it*, she told herself. *I will.*

Once they had finished their meal, he cheered her by refusing Bishop Peel's offer of a ride up the hill in his trolley with him and his two grown daughters. That saved Vera having to pretend to be British with the proper Peel girls.

"Thank you very much, my Lord," Justin said. "We do enjoy stretching our legs in the cool of the evening."

They saw the bishop and his family off, propelled home by his trolley boys in white twill uniforms trimmed with the prelate's signature magenta.

Vera and Justin went hand in hand up the sandy street. The gibbous moon shone on the huge mango and baobab trees in front of the cathedral at the top of the hill. She always felt like a little girl when they walked like this; he was so much taller than she. She let go of his hand and pulled his arm across her shoulder, feeling sheltered with his body near. She loved him so. "I feel I have to tell you something else," she said very gently. "Something that feels like a betrayal."

He stopped and turned her so that the moonlight was on her face. He looked into her eyes. She held his gaze. He kissed the top of her head, and they continued up the hill. "Okay, out with it, you minx."

She let out a sigh. "Katharine Morley suspects her brother of Majidi's murder." She spat out the words and then gulped in some air. "She says he has been acting very suspiciously of late."

"He is not the killer," Justin said.

He seemed so definite about it that she was taken aback. "You know this for certain?"

"He made a statement to me that explained his whereabouts."

"Where was—" She didn't complete the sentence. She guessed the truth. "He was someplace else, someplace disgraceful for a missionary to be. He could not tell Katharine."

His arm across her shoulder stiffened. "I have told you enough to set your heart at ease. I cannot reveal what he told me. It would…"

She squeezed his hand. "You are my man of honor," she said. Her heart was full of him. "Remember when you told me about the conflict between being a gentleman and being a policeman? It is happening for you again, isn't it?"

He stopped and held her. She raised her face to him and accepted his soft, delicious kiss. He took her breath away.

She nestled her head against his chest. "I have changed," he said as if he were confessing a fault. "I have felt it keenly since we returned. I am duty bound to do certain things, but I cannot think of doing only my duty. I came into the police force thinking that serving justice and serving King and Country were the same thing. How naïve I was. I no longer care to adhere to the letter of the law. I will keep my word and see out my time here, but on my own terms. I am not sure what I will tell Egerton in the morning, but it will not be everything, not anymore. He despises Morley. But I mean to protect Morley as far as I think he deserves it. If the officials of the realm can compromise with the letter of the law, so can I."

They stood in the shadows at their garden gate, embracing. She felt it then. *This* was the reason she wanted him off the force. Because her Justin was not a man to follow rules, British rules, when they meant that iniquity rather than justice would be served. A picture fell into her head of their tossing his uniform onto a bonfire. "Oh, my darling, my darling," she whispered.

He kissed her. The sky above them was full of stars.

CHAPTER

12

In the cool of the following morning, with a few of the brightest stars still visible over the town, Justin Tolliver left home. Invigorated by the almost cool air, he jogged to the police barracks, where he asked the askari on duty at the desk to wake up Kwai Libazo.

As Tolliver expected, the boy Haki appeared when Kwai did, which meant he was living there—against all regulations. It pleased Tolliver that what he had said to Vera the night before was true. He no longer felt obliged to put a stop to Libazo's kindness to the child just because British rules said he should. Instead, he gave the boy a coin and sent him off to find some breakfast.

"We need to go to the bazaar," Tolliver said.

The look on Kwai's face was like nothing Tolliver had ever seen there. His breathing quickened as if he were the one who had been running. But "Yes, sir," was all he said.

Tolliver remembered that Libazo had resented something Abrik Singh had said about the brothel. And that he had found the Arab dagger there. Whatever was going on, Tolliver hoped that Libazo had not taken up with one of the prostitutes.

It was fully light by the time they approached the souk. Along the way, Kwai had said nothing. His mind was full of what had passed between him and Aurala in that room of draped green silk the day before.

He had gone to her and let her take him into the room. Whatever else he thought, he could not stop himself from making sex with her. If he had to pay her, he would. He was sorry for the way he had been dressed. He had wanted to go to her for the first time in his Kikuyu *shuka*, not in his uniform. But once she was in his arms, no other thoughts were possible.

Afterward, he had poured out his questions to her. "Why are you doing this? You are too beautiful to be doing this."

She had touched his face, lightly, with what seemed like real affection. "You are not the first man to say that."

He looked away. "I do not want to have to buy your time." He struggled to keep the accusation out of his voice. The whole business confused him. If he were just a Kikuyu or Maasai tribesman and she just a girl, the custom would be for him to buy her from her father in exchange for goats or cattle. Was paying to be with her here so different from paying to have her as his wife? But he knew it was, because if he had bought her from her father, she would be his and only his and that was what he wanted her to be.

She had risen up and sat cross-legged beside him. "Up in Somalia, my sister was taken away by bad men," she said. "People told me that they had taken her to Mombasa. I ran away to find her. She was my only friend. It is—" She had stopped and studied him for a moment. "Why do you want to know this?" she had asked.

There was only one answer. And he did not know how to give it. A tribal girl would expect him to buy her from her father for cows and goats. A British girl would expect him to ask her father's permission and to take money along with the girl. He had no idea what a Somali girl's family would expect him to do. But he and Aurala were no longer part of any such family. They were alone in this world. Except for each other. "Because I want you to be my wife," he said before he knew he was going to.

Tears came into her eyes. "You are in earnest, aren't you?"

He took her hands in his. Her fingers were long and beautiful, like everything else about her. "Yes," he said. "I am in earnest."

She seemed confused. But then her eyes registered realization. "This is about Majidi, isn't it?" she demanded, shocking him.

"The dead man? No. Why would you think that?"

"What other reason could there be for you to say you want to marry me?"

Her words made him angry. "You don't see me," he said with more heat in his voice than he intended. "I am not the sort of man who would say such a thing to get information. I am a man who wants to be yours. Who wants you to be his. That is all. Will you or won't you?"

She had looked at him for a long time, gazing into his eyes as if she were reading a book, and then putting her hand on his chest.

Her face had been grave when she finally spoke. "You must wait and let me ask some questions of my sister. We will talk of this again another day." And then she had made love to him again, and she had wept when it was over.

She had not taken any money from him. Before he left she had given him one of the bracelets from her arm. He had it now in the left breast pocket of his uniform shirt, and here he was, arriving at the bazaar with Tolliver.

It was very quiet. A few of the Hindu Indian stalls were open for business, but the Muslims were all in their mosques, because today was Friday, their holy day.

When Kwai spoke for the first time that morning, he reminded Tolliver that the place where they were going was run by Somali women and that it might be closed.

"I don't think they stop work in brothels for religious reasons." Tolliver laughed, but the look Kwai gave him dissolved his glee.

The rear of the market was very quiet. The bookstall was still locked. The door to the brothel was closed, but a single electric lightbulb burned before its entrance. Tolliver rapped on the door and within seconds both Leylo and Aurala Sagal came to let them in. Aurala Sagal confirmed Tolliver's fears by going immediately to Kwai Libazo's side and taking his hand. She was almost as tall as he, elegant and seductive in a way he was sure Kwai found irresistible.

"We are here to ask you some questions," Tolliver said to the older of the two.

Leylo bowed. "My sister wants to tell you what she knows," she said. Her stance was stiff, as if she were trying to be brave, but her voice shook. "I think that she is going to be killed if she speaks the truth to you. I think I will be killed too, even if I do not speak the truth to you. The people who don't want you to know the truth are dangerous to us. They know where we come from. They have warned us that if we give testimony, they will tell our father where to find us. He will send our brothers to kill us for what we have been doing here."

Libazo further astonished Tolliver by protesting, "But you were brought here against your will. Why would your father punish you, and not the men who stole you and brought you to this place?"

"It is the way of our people," Aurala said. "The only way the men of our family can restore their honor after what we have done is to kill us." It was impossible to know if she herself believed in that code of honor. It was only clear that she knew it was inescapable.

"Unbelievable!" The word slipped out of Libazo's mouth.

It made no more sense to Tolliver than it did to Libazo. "No one saw us come in," Tolliver said. "Take us in the back and talk to us out of sight. We will do everything we can to keep it a secret that you have given evidence."

When Leylo moved toward the room draped in green, Aurala objected and parted the red curtains farther on. "In here is better," she said. She was still holding Libazo by the hand. They sat side by side on the bed. Leylo drew a chair forward from the corner of the room for Tolliver. She refused to sit.

"Someone has reported," Tolliver said, "that the man behind this—this operation, is—ah, was Khalid Majidi. But I have also been told that it was the bookseller across the way, the one whose nephew threatened the Grand Mufti, that he is the real owner. Please tell me which of these is the truth."

Leylo Sagal fidgeted but did not answer.

"Majidi is dead," Aurala said, looking sharply at her sister.

"You must speak if you can," Leylo answered. "I am too afraid." She went into the corner and kept her back to them.

Tolliver knew that he should insist on her giving her own statement, but he could not bring himself to force such a thing from a woman so terrified.

She was moving slowly toward the opening in the drapery.

"You may go for now if you promise to wait outside," Tolliver said.

"I will not go far from my sister," Leylo answered quietly.

Tolliver nodded his assent.

Aurala looked after her with the look of child being abandoned by its mother. Her hand tightened on Libazo's; he covered it with his other hand. Tolliver thought how his sergeant had been in Mombasa for such a short time, and wondered what could have passed between the two of them in so short a time to endear them so profoundly to each other. But being a man in love himself, Tolliver was sure he knew.

"How old are you?" He had no idea why that was the first question that dropped from his lips.

"I am fifteen," she said. She straightened her back as if to make herself taller, older.

"Please tell me what you know about the question of the bookseller and Majidi."

"The bookseller tries to be known as the owner of us," she said. Her eyes were downcast as if she were pleading guilty to a crime, or confessing her sins to a priest. "But it was always Majidi who came to take the money. He came through the back door. No one came through there but him. To get the money." She raised her eyes to Justin. "We had no choice but to do what he said." Tears ran down her cheeks.

"How many work here?"

"More usually, but only four now."

"Where do the girls go when they leave here?"

"The bookseller says that they are taken away to have babies, or because they have become sick."

Libazo's neck and jaw visibly stiffened, but he did not speak. He is afraid for her, Tolliver thought. And for himself.

"How long have you been wor—how long have you been at this place?" Tolliver asked her, hoping to relieve Kwai's concern.

A sad, knowing smile flitted across her face. "For four months. I am well. I am not sick. My sister was very careful which customers...who she sent me to."

"What do you think will happen to you now?"

"We do not know," Aurala said. "We have not known what to do. Before, we had the bookseller watching us. And Majidi coming to collect the money and giving us food. When the bookseller went to prison, Majidi told us he was having us watched by someone we would not see until we tried to do something wrong. Then we would die. After Majidi died, no one came. We kept some of the money, but only enough to eat. We put the rest of it in Majidi's box, the way we always have."

"Can we not—" Libazo started to ask a question, but Tolliver held up his hand to stop him.

"Please go and bring your sister to me," Justin said, trying his best to hide his sympathy for the girl. He watched her walk out. Her gait was very alluring but seemed unintentionally so, only the natural motion of her limbs. Men like him were meant to despise girls like her. But men like him also made love—not that one could call it that—with them. He understood lust. But he did not understand lusting after a woman whom one also despised.

The speed with which she and her sister returned could only have meant that Leylo had been standing just outside in the corridor.

Tolliver stood up with his legs apart, taking his most authoritative pose. He hated to intimidate the poor woman, but she had too many reasons to hide the truth. "Who has been in charge here since Majidi was killed?" he demanded of Leylo.

"I don't know. We have carried on as before. No one has come to take the money. And no one has brought us food. I have used some of the money I collected to buy us food."

"The rest of the money?"

"It is in the locked money box. Where I put it for Majidi."

"Show it to me."

"It is in the room near the back door. The other girls are sleeping in there now."

"Bring it to me then."

"It is attached to the wall and locked. Only Majidi has—um, had the key. We put all the money we receive in there. That was what he told us we must do. He said he would kill us if we did not put every rupee in that box."

"How would he have known if you kept some back?"

"I don't know," she said. "But he seemed to. He counted it and if it was not enough, he always knew. He would always say, 'There should be thirty rupees and there are only twenty-seven.' If he was wrong, he would not accept it. He always blamed us. And punished us. Even if we had done nothing wrong."

Tolliver remembered all the ledgers in Majidi's office. If he had kept careful records, it would not be difficult for him to predict the number of customers and, therefore, the amount that should have come in on any given day.

Tolliver relaxed his pose. "Do you want to continue here?" He directed this only to Leylo. He did not want to ask Aurala the question that Libazo alone should ask her.

"We have nowhere else to go. No one would take us in."

"I will get Majidi's keys and open the box," Tolliver said. "The money in it will belong to you and the others. If you carry on here, will you have enough to live on?"

"If we keep it all for ourselves?" It was a notion that seemed to fill her with wonder.

"Yes, of course," Tolliver said.

"We will be rich," she said.

Libazo was looking from him to Aurala and back again.

Tolliver drew out his watch. "I will wait for you outside for two minutes," Tolliver said to his sergeant. "I have to meet Hastings at headquarters." He went out and left Kwai with Aurala. If the poor blighter was in love with the girl, how could it hurt anyone if he had a minute to talk to her?

After his encounter with A.D.S. Tolliver in the billiard room at the club, Carl Hastings had spent the rest of the evening, and into the wee hours of the morning, trying to figure out what Tolliver might know and why the policeman wanted to speak to him about the murder of Majidi. Of course, the young prig might suspect he was the killer. Which was absurd. The British gossip mill seemed not to know the slightest thing about, nor care about who might have slain the ivory dealer. *Not any of our concern if one wog wants to kill another* was the typical response.

Still, the young A.D.S. seemed to have something up his sleeve, though how could he know anything substantive about Hastings's dealings with Majidi? With Joseph and Majidi dead, the only living person who knew the details of Majidi's operation and Hastings's part in it was the eunuch Ismail al Dimu, and there was no reason in hell for him to go reporting anything to the police.

Then, just as Hastings was falling asleep, he sat bolt upright and nearly shouted. That letter he had received from the now-dead slave had been in English! How could he have forgotten this? There was enough information in the letter to make a person suspicious. *The secrets you and I share about Majidi and the work you and he do together*, it had said. Even if Joseph had told his scribe nothing more than that, it was enough to cast mistrust on the man to whom the letter was addressed: Mr. Carl Hastings, who slept not a wink the rest of the night.

The following morning he sweated his way to meet the policeman. His mind reeled over the impossibility of ever finding out who had helped Joseph write that letter. By the time he arrived at the police headquarters, he was fit for nothing but a change of clothes and downing an entire bottle of whiskey.

As it happened, he saw Tolliver striding toward the fake Greek building from the other direction. Sanctimonious, he looked. Filled up with himself. They said he was the son of an earl. Well, this country was full of them—second sons of this or that. Acting as if they owned everything. Which in large part they did. But most of them were doing nothing at all useful. This one was walking along deep in conversation with that nigger constable he seemed always to have at his side.

Hastings hailed the young snot as if he were a friend and held the door with a smile. "After you, Mr. Tolliver," he said.

Ever the gentleman, Tolliver deferred to Hastings.

Hastings entered and then to his surprise and delight, overheard Tolliver and his sergeant give the one piece of information he most needed. Tolliver turned to his blackie and said, "Have you found Gautura's friend whom you were looking for, the one we heard about from the missionary?"

"Juba Osi?" the askari asked. "No, sir. I can go now and continue to look. I'll take a couple of the boys with me, if you can spare me."

Hastings was sure he had the answer to the question that had been burning him—the name of Gautura's letter writer, served up to him on a silver platter. Being a slave, Joseph Gautura was unlikely to have other confidants besides this kinsman. Juba Osi was very likely the person he had gone to when he needed help. What a stroke of luck. That dolt Tolliver had no idea how helpful he was being. Bully for me, Hastings thought. Bully for me.

"Bring Osi here, if you find him," Tolliver ordered.

"Not if, sir, but when," the arrogant little shit said before he marched back out the door.

"I will call for you in a moment," Tolliver said to Hastings, indicating a bench where the man could wait. He mounted the stairs two at a time.

Hastings sat in his sweat-dampened clothing and stewed. How much longer would he have to wait? He had to find this

Juba Osi quickly and do away with him before the native squad got hold of him. He doubted they could find the sod quicker than he. All he had to do was convince the sweet young A.D.S. to let him go. And quickly.

Tolliver learned two astonishing things when he reached his desk to prepare for his interrogation of Carl Hastings.

Two sealed envelopes awaited him, both with *Tolliver* scrawled on them in Egerton's commanding hand.

In the first was a report written on paper headed: *The Protectorate of British East Africa, Office of the Treasurer.* It gave the totals of the cash confiscated from the safe in Khalid Majidi's shop: 7,173 rupees in paper money, 4,360 pounds sterling in bills, and also coins of various nations equivalent to another 415 rupees. The report was signed by Deputy Treasurer Michael Linane.

A quick calculation told Tolliver that the pound notes alone amounted to a bit more than seventeen years' worth of his current salary. It was a sultan's ransom. Impossible to imagine where the ivory trader had come up with such an amount. Most perplexing of all: the person who had killed him had left it behind. Incomprehensible.

It took Tolliver a moment to catch his breath and open the other envelope. A note inside informed him that Miss Katharine Morley, the sister of the Reverend Robert Morley, had come to see Egerton and demanded that he arrest her brother for the murder of Khalid Majidi.

Once he recovered from this second jolt, he wrote a note to Vera, telling her what Katharine Morley had done and asking her to go to visit the woman and try to calm her. Writing to Vera eased his own tension. He put the note in an envelope and took it to the desk in the entry hall. "That boy who hangs about with Sergeant Libazo," he said to the Indian clerk at the desk. "I saw him outside a few moments ago. Please take this to him and ask him to deliver it to my wife forthwith. The direction is on the envelope, but the child probably cannot read. Be sure he knows the way. And give him this." He handed the clerk a generous coin.

Tolliver then collected Hastings from the bench and took him up to his office. The man seemed entirely too happy to be invited to give a statement. Men brought in for questioning were ordinarily made nervous or were put out by the very idea. Tolliver recalled how testy Hastings had become at having to wait for the Grand Mufti to disembark before he could go ashore. Yet he had waited here nearly twenty minutes in perfect good cheer.

Tolliver decided that the English ivory hunter was only acting the part of a man going on a picnic.

Hastings smiled broadly as he followed Tolliver up the stairs. He was determined to show the sanctimonious puppy what a model of an educated Englishman he was dealing with. He knew Tolliver's type. He had suffered them on three continents. All swollen with their own superiority and sense of privilege. They became extremely annoyed when circumstances forced them to earn their own coin.

Hastings smiled, took a seat, hoped to be offered a cup of tea, and smiled all the more once he was denied that courtesy.

Without preamble, Tolliver folded his hands in front of him and said, "I understand you had an intense dislike for Khalid Majidi and might have had reason to do him harm."

Hastings sputtered, shocked by the audacity of the statement. It took him six too many deep breaths to be able to say anything coherent, especially under the impertinent inspector's steady blue gaze. He thought only of telling Tolliver he was out of his mind. When he finally had enough air in his lungs, he managed a laugh. "Where would you have gotten such an idea?"

Tolliver relaxed his posture. "Suppose you begin by telling me what your relationship was with Majidi." He picked up a pen from the desk as if it were a weapon he could wield. It was.

"I hunt ivory. I sold my takings to Majidi. We had a business relationship."

Tolliver's blue eyes seemed to be calculating, as if measuring Hastings for a suit, or a coffin. "Where do you hunt your ivory?"

His voice was chatty, as if he were asking a casual question, but it made Hastings's guts tremble. What exactly did this upstart know? How much of the truth had his informant, whoever he was, given him? If they had not yet found Juba Osi, who could the squealing pig be? The truth fell out of Hastings's mouth despite himself. "I hunt up in the Mau Forest."

"I was up in that area last year," Tolliver said, as if they were trading stories at the bar at the club. "I was tracking a murderer."

Hastings got ahold of himself. "Did you catch him, I hope?" Two could play this game.

"In a manner of speaking. Did you come to Africa to hunt professionally?" The questions had turned much too friendly. Tolliver either knew more than he was revealing, or he was fishing with suppositions as bait.

"Not at all. You have probably already heard. I went belly-up trying to grow flax, didn't I? It must be all over the gossip mill."

"I had heard something to that effect," Tolliver admitted, "but I am a policeman. I have to deal in facts, not rumors."

Happy that he had reduced Tolliver to mouthing platitudes, Hastings made a move to finish this charade. He needed to get out of this building quickly so he could silence Gautura's scribe once and for all.

He gave Tolliver his most charming smile. "So you can see, my boy, that I was forced by circumstances to take up ivory hunting, since I had no capital at all. Majidi provided me with an outlet for the ivory I took. Why would I harm the man who gave me the means to my paltry living?"

"Wait here for a moment," Tolliver said, and walked out of the office.

Waiting was an affront that Hastings could not bear. But he did not know if he could actually get away if he tried to leave immediately. He drew out the watch at the end of the chain that stretched across his belly. He would give the young snotty-nose four minutes.

Tolliver walked as nonchalantly as he could out of the room and took his time closing the door behind him. Then he sped down the stairs to the desk, wishing he had Kwai nearby and then relieved to find Abrik Singh on duty. "Who do you have here who is trustworthy and bright?"

Abrik blinked at him for a moment and then said, "My brother is upstairs delivering the dispatches."

"Is he canny enough to follow a man without being detected?"

"He is in uniform."

Tolliver looked about him. There was no one else. "He will have to do. Carl Hastings is about to leave my office. I will keep him a few more minutes. Get your brother and send him outside and tell him to follow Hastings. I want to know where he goes."

"Yes, sir."

"And send a runner to Fort Jesus. I am going to go there in an hour. I will want to interrogate the bookseller from the souk and his nephew, but separately."

"I understand, sir."

When Tolliver got back to his office, Hastings was standing, looking at his watch, and tapping his foot. Tolliver found his overwrought sense of personal dignity ludicrous. He was a nobody, really, and yet he seemed to think he had the right to judge others, to demand a regal level of respect, and then he had the gall to think he could put on a sham act as the cooperative citizen and get away with it. Tolliver did not want to think the man guilty just because he disliked him, but Hastings's snobbish attitude made it difficult to be fair.

"Thank you for waiting," Tolliver said. "I appreciate your cooperation. Do you have any plans to go off hunting in the next few days?" Tolliver tried his best to sound only mildly curious.

He had a lifetime of training in how to be polite to people who did not really deserve it, but he had never been as good at it as his mother thought he should be. The haughty look he got from Hastings proved he had been unsuccessful again.

"I am free, white, and English," Hastings said, actually putting his nose in the air. "I will do as I please."

"Certainly," Tolliver answered. "You may go," he added, pretending that he could keep Hastings if he wanted to. Not that he could. Not without evidence. He feared the man would disappear from Mombasa before the facts emerged.

The little Swahili boy who approached Vera's front gate had a confident, worldly-wise look about him, far in excess of what one would expect in a child so young. Vera was standing in the front garden, trying to decide exactly how far away from the front corner of the bungalow she wanted to plant a frangipani sapling. To her amazement, the boy came through the gate without asking permission, marched up to her, and, with a graceful flourish, but without a word presented her with an envelope. Her name and the address of the bungalow were written on it in Justin's gentlemanlike hand.

"Thank you, boy," she said. "What is your name?"

"Haki," the boy said, standing at attention. "I work for the police."

What a charming child. She asked him to wait while she went inside and brought out a coin for him. When she returned he took the coin, saluted, and ran off.

The contents of the note disturbed her. Poor Katharine must be beside herself to be betraying her brother in such a way.

How could she march into the police with such a demand unless she was positive of his guilt? Perhaps not even then, except to save the life of an innocent. Justin was convinced of Morley's innocence. Did Katharine know something that Justin did not?

She gave the gardeners their orders, pointing to a spot she feared would turn out to be too close to the house, but not caring since she would not live there long enough to see the tree fully grown. She sped inside, changed as quickly as she could, and made her way with all due dispatch to the Mission, worrying along the way that Katharine would not be there when she arrived, or that Robert would be with her and want to know what they had to discuss. Suppose she were forced to reveal to Katharine her brother's peccadilloes. Justin had not told her the whole truth, but it was very easy to guess at it. Katharine was exactly that prudish type of woman who would be shocked at the very thought of anyone having sex with anyone.

The oppressive heat along the way made it nearly impossible for Vera to gather her thoughts. As she approached, she was happy to see Katharine alone, sitting on the veranda with a book.

As Vera crossed the lawn, formulating her greeting, suddenly her head swam. The sun seemed to grow brighter. She reached out, but there was nothing to grasp. All went blank.

Kwai Libazo's inquiries about Juba Osi all pointed in one direction. The only likely place to find Gautura's tribesman was in the native sector on the outskirts of the town center near the Kilindini Harbour.

By midmorning Libazo was making his way uphill, past the Gymkhana Club and the small European cemetery. At the top was a sprawling open-air market full of noisy traders. The buyers were largely Swahili women, many wearing veils. They refused to acknowledge, much less speak to the tall, exotic-looking askari stranger who spoke Swahili with an up-country accent.

No one seemed to want to tell him anything, and he was beginning to think he should come back without his uniform. He stopped to buy some biltong and a beer, to give himself an excuse to speak to the seller. He chose an elderly one. The tooth-less woman, who evidently could not eat the chewy product she sold, looked him up and down and called him "handsome *polisi*." He gave her his best smile, told her that her beer and the biltong were excellent. He continued to converse with her while he ate and drank.

"Everybody comes to my stand," she told him.

"I am sure that is true. Your products are very tasty."

"I have not seen you here before."

"I have not been here before, but I will be sure to come back when I need a snack."

"I will give you a discount."

He smiled again. "I came here because I have some news to bring to someone who lives in this part of the town, but I cannot find him."

The woman denied knowing Juba Osi, but she left him to "guard" her stand while she went and asked if her friends nearby knew where Juba Osi lived.

Carl Hastings left the police station and made directly for the native quarter. He had not spent the past two years in this godfor-saken town without learning his way around. When Tolliver had ordered his askari to find Juba Osi, his tone of voice told Hastings that none of them had the faintest idea where to look. Hastings, therefore, felt sure he would get to Gautura's kinsman first. Though he sorely wanted a gin and quinine, he could not chance Osi being found and taken into custody before his trap was shut for good.

As it was, Hastings was forced to part with five rupees before anyone would tell him where to find the bloody little son of a whore.

Tolliver entered the prison in the old Portuguese citadel with an excitement brought on from his sense of its history. There were many structures in his native Yorkshire that were older than this place's three hundred years, but the site recalled the imaginary battles in the books he had read as a boy, which had given rise to his fascination with the exotic, the long-ago and the faraway. On rainy days in his father's library he had pored over old texts and maps that smelled of dust and adventure. He shook his head and smiled to himself. Sometimes he still felt like a little boy inside.

When he got to the interrogation room, a massive native policeman stood guard over the bookseller's nephew—the man who had been arrested for threatening the Grand Mufti and had then escaped from the courthouse. Tolliver questioned him for a good half hour, but in the end, he failed to get any information about Majidi from the young man. All he would tell Tolliver was that he must get the facts from his uncle. Tolliver hid his frustration and had the huge askari take away the boy and bring him the bookseller.

The uncle was a small, slight man with a surprisingly round belly that protruded from the front of his long midnight-blue gown so that the buttons gaped and threatened to pop off. It was the kind of garment one would see only on a Catholic priest in England. There, it would be black, but this one was a midnight shade of blue. The man's face and long black beard were cleaner than Tolliver could have imagined he could keep them while in prison. Tolliver feigned an inability to speak Swahili and interrogated him through the interpreter. He understood quite well what was being said, but the ruse gave him a better opportunity to observe the prisoner objectively.

"The general belief in the Arab community is that you are the owner of the brothel across the way from your bookstall in the bazaar. Do you own that place?"

"Since coming to this prison, I have heard that Khalid Majidi is dead. Is this true?"

"I am here to ask the questions; you are here to answer them."

"If Majidi is truly dead, I will answer your questions. If he lives, I will not."

Tolliver relented. In this case, he would rather have the answers willingly than try to extract the information by intimidation. "He is quite dead."

The man sized up Tolliver for a second, seeming to assess the truth of the information. He took in a deep breath. "The brothel across from my bookshop employs Somali women who are from Muslim families. It is a disgrace what they are doing there. I would not want to have anything to do with such a disgrace."

"Then how is it that your name is attached to the operation, and why is it that your nephew threatened the Grand Mufti when he condemned that brothel and called for it to be closed?"

"Majidi held a great deal over my head and over my family. He knew some things about us that would cause the Shari'a court to take away all we had—our possessions and our good name. There are people who would want to kill us if our history were revealed. In exchange for his keeping our secret, he forced me to pretend that I was the man behind the brothel. And he was the one who insisted that my nephew silence the Grand Mufti. He said if the Grand Mufti's words made the police close his brothel, he would punish me by revealing my secret."

"It makes no sense. Why would you go along with pretending that you owned a brothel to save your reputation?"

He gave Tolliver a world-weary look, as if only a child would need an explanation. "There are secrets and there are secrets, Mr. Policeman. I could never have allowed Majidi to reveal what he held over me."

"Even if it meant participating in the assassination of such an important figure in your religion?"

"The Grand Mufti is a Sunni; we are Shi'a."

Tolliver had a vague notion that there were sects of Islam, but he had no idea of their meaning, much less their origin. "How can that be a reason to kill a man?"

The bookseller laughed so bitterly that it was almost impossible to call the sound he made an expression of mirth. "Have not the English Protestants and Catholics been killing one another for centuries?" He took his hands out of his lap and folded them on the table in front of him. "My nephew was sent to intimidate the Grand Mufti, not actually to kill him."

"You are going to have to tell me—" Tolliver started to say. But his eyes focused on the man's hands. They were very small, like a woman's really. His fingerprints might appear too small to be thought a man's. Like the ones on the murder weapon. This man was bound to Majidi in some terrible way. He certainly had motive enough to kill the person who was forcing him to do heinous things against his will.

Tolliver was about to stand up and order his fingerprints to be taken, but then he realized that at the moment Majidi was murdered, this man had been locked up in prison.

He had begun to formulate his next question when a painfully bright flash of insight stopped his thoughts and his breath. Those small fingerprints on the murder weapon were likely a woman's. He and Egerton had both dismissed that without ever logically considering it. And yet the person who found Majidi's body was a woman... And one who quickly disappeared from the scene. Katharine Morley. She, who had now demanded that her brother be arrested for the crime. Inconceivable as it seemed, that pinched maiden lady might actually have taken the man's life. And Vera was on her way to visit a woman who could very well be a murderer.

"Lock him up again!" he called out to the guard, springing to his feet and out the door.

He had sent Libazo on a search of the dead slave's tribesman. There was no one about whom he knew or could trust. There was nothing for it. In the heat of the day, completely on his own, he ran with unholy speed toward the Mission.

Kwai Libazo became confused as he followed the biltong seller's directions to the dwelling of Juba Osi. Like every tribal village Libazo had ever visited, Mombasa's native town was a helter-skelter arrangement of huts and shacks. Everywhere about, chickens scratched the red dirt and children raised a joyful racket. He was looking for a roundel with a corrugated roof near a tall palm, but there were three such places in the direction the woman had indicated. He approached two girls dressed in English fabrics wound tightly around their bodies. One was sitting in the doorway of a hut that looked as if it were held together with coconut rope. The other stood behind her, fixing the seated girl's hair. When he asked for Juba Osi, neither of them spoke but they both pointed to the same hut.

As soon as he looked that way, Libazo was taken aback and put on his guard. At that moment, a tall, portly white man, in typical Englishman's clothing, a man he had only just seen at headquarters, was standing in front of Juba's doorway speaking to someone just inside the door. Kwai moved slowly toward him, trying his best not to draw the man's attention. He was almost upon him when he saw another askari, one he did not know, peering out at the Englishman from behind a nearby hut. The other askari looked startled when he noticed Kwai.

Kwai instantly signaled to him, pointing to himself and drawing an arc with his fingers to show he would come around behind the building, and then raising his palm to signal the other policeman to go back into hiding.

Carl Hastings faced Juba Osi in his doorway and realized he had to proceed with care. The man, who greatly resembled his tribesman Joseph Gautura, was holding a large knife with which he had been fashioning a bowl out of some sort of wood. Osi was broad-shouldered and though shorter than Hastings, gave the impression of being very much stronger. Hastings had a pistol under his jacket, but drawing it here in broad daylight must be a last resort. The first thing he needed to do was to find out if this was the blighter who had written the letter. Then it would just be a matter of luring him to a place where he could safely shoot him and leave him to rot.

Without entering the hut, he greeted the man and said that he needed to employ a native who could write English, that he needed such a person for his business.

All he got for his trouble was an answer in Swahili that Osi did not have any English. Hastings did not believe him, of course. The bastard must somehow have divined that Hastings was the recipient of Joseph Gautura's letter. These natives were sometimes not as stupid as they looked.

Hastings switched to Swahili and tried a different tack. "Still, I can use a strong man like yourself."

"For what sort of work, Bwana?"

Hastings was casting about for what to say next when a voice from behind him said in Swahili, "Are you Juba Osi?" in a very commanding tone.

Osi looked terrified, and Hastings spun around to see two black policemen approaching—one of them tall and looking as strong as a gorilla. He was, Hastings was sure, the very man Tolliver had sent to look for Juba Osi. "Good afternoon, Colonel," the ape said in English to Hastings.

"What do you want?" Hastings blurted out in his own best commanding tone. There was no way he would be able to spirit Osi away now without a scene, and if they got the savage back to headquarters, he would squeal whatever he knew like a sewer rat.

In desperation, Hastings was trying to figure out how much of a bribe he could offer these two to let him deal with Osi when the tall one said, "Juba Osi, we are here to arrest you for the murder of Joseph Gautura."

Osi screamed and began to prattle on at such a rate that Hastings could make no sense of it, except that the blackie was declaring his innocence.

Tolliver's tall, overconfident sergeant handcuffed Osi nonetheless. "If you are not guilty, you will be freed," the sergeant declared. Osi continued to plead and shout.

Then the uppity askari had the temerity to ask what Hastings's business was with Juba Osi. "None of your goddamned concern!" Hastings spat out in his face. "Watch your manners, you stupid savage, or I will have your head."

Hastings marched off shoulders squared, determined, confident. But his brain seethed with fear, with a compulsion to run. He had to find that ball-less Ismail al Dimu and get some money out of him. He would pretend to be carrying on with the hunting expedition they had planned with Majidi. But then he would go overland—into Ethiopia, or Egypt. He did not know what he would do after that, but he would have to be far away now that the authorities would learn what Juba Osi undoubtedly knew.

CHAPTER

15

Justin Tolliver arrived at the Mission grounds out of breath and soaked with sweat. Getting to Vera was his only thought. Much as he wanted to be angry at her for involving herself where she did not belong, every fiber of his being knew that if he lost her, he himself would be lost. And he was the one who had sent her here! As he crossed the lawn, he shooed a troop of baboons out of his way and called for Vera.

Robert Morley came rushing out of the schoolroom to the left of the house and met Tolliver as he arrived at the veranda.

"Where is my wife?" Tolliver demanded.

"She is lying down. My sister is attending to her. I am sure she will be fine."

"What do you mean? What has happened to her?"

"She has had a fainting spell is all. Happens all the time to women in this heat."

"Vera is not the sort of woman who faints. Bring me to her immediately!"

Morley looked surprised. "Really, I am sure it is nothing. We insisted she lie down in an excess of caution."

"My God, man…" Tolliver could not stand it for another second. He rushed through the door and shouted Vera's name.

Morley followed him. "Now, see here…"

Tolliver ignored the missionary and made immediately for the hallway that seemed as if it must lead to the bedrooms. The sister was standing at one of the doorways and turned a disapproving face to Tolliver. "She was sleeping, but you have wakened her. Why are you shouting?" She sounded like a schoolteacher scolding a bad boy.

"Move aside," Justin said. Never in his life had he spoken to a woman in such a tone, not even a parlor maid. Morley came up beside him, still sputtering.

Vera lay on the bed looking a bit dazed. He ran and knelt beside her. Her hand was cool. "Tell me, Vera," he said, "what has happened? Are you all right?"

"She fainted as soon as she arrived," Katharine said from the doorway. "She hadn't said a word to us. She just passed out in the middle of the lawn."

He did not believe her. His heart was pounding. "Leave us alone."

"Well, I never—" the missionary said. Brother and sister both grumbled as they moved away, but they left the room.

He took Vera in his arms. "Tell me precisely."

"It was exactly as Miss Morley said. I never reached her even to say hello. I passed out on the lawn. They think it was the heat."

"Are you sure she did not give you something to make you ill? She did not try to hurt you?"

"She did not. Why ever do you think she would? Really, Justin. I can't imagine that she—"

He did not want to but he blurted out what he feared. "I have reason to believe that Katharine Morley killed Khalid Majidi," he said as quietly as he could.

At first, Vera gave him a look of complete disbelief, but then she blinked for a moment and sat up. "I can't—"

"Can you move now? I think it best if we talk about this elsewhere."

"Yes. I am fine now. Absolutely fine. They insisted on putting me to bed, but all I needed was a brief sit-down and a glass of water. I assure you there is nothing wrong." She proved it by springing up from the bed in that light, graceful way of hers. Sometimes she seemed to him more fairy creature than real girl.

On their way back to Mombasa he explained to her about the small fingerprints on the murder weapon. The whole notion of fingerprints amazed her. "So if Inspector Patrick went into the Morleys' guest room right now, he would be able to tell that I have been there?"

"If you touched anything, like the bedpost or the door handle."

"The bedclothes? Or the vial of smelling salts on the bedside table?"

"Not the bedclothes. Perhaps the smelling salts."

They were on a small ferry, crossing over to Mombasa Island. He put his arm around her. "I am going to have to ask Katharine Morley to give her fingerprints," he said. "I don't like to do it."

"It will cause an awful lot of talk. I am afraid of what that will do to the reputation of Father's friends."

"I will try to keep it from the gossipmongers, but you know how news gets out and travels."

"Yes, I do."

"When will you do it?"

"Not until tomorrow. There are a lot of other details for me to collect. And I want to see you safely home first."

"I am fine. How many times do I have to tell you?"

After returning Vera to the bungalow, Tolliver hurried back to headquarters, where Juba Osi had been brought in for questioning.

"Where is Sergeant Libazo?" Justin asked the askari who was guarding the witness. The man shrugged but didn't speak.

Anger prickled at Tolliver. Kwai, he suspected, was off with his Somali lady of the night. If he was, there would be no hope of saving his position. The services, military and police, had very little tolerance for men going absent, even when they were legitimately sick. Absence without leave meant the stockade and then dishonorable dismissal, at best. Execution was a possibility. Tolliver's heart sank at the prospect of having to arrest his sergeant for dereliction of duty.

Another askari, who turned out to be Abrik Singh's brother, soon found Tolliver and allayed his fears. He and Libazo had converged on Juba Osi's hut, where they had found Carl Hastings. Kwai had decided to follow the Englishman. Tolliver's declining admiration for Kwai made a quick about-face. There were European men on the force getting paid twice as much who were not worth half of Libazo.

Juba Osi, sitting handcuffed in Justin's office with a Goan guard standing over him, was frightened half to death, but also incensed. "They told me that they were arresting me for the murder of Joseph Gautura," he told Tolliver. He looked as if he might weep. "Joseph was my friend and my kinsman. I could not take him to live with me. Our Shari'a law gave me the way to free myself from slavery. But I am afraid my old master will force me to go back. He can take me to Shari'a Court and give such behavior as a reason to take me back. You know he still can. And he can claim my children under the Shari'a. I could not keep Joseph in my house while his master was looking for him, but I did not want to see him die. Never," he said emphatically. "Never."

Justin regretted not keeping the arresting askari close by. He needed to know why they had told Osi he was being arrested for Gautura's murder. Libazo must have had a reason.

"There must be some evidence against you," Tolliver said, though he had no idea what that might be. "The best way for you to convince us of your innocence is for you to tell us all you know."

Osi stammered and stuttered his way through several minutes of repeated denials, claiming that he had been minding his own business when the first stranger came to his door.

"What did the stranger want?" queried Tolliver.

"He said that he wanted to hire me, because he thought I write English. I cannot, Bwana. I cannot write English. Joseph could write English, but I cannot."

"Yes, I understand. And then what happened?"

"He said he wanted to hire me for other work. I need work. But I would not go with him. He does very bad things, things that could make a man suffer prison."

Tolliver knew that Carl Hastings was not on the up-and-up. Now he was going to find out exactly how low he had sunk. "What things?"

"Majidi will kill me if I say."

"Majidi? What has he got to do with this?"

He held up his shackled hands. "I am going to die anyway, yes?"

Tolliver considered him for a moment. What Juba Osi knew could answer all the riddles that Tolliver had been trying to solve for more than a week. "Unlock the handcuffs," he said to the Goan guard, "and bring us a pitcher of water and two glasses. Make sure it's boiled water."

The guard looked at him in disbelief. Guards were not used to seeing the English be polite to natives.

"Now, please," Tolliver said gently.

He turned back to Osi. "Listen to me," he told the witness after the guard had freed him and gone out to fetch the water. "Majidi is dead. He cannot hurt you. You must tell me everything you know about Hastings and his dealings with Majidi. I already know, Mr. Hastings told me himself that he dealt with Majidi. Hastings is an ivory hunter. I believe he sold his ivory to Majidi. I see nothing troublesome about that."

Tolliver also knew that Hastings was hard up for cash, but the man's financial predicament must have been far worse than Tolliver imagined, considering what Osi said next.

"Joseph Gautura was more than Majidi's slave. He was the one who went between Majidi and the men that did his bidding. Majidi did not do the awful things. Never. He always found a way to force other men to do them. Mr. Hastings was one of those men."

"He did Majidi's bidding, you say? In the way he traded ivory with him?"

"That is right, Bwana. He sold some of his ivory to Majidi here in Mombasa, but the other ivory he transported to Malindi, along with the other cargo."

All Tolliver knew about Malindi was that it was a town north of Mombasa on the coast, but with a port much smaller than the ones here. "Why was some of the ivory shipped from Malindi?" Tolliver thought he knew, but he needed to hear it from Osi's mouth.

Osi regarded Tolliver with disbelief, as if the policeman lacked a grasp of the obvious. "It is a small place, away from the authorities here. It is where the contraband goes."

"Yes, certainly. So you are saying that the ivory for which the hunter had a license came here to Mombasa, but that he shot more than he was licensed for and shipped the illegal ivory from Malindi?"

"Yes, Bwana."

This confirmed Tolliver's suspicions that Hastings was breaking the law. But Osi still seemed to be holding something back. "They were breaking the law in another way, weren't they?"

Osi bowed his head. "Yes."

"How, man? You must tell me."

"Another cargo besides ivory, Bwana."

Tolliver suppressed a curse at the time this was taking. "What other cargo?" he demanded as evenly as he could. *"What else were they shipping out of Malindi?"*

Osi bit his lower lip. "People," he muttered barely audibly.

It took some effort for Tolliver to keep his jaw from dropping. "What do you mean by *people*?"

"African people." Osi stated it as if he were saying the only plausible answer.

"Slaves?" Tolliver didn't even attempt to maintain his cool exterior now. His anger came out full force. "Slaves?" he shouted. "You are telling me that they have been trafficking in slaves? Tell me exactly what Gautura told you. Tell me everything that you can remember that he said. Everything!"

"He said that Mr. Hastings went hunting for ivory in the area of Mount Elgon. That he shot many more elephants than he was allowed. That he hired many porters from among the people who lived there. Then he took porters to carry the ivory to the coast. And he took young girls and little boys. When they got to the coast, the porters and the children were loaded on dhows and shipped away with the ivory."

Tolliver's breath shook with rage. "You are certain of this? Absolutely certain?"

Osi's next words came pouring out in a flood now that the dam was broken. "It was why Joseph stayed with Majidi. He had the money to buy his own freedom, but he did not. He was worried that he knew too much. He not only saw the slaves being shipped from Malindi, but he oversaw their loading onto the dhow. And he knew everything Majidi and the Englishman talked about. And what Majidi said to the Arabs that he controlled. Joseph hid from Majidi that he knew English and Arabic. Joseph thought he was safe because of this, that Majidi must think he did not understand all the wrong things that Majidi did. But he did know them. And sometimes he feared that Majidi knew how much he understood. Joseph was afraid Majidi would begin to fear him. Majidi killed anyone he feared."

"Then why did Joseph run away?" It seemed to Tolliver that if all Osi was telling him was true, Gautura had signed his own death warrant by leaving Majidi.

"Joseph said that to be a good man, he had to stop helping Majidi, who did only evil things. He said he was sick in his heart to help such a bad person. To help him turn men into slaves. To turn children into slaves." Osi picked up his glass to drink, but it was empty.

"So he ran," Tolliver said.

"Yes, to the English priest," Juba Osi said. He spat out the words as if they disgusted him. "He said he could protect Joseph, but Joseph went to him only to be murdered. He did not keep Joseph safe." He looked as if he would begin to weep again.

Tolliver considered how he could keep his witness safe. He had no idea how extensive Majidi's criminal circle was, and who might be left to exact revenge once Hastings was arrested. He did not want to jail this terrified ex-slave. Nor did he want to see him go free and be killed by those who would silence him with a knife to the throat.

"I am going to keep you in this building," he said. "I will get them to bring you something to eat. I have to make sure you will be safe before I let you go. Do you understand? I do not believe that you killed Joseph. But I do believe that there are people in the town who could mean you harm."

Osi dropped his hands in his lap and sighed. Like all the other natives, he had little reason to trust an English policeman. Tolliver would make sure that he became convinced.

As soon as Justin had left Vera at home and sped off to his investigation, Vera sent a note to Katharine Morley. She apologized for Justin's brusque behavior at the Mission and invited Katharine to tea. There were flowers in a bowl in the center of the cloth. Lovely china cups. And sparkling glasses ready to receive cool lemonade to refresh the visitor as soon as she arrived. The teapot ready with the leaves to brew the beverage that Katharine loved. Some freshly baked currant scones. Everything to put Katharine at perfect ease. By the time the afternoon had begun to cool, Vera was ready to extract from Katharine what Justin would need to prove once and for all whether Katharine Morley had murdered Khalid Majidi.

Tolliver went out to the street in front of the police headquarters and looked about him. He hoped he would see Kwai, though he knew it was unlikely. The boy, Haki, sat on the ground near the door, with his back against the building. He shook his head but did not speak when Tolliver asked him if he knew where Kwai was.

Tolliver found another askari who knew what Libazo looked like and told him to take three or four others and go look for him. "Do not speak to him or give away his position by anything you do. Just take note of where he is and then come and find me," he told them. He took a constable with him and went to the club to see if perhaps Hastings had returned to his room there. One could often find him in the bar or in the billiard room.

When Tolliver did not see Libazo anywhere in the vicinity of the club, he concluded that it was unlikely that Hastings was inside. He went in anyway and found he was correct. No one had seen Hastings since early that morning.

Tolliver returned to headquarters, dragging his feet. He would have to report to Egerton. The D.S. was not as one-sided in his opinions as others Tolliver had reported to, but he would object strongly if Kwai Libazo tried to arrest an Englishman. Europeans were never, never taken into custody by Africans. Tolliver knew that he had to be the one to arrest Hastings, so he must be there when the man was found. The town was not so very large. Kwai was on the man's trail. But there was no way of knowing where that had led him.

As Tolliver reentered police headquarters, his thoughts were so distracted he did not notice that Haki was no longer sitting in his accustomed place. As Tolliver knocked on Egerton's office door, he would have been heartened if he had known where the boy had gone.

It had been nearly two hours since Carl Hastings had entered a small nondescript building near the entrance to the bazaar. From the beginning of his service on the British East African police force, Kwai Libazo had gotten used to staying with the task at hand for as long as it took to accomplish it. He felt it was bred into him from his Maasai ancestry to be able to withstand hunger and thirst.

Hastings had come here straight from his encounter in the doorway of Juba Osi's hut. Kwai stood with his back to a wall, behind the stall of a street vendor, a place where he could observe the door, but where he was sure anyone entering or leaving would not notice him. Not that anyone at all had come to or gone from the house, which lacked any window overlooking the street.

The peddler sold lacquered trays and was doing no business at all. Kwai wished the man had had the sense to sell fruit or those pieces of cooked meat on a stick that were so delicious and available on almost any corner in the town.

Across the narrow street, in front of a small Hindu temple, a man in a turban sat blowing into an instrument made from dried gourds. He was charming a cobra that rose from a basket and danced and swayed. Kwai felt that if he kept watching the snake, he himself would soon be dancing and swaying. He turned and peered between the vendor's goods at the door.

It occurred to him that his vigil here could be useless. He did not have any real understanding of that Englishman's role in the investigation. He had followed him because he thought it extremely curious that he had been in the police station and then had gone to see the very man who was a kinsman to Joseph Gautura. Something inside Kwai had told him not to let the Englishman know the real reason Tolliver had sent him to find Juba Osi. He had taken it upon himself to pretend he was there to arrest Osi. It was the only way Kwai Libazo could think of to get Osi away from the Englishman. No African askari could otherwise challenge any Englishman. By being here Kwai was breaking several written and unwritten rules. He was at risk of being expelled from the force for taking it upon himself to follow an Englishman.

This thought made him afraid, but he told himself over and over the word A.D.S. Tolliver had used the previous year when he presented Kwai to District Superintendent Jodrell, as a candidate for the rank of sergeant. The word was *initiative*. He and A.D.S. Tolliver had had many talks about the border between the lands of *initiative* and *overstepping*. Libazo was not at all sure which land he was in at the moment. He wished another constable had happened by while he was standing there, so he could send a message to Tolliver to come and speak with him. This afternoon he had a lot of sympathy with the settlers up in Nairobi who always complained that there was never a constable nearby when one was needed.

Libazo was pulled from his doubts by a tug on his arm. It was the boy, Haki. "Not now, child," Kwai whispered. "I am on duty. I have told you about duty."

The boy stood at attention and saluted. He had the sense to whisper too. "Yes, my sergeant," he said. "It is for duty that I am here. Your captain is looking for you. You must come away now to him."

Libazo glanced from the child to the door, back and forth, afraid that the moment he took his eyes away the Englishman would come out. The rules said he should follow Tolliver's wishes and go with Haki, but he thought it even more important to keep his eyes on the Englishman. "Did A.D.S. Tolliver send you for me?"

"No. He sent other policemen. But I am the one who found you." He smiled with great pride.

"Listen to me, boy," Libazo said. "You must go to the police headquarters and tell Mr. Tolliver where I am. Bring him here with you. You must be quick. If I am not here when he comes back, it is because I am following the Englishman. Can you remember this exactly?"

"Yes, sir," the boy said with another salute.

"Go as quickly as you can," Libazo told him. Glancing over his shoulder as the boy sped away, he saw the child skirt a camel and slip his little body through the throngs on the street faster than any man could have moved along.

CHAPTER 16

The shadows were lengthening outside D.S. Egerton's office window, but his temper was getting shorter by the moment. "And you actually believe that we should arrest one of the king's subjects based on the hearsay evidence of some black beggar?"

Ordinarily, Egerton was more even-tempered. But it was late on a Friday. Perhaps he was fatigued.

Tolliver drew his chair closer to the desk between them. "I was not suggesting that we immediately charge Hastings with Majidi's murder. We don't want the force to come in the way of criticism for that. On the other hand, we can't let him escape if he is guilty. That would give us a terrific black eye."

Egerton gave Tolliver a dyspeptic grunt.

Tolliver pressed on. "Hastings has already told me that Majidi was holding his indebtedness over him. That would give him a motive to kill Majidi. Now Hastings has been found with another witness, this one in the case of the dead slave Joseph Gautura. I think that gives us grounds to bring him in for more questioning."

"Hastings's debt was not to Majidi, you know," Egerton offered.

"I did not," Tolliver said. "He merely told me that, because of the debt, he needed his trade with Majidi or he would wind up in prison. Do you know who he owes and how much?"

Egerton leaned into the conversation now. "Based on what you've told me about your previous conversation with him, I made some inquiries. He has bank loans that have been in arrears for some time. The total, principal and back interest, is twenty thousand pounds."

"Good heavens. How could he have dug himself a hole so deep?"

"It seems, given his background, he was well thought of by a number of people. Three different bankers loaned him money and let him string them along."

"Well, you must see, sir, that—"

Egerton had left his office door open, and a ruckus below in the entry hall disturbed their conversation. They both went to the balcony, which overlooked the source of the noise. Below, the child Haki was raising his voice and struggling to get out of the grip of Sergeant Singh. "Let me tell him. I have to tell Mr. Tolliver," the boy was shouting. "Sergeant Libazo—"

"You will do nothing of the sort, you disgusting little monkey."

Tolliver started for the stair. "No, Tolliver," Egerton said. "That child does not belong in the police barracks."

"Begging your pardon, sir," Tolliver said, failing to suppress his impatience. "He may very well know where Libazo is."

The noise continued below as Singh dragged the child to the front door.

"Hold him, Singh! I am coming down," Tolliver shouted. He turned to Egerton. "Really, sir. This could be very important."

Egerton threw up his hands more in exasperation than agreement.

Tolliver jumped down the last three steps to the landing and took the rest three at a time. As soon as he reached the ground floor, Haki stopped struggling. "I have found Kwai Libazo, Bwana."

"Singh," Tolliver said, pointing to the guard beside the door, "let that constable take your place. You come with me."

Singh looked positively gleeful at the prospect of getting away from desk duty.

The boy took Tolliver by the index finger and fairly dragged him to the spot where he had seen Libazo. Singh followed along. But when they got there, Libazo was gone.

Carl Hastings was given no choice but to storm away. No amount of cajoling would convince the bastard al Dimu that they could become very rich if they cooperated with each other. With Majidi out of the way, they could take over everything themselves.

Hastings had started out offering the man, if one could call him that, twenty-five percent of the profits, a cut he considered generous since he would be the one taking all the risks of life, limb, and freedom. As he upped the eunuch's percentage, he thought he was making headway, but then it became clear the blighter was just prolonging his agony while sipping copiously the good whiskey Hastings had brought him as a gesture of friendship. Al Dimu never budged an inch, not even when Hastings clearly pointed out that Majidi never did a stroke of work himself. That he caused others to break the law. All he did was make threats and take the profits.

With that, the desexed towelhead had stood up and assumed an air of righteous indignation. He sanctimoniously announced that he would have nothing more to do with Hastings, that their business dealings had come to an end the moment Hastings murdered Majidi.

What an outrage! "Why would I have murdered Majidi? He was my partner in business. I needed him as much as he needed me," Hastings shouted, so loudly that he became afraid he would be heard out in the street.

Majidi had been Hastings's only chance to crawl out of the hole he was in. But he was not going to say that to this capon. He would gladly have strangled the upstart on the spot, if he were not bigger, taller, younger, and stronger. He would have shot him, but the pistol's report would have brought in a thousand of the eunuch's neighbors.

The best Hastings could do to express his anger was empty the meager remains in the bottle onto the man's desk and storm out of the building.

Without thinking, he made his way toward the train station. His brain buzzed with desperation. There was only one way out for him now. He could not carry on pursuing ivory. Legal ivory would not earn enough. He could not sell the illegal stuff without contacts in the Arab world, and his only contact had been Majidi. Surely there were others who bought and sold as Majidi did, but Hastings had no safe way of finding such traders. Merely asking the question of someone he did not know well could put him on the wrong side of the law.

He loathed the very idea of it, but he had to do what others had done before him. Change his identity. Start over elsewhere. They would be watching the ports. The easiest way out of the country would be through the interior. Uganda by rail. Then out to a coast, any coast. Then where? Godforsaken New Zealand? Even Australia. Anywhere but here. This place had beckoned as the choicest on earth for an Englishman looking to get rich. Bloody hell is what it had actually turned out to be.

He plowed through the streets that smelled of donkey dung and human sweat, cursing under his breath and so frightened that he was in danger of soiling himself.

"Hastings must have left the building. Libazo must have followed him." Tolliver was thinking out loud.

"Yes," Abrik Singh and Haki said in unison. "But where?" the boy added.

Tolliver put his hand on the child's shoulder and addressed Sergeant Singh. "I will go to the club and see if Hastings went there. He will eventually. You go to the police station at the end of the Ndia Kuu and get the boys there to spread out through the town to find Hastings or Kwai. Bring word to me at the club if either of them is found."

Singh saluted and sped off.

"I will search too," Haki said.

The boy's bones under Tolliver's palm were so small. He seemed so delicate. "No," Tolliver said. "I want you to come with me. I may need you to take a message for me. You will stand by near the club in case I can use you."

Tolliver scanned the streets and alleys as they moved along. It was dark now. The electric lamps along the streets cast only small pools of light. Anyone could be lurking in the unlit places, made darker by contrast with the blue light of the lamps.

Hastings was not at the club. Tolliver went out and sent the boy with a message for Vera that he would not come home for dinner. She would be lonely without him. He told himself she needed to be resting after her fainting spell.

He took up a position at the end of the bar where he could see the front door, ordered a weak gin and quinine, and sipped it while he waited. He considered whether he should speak to the management of the club about Hastings, but decided against it. This place was owned and run by a private company. The members got to make the rules about who could and could not join, that sort of thing, but he did not trust the management to put law enforcement ahead of the reputation of their establishment.

As it turned out, his vigil was much shorter than he imagined it might be.

Kwai Libazo arrived first, breathless. Tolliver brought him inside to the consternation of the Indian doorman, who himself would not have been allowed into the club if he had not worked there. Tolliver drew Kwai inside the cloakroom, where they could keep an eye on the door.

"He is coming this way," Libazo said, gulping air. "He is not fit enough to move fast, but he is hurrying."

"What have you found out about him?" Tolliver asked, trusting Libazo to give him the salient facts quickly and without embellishment.

"When he left the eunuch's house, he went to the train station, first to the ticket office and then to the bar. While he was drinking I asked the clerk. He bought a second-class ticket on the next up-country train. It leaves at noon tomorrow."

"The ticket agent told you that?"

"Yes, sir. I told him that Hastings was my captain's father, that I was not sure if he was going to buy the ticket or if I should purchase it for him."

Tolliver chuckled. "That was excellent, Liba—" At that second, the door opened and Hastings entered. Tolliver stepped forward and blocked his way. "I wonder if I might speak to you privately," Tolliver said quietly.

"Absolutely not!" Hastings fairly shouted.

Tolliver felt Kwai move closer behind him. Tolliver kept his voice low. "Please, Mr. Hastings," he said. "I do not want to embarrass you any more than is necessary."

"Then move out of my way and let me go by."

Tolliver raised his voice to a normal pitch. "I am trying, sir, to spare you and the club members the embarrassment of seeing you arrested and dragged away forcibly. But I will do that if you make it necessary."

"Exactly what is this about?"

"I want to speak to you about the murder of Khalid Majidi."

"I have given evidence in that case." He began to reach inside his jacket. "I am not going—"

Tolliver grabbed Hastings by the wrist, twisted his arm, and pushed him to the floor. The big man went down with a loud groan.

Behind them in the bar someone exclaimed and ran toward them. Libazo headed the intruder off. Tolliver held Hastings down, reached inside his pocket, and took out a pistol. "Come with me now, Mr. Hastings. You are making a scene."

"And you are making a mistake," Hastings shouted for the obvious benefit of the onlookers behind Tolliver. But then the big man came to his senses, hefted himself to his feet, turned on his heel, and let Tolliver escort him out of the building.

They went directly across the road to Fort Jesus. Since Hastings was an Englishman not yet charged with a crime, Tolliver would ordinarily have interrogated him at police headquarters, but he was tired and hungry and disgusted with Hastings's attitude. And the man had already purchased a railway ticket out of town. It would be folly to give him a chance to escape.

Hastings blustered and complained all the way, taking his anger out on Libazo, calling him a string of names, each more insulting than the last. For all Libazo reacted, the bloody bully might have been reciting the names of the kings and queens of England. Tolliver had never been more proud of his sergeant.

They marched Hastings to a small room off the corridor that led to the cells. It contained two chairs and table. The corners were stacked with boxes of tinned bully beef, sacks of cornmeal—staples of the prisoner diet, and a barrel of oil for hurricane lamps, one of which dimly lit the space.

Libazo took up a guard position at the door.

Once Hastings and Tolliver were seated, but before Tolliver had the chance to ask a question, Hastings resumed his bluster. "Are you going to take the word of that black savage Juba Osi against the word of an upstanding Englishman?"

Tolliver nearly laughed aloud at the man's foolishness. It was no wonder anything he attempted went belly-up. "Do you understand what we now know about your illegal traffic in slaves and ivory? As I see it, you had ample reason to do away with Majidi, since he could reveal your crimes. He kept proof of your deeds, but you had none of his. He did that to everyone who worked for him, I understand. Killing him was your only way out."

Hastings pounded his fist on the table between them. "Balderdash! Majidi could not have given me up without confessing to the same crimes himself."

Tolliver put his forearms on the desk and leaned forward the better to see Hastings's face. "Then you admit that you have been taking unlicensed ivory and capturing and shipping slaves? Have I understood you correctly?"

Hastings sagged. He seemed to understand that he was well and soundly on the hook for very serious crimes. "I did not kill him."

"Why should I believe that?"

Hastings clicked his tongue. "I need money. You know that. Well, word has gotten 'round that a fortune in cash money was found in Majidi's open safe when he was murdered."

"Exactly how do you know this?"

"Everyone knows it. It's been the talk of all the white men's bars. The lads are dreaming of what they would do if they had all that lucre."

"And how is that relevant to your activities?"

"Be sensible, man. You know what a hole I am in. If I had bashed the bastard, I would have taken the money. Why would I have left it behind? It is the lack of money that is the reason for it all. I am not saying that I would have bashed him to take the money, but if I had killed him, why on earth would I have left a fortune behind?"

It was a point Justin had pondered about the murderer. Whoever had killed Majidi was not after the money. And Hastings did seem incapable of leaving a fortune behind.

"For now," he said, "I will charge you with slave traffic and hunting violations. I will have to see about the murder charge." He looked at Hastings's fingertips. Like the rest of the man, they were big and thick. They were certainly not the fingers that had held the box that killed the ivory dealer.

"You cannot prove I did any of those other things." He seemed to be attempting to laugh, but it came out more as a bark.

Tolliver stood up and grasped the door handle. "We will begin to gather evidence. In the meanwhile, you will stay here as a guest of His Majesty."

Hastings leapt to his feet. "See here," he sputtered, but Tolliver left him to fume, instructing Libazo to get him something to eat and put him in a cell.

Tolliver drew his watch out of his pocket. It was nearly ten o'clock. All he wanted was some dinner, and a nap, and then his wife. In the nighttime cool, he jogged home.

When he arrived, he heard Vera at the piano before he reached the garden gate. She was playing and singing one of those popular songs she had learned on the ship: "On Moonlight Bay." She always wanted him to play and sing those new songs with her. He found most of them silly or maudlin, though, and much preferred playing duets of Bach or Schubert. But tonight, this seemed just the thing. He stood outside the open window and began to sing along through the mosquito netting: *"You have stolen my heart, now don't go 'way..."*

The piano playing stopped, but her voice grew louder. They met at the front door and sang the final words together. Justin thought to sing the harmony but Vera deepened her alto to harmonize with him, and he did her one better by taking the melody up an octave and singing it falsetto: *"—love's old sweet song, on Moonlight Bay."*

She laughed and kissed his mouth at the same time. "I have a surprise for you," she said.

He put his sun helmet on the small table near the door and undid his jacket buttons. "I hope it has something to do with meat."

"Not at all. Wait till you see. Follow me." She turned and fairly danced to the door at the end of the hall, which led to the veranda and the back garden.

There was a paraffin lamp burning on the outdoor table where they took their meals in the daylight hours. Scores of flying insects flitted about it.

She turned her palms up and indicated a tall green glass tumbler next to the lamp. "Ta-da," she sang out.

He reached for the glass.

"Don't touch it," she cried. "On that glass are Katharine Morley's fingerprints."

Kwai Libazo had changed out of his uniform into a Kikuyu *shuka*, the simple orange-brown cloth tied at the shoulder that he had always worn before he became a policeman. He wanted Aurala Sagal to see him for the man he was, not for the function he fulfilled in the British government. He found her exactly where he had asked her to meet him, near the small Catholic school across from the police barracks. In the light of the waxing moon, he took her by the hand to a hut on the cliff overlooking the sea, one that some Swahili fishermen used only during the day.

The men who owned the hut had agreed that if he left them "gifts," he was free to go there after the sun went down. His gift for them this night was three bottles of beer. He also carried a lantern and a rough army-issue blanket.

Kwai and Aurala hardly spoke as they walked along. His thoughts were consumed with desire. The moonlight made a path upon the water.

He had removed his sandals and untied the knot that held his *shuka* at his shoulder. Glancing into Aurala's glowing eyes, he spread the blanket on the floor and covered it with the *shuka* cloth. Then slowly and carefully he unwrapped the silken cloth from her body. Nothing was softer or smoother than her skin.

He lost himself in the pleasure of her.

The moonlight was gone before he became aware again of anything but the taste, the scent, the feel, the joy of loving her.

When he raised his head and looked about him, he said, "It is dark outside," as if it were a great surprise to him.

She laughed, a liquid noise like the water in the fountain in front of the Treasury Building. "You are a very desirous man," she said, still laughing.

He did not know if she meant that he desired her, or that she found him desirable. He lay back and took her in his arms, wanting nothing for the moment but to lie next to her and breathe in the air of the ocean that was soft and tasted of salt.

"How old are you?" she asked after a while.

"I am twenty-five," he said.

"And yet you are not circumcised."

Her words froze his heart. Suddenly nothing was right with this night. "Why do you say that?" He could hear his own voice shaking.

She sat up. "I am sorry. I should not have said it. Please don't be angry. I only asked because I am not cut either. You know that the Somali cut their girls before they marry."

"The Kikuyu and the Maasai do that too."

"I ran away to find my sister before they cut me. I want you to know this, even though I think it will make you not want me anymore."

"Nothing will stop me from wanting you." He wanted to add *especially not that*, but he did not know what that would mean to her. Instead, he explained that being half Kikuyu, half Maasai meant that neither tribe accepted him as a warrior. "That is why I was never circumcised."

She kissed him with her lips, with her tongue, and gently with her beautiful teeth. "You are perfect," she said.

The Idol of Mombasa

Because he could not do or say anything else, he loved her again. When he felt her body respond to his, he rejoiced that they had not cut her. He wondered why any man who truly desired a woman would want her not to respond as Aurala did to his touch.

When the horizon became visible where the sea met the sky, he knew they must soon go. He offered her some water and drank some himself.

"This is a good place for us," she said. "I like to be here where we can hear the sea and feel its breeze and smell its clean breath."

"Any place I can be with you is a good place for me," he said. "I am sorry to leave you, but I must report for duty."

"Can we walk together into the town?" she asked.

As they did, she told him about her sister and the silk shop. That her sister did not want her to do such work anymore. "She never wanted me to. But Majidi said that I must or he would kill us both."

"I am happy he is dead then. I would kill him if he were still alive." He said it with conviction. But he wondered if it were really true.

"With the extra money that my sister and the other girls are keeping, we have enough to take a little house in the native village, but most of the Swahili are Muslims. They will not have us near them. We are the worst of sinners. We cannot live among them. So we are still living in the souk."

He took her hand and held it as they walked along. He did not want her to live there, but he did not have enough money to pay for another place to live. He was required to live in the barracks. They had only the fishermen's shack for the times they could make sex together in the night. For the first time since he had seen her, he longed to be back in his home country, where the tribal people could be cruel but did not have such rules about boys and girls.

"Perhaps," she said, "after the Grand Mufti leaves, things will calm down. It is since he is here that the people are trying so hard to be holy."

"The G.M. is very important. All of the English are very worried that he will be hurt. Or even just displeased."

"I think he is a good man," she said. "I don't think he knows how the men take his words and turn them into things they think they must do. I, of course, have not heard him with my own ears, but they talk about his words. Then they twist them into commands. The next thing you know they are talking as if the Grand Mufti told them to kill someone."

Suddenly, Libazo thought that what she was saying was important, not only to her but to him, the sergeant. "Tell me the things he says and the things they do."

"I have heard them talking as they walk in the souk. They say that the Grand Mufti spoke in the mosque and said, 'Take yourself seriously as followers of the Holy Prophet.' And then they begin to discuss Majidi. That he worships only money. That he does things that are against the Shari'a law only to get money."

"Shari'a?" It was not a word Kwai Libazo knew.

"The law of Islam," she said, "the law of my people. They speak as if that is what is important to them, but I think that many of them hate Majidi only because he has so much power over them."

"Where does his power come from?"

"I do not understand exactly." She stopped now. They were near the bazaar. "I have to be careful not to be overheard," she said. She lowered her voice but went on. "Majidi had a lot of people who did what he wanted, who made money for him. He did not do the evil things. He forced others to do them."

"How?"

"Leylo says that he tempts them to do something bad, to do it for a great amount of money. He keeps the proof that they did this bad thing. Then he threatens to expose them for what they have done if they don't continue to obey him."

"What sorts of things could be so bad that they will do his bidding against their own beliefs?"

"I don't know. Bad things. He gets them into debt and then forces them to earn their way out. Many have gone to capture Somali girls up in the north, Muslim girls, to bring them here to work for him. Spoiling them for a life as a woman of Islam. That is how he got Leylo."

"He did that?"

The dawn had broken. People were beginning to move in the streets. In the pale light, he saw her bring her finger to her lips. She whispered. "Not to me but to my sister and to the other girls at the shop."

He saw what it meant. "So Majidi told the bookseller that he must stop the Grand Mufti's preaching."

"I think he was afraid one of the men he commanded would be inspired by the Grand Mufti's words, that he would betray Majidi to the Shari'a court."

"But someone killed him instead. And I think it must have been for his disrespect for the laws of your religion." It was an impulse Kwai understood. Once he had joined the British police force and begun to work with A.D.S. Tolliver, he had devoted himself to serving the rule of law and justice. He understood fully how a religion could be based on the law. But this would mean here in Mombasa there were two kinds of law—the law of the Arabs and British law... And they did not move men in the same direction. Not in the same direction at all.

She gripped his hand and looked into his eyes. "My sister says that those men of Majidi's, to prove how holy they are, have also sent word to my father, telling him where Leylo and I are. That means my brothers will come after Leylo and me. They will want to kill us."

Kwai believed her. Suddenly his heart was beating as fast as it did when he kissed her. "When? Do you know that they are coming? I must hide you. They must never find you." Every bit of him was suddenly alert, as if he were prey near a hunting lion in the wilderness. As if he were about to be eaten alive.

"Leylo told me they were just saying those things to frighten us. But I saw true fear in her eyes. She is the one who is lying, to stop me being afraid."

He looked up. The sky was already bright. He would be late reporting for duty. If he was dismissed from the police force, how could he keep her safe? But he did not want to go from her. He did not want to let her out of his sight.

"You must go to your work," she said. There was not a hint of hesitation in her voice.

"I will find a place for you to hide. I will—you must—"

"Go," she said. "I will hide in the Hindu shoe seller's stall if they come today. But I am sure it is too soon. They will not get here so soon." She put her hands together and bowed her head to him, turned her back, and walked away. She did not look back, and he did not follow. He had no place to hide her. He wished he could put her inside his own body and keep her where no one could hurt her.

A couple of hours later, Inspector Patrick put down his magnifying glass and turned to Justin Tolliver, who had been forcing himself not to pace while he waited for the result. Patrick picked up the glass tumbler and handed it to Tolliver. "You can return this to your clever wife," he said. "The fingerprints on this glass do not match the fingerprints on the murder weapon."

"Well, that's a relief! Now I won't have to arrest a missionary woman for murder."

"That is if those truly are her fingerprints on the glass," Patrick said rather drily.

Tolliver opened his mouth to express his indignation. He had told Patrick that it was Vera who had obtained them. Did this fingerprint expert think Vera would lie about such a thing? But Tolliver bit his lip. *Would* Vera lie about such a thing?

"Please don't take offense," Patrick said. "It's how a chap in my line needs to think. Narrowly about the observed facts."

"No offense taken," he said as lightly as he could. "I will do what I can to confirm." He turned away to hide his grimace. He did not want Patrick to think his wife would fabricate evidence. He wouldn't want any other sort of wife than the one he had, but he preferred that the men of the force think her just another British woman, which she certainly was not.

He left Patrick to write his report, went to his own desk, and wrote out a request to the district commissioner at Malindi for any evidence about the shipping of contraband ivory or slaves. He thought he might interrogate Hastings again, to see if he could get him to come clean. But then Egerton arrived looking like the wrath of God. He closed the office door with a thump.

"Tolliver," he said, "the commissioner tells me that you have arrested an Englishman."

Tolliver indicated the chair next to his desk, but Egerton remained standing and paced the small space like a tiger in the zoo. "You know full well that you must report such an action to me. I hope you have a good explanation for why you did not do so before the commissioner's question caught me by surprise."

"It happened very late last night, sir. I have credible evidence that he and Majidi were dealing in illegal ivory and worse—trading slaves out of Malindi. I have just finished sending off a letter by runner mail to District Superintendent Longworth up there, asking him to look into it from his end."

Egerton placed his fists on the desk and leaned over it. "I have it that your so-called evidence is the word of an African." Egerton's voice was full of exasperation.

Tolliver forced himself not to pull back. "A freed slave named Juba Osi, sir." He'd be damned if he would let Egerton force him to drop this investigation. "Sir, the rules say we are not supposed to use a double standard. Yet we arrest blacks for using abusive language on the mere accusation of a white. Hastings is alleged to have committed egregious crimes. We have to take what I have learned seriously or we will look like a passel of fools instead of a competent police force." He closed his mouth and held his breath.

Egerton glared at him from mere inches away. Justin looked into his eyes calmly, without challenge. Egerton shook his head and sighed. "Your file says you are sensitive to native relations. I did not take that to mean that you preferred the word of a black to a white."

"I prefer the evidence that seems to point to the truth, sir." Hearing what a prig he was being, Justin realized he'd better let the D.S. save face. "Really, sir. I do believe we have a good case against Hastings. When I confronted him with what I had been told, he did not deny it. He merely said that I would not be able to prove it. I am taking the opportunity to try."

"But you are holding him in prison in the meantime, on the word of an ex-slave." Tolliver did not wince, though Egerton's tone was accusatory, as if Tolliver had burned down the town to rid it of a mouse.

"He had bought a ticket to Uganda on today's noon train."

"We can't look as if we prefer the blacks to the whites."

Tolliver bit back an oath. "But we must prefer truth to lies, and the rule of law to everything else." Tolliver no longer cared how sanctimonious he sounded.

At that moment, Kwai Libazo arrived looking as if he were bursting with news.

"I promise, sir," Tolliver said to Egerton, "that I will clear up the issue of Hastings as quickly as possible. I will release him if I don't have a corroborating report from Malindi within a few days."

"See that you do," Egerton said, as if he had the upper hand, which by virtue of his rank he did.

As soon as he had gone, Libazo reported what he had learned about Majidi and his machinations. "Given Mr. Majidi's evil actions, I think, sir, that it must be one of the Arab men who killed him. Do you not think this could be true?" He looked to Tolliver as if he expected to be congratulated for what he had found out. But Tolliver had no idea how he would go about discovering who among the men in the Arab community had done the deed, if in fact one of them had.

In a flash of insight, it suddenly occurred to him that if the fingerprints on the murder weapon were a woman's and if Majidi actually had captured the women of the brothel and forced them into that way of life, one of them might have taken her revenge against her captor. Prostitution was against British law. But as long as the women did not disturb the peace or break other laws, the British police left them to themselves. The story would be very different if the charge were murder.

"We will have to arrest the women in the silk shop," he said to Libazo. "Take a detachment of men there and bring them all to Fort Jesus."

He expected Libazo to be angry, unwilling, expected him even to rebel against the idea. Instead, he looked entirely happy at the prospect of arresting a woman in whom he seemed to have a love interest. There were times when Tolliver thought he was beginning to understand his sergeant. And then, in one stroke, the man would destroy that illusion.

Kwai Libazo obeyed orders. In this case he was more than happy to do so. Aurala would be safe from her father and her brothers while she was in police custody. It was an answer to his prayers.

For extra protection while transporting her and her sister and the other girls, he went to the police barracks and chose four askaris, making sure that none of them were Somali. As he marched the men in the direction of the bazaar, his mind raced. He had to make sure that Aurala Sagal was not convicted of a crime. In prison, women were supposed to be separated from the men, but all too often they were not. He did not want to think about what the guards made girls do.

For now at least, being under arrest would mean that, if her brothers came intending to defend their family honor by killing her and her sister, they would have to break into the prison to do so.

Tolliver had Inspector Patrick waiting at Fort Jesus with his fingerprinting apparatus as soon the silk-shop girls arrived. The women found the procedure curious, but they cooperated, as he would have expected.

While Patrick went off to his laboratory to compare their fingerprints with those on the murder weapon, Tolliver proceeded to question them one by one. Leylo Sagal, the eldest, quickly confirmed that she had been kidnapped from a coastal town called Shaka, just over the border in Somalia. She had been a young wife, married only a few months. She was happy to speak at length of the meanness of her husband's first wife, of the mixture of fear and relief when she was taken away from what would have been a lifetime of misery. She said her life in the silk shop was neither better nor worse than she would have had, but when he tried to prompt her to describe her life after the abduction, she pursed her lips and looked away. No amount of coaxing on Tolliver's part could persuade her to look at him, much less open up.

Nyah, the second girl, would tell him nothing at all, not even to confirm that she too had been kidnapped.

Aurala Sagal was entirely cooperative. She had not been kidnapped, but had followed her sister of her own accord. But when Majidi discovered her arrival, she became his captive. She told Tolliver the names of more than twenty men who had been in thrall to Majidi, any one of whom might have wanted to kill him. "The Grand Mufti is one of the highest persons of the law of Islam. I hoped very much that the Grand Mufti would learn how evil Majidi was and kill him." She raised her head and looked Tolliver right in the eye. "Every night of my life here, I prayed for the courage to kill him myself."

Her defiance made her all the lovelier. Tolliver saw exactly why Kwai Libazo was so taken with her. She was beautiful, with chiseled, refined features and a melodious voice, all animated by her lively spirit and the sparkle in her eyes. But he wondered at her lack of guile. She was here being questioned about the very murder that—by her own statement—she had wished to commit. He could not blame her for longing to free herself from captivity, to escape from a life that debased her. Sheltered from the world as she must have been as a girl child, she had had the pluck to run away from home on her own to find her sister and try to save her. When he questioned her in the silk shop, she had told him she was only fifteen. She seemed so womanly much of the time. But now she had revealed her thoughts as no canny adult would. It seemed a childlike thing to do.

Almost as if she had read his mind, her determination deepened. "Majidi deserved to die," she said.

Tolliver did not know what to think. Girls her age were considered children in England. Not so in Africa. Yet how, at such an age, could Aurala Sagal have been condemned to work as a whore? That was how he was supposed to think about her. Every ounce of his English mores and morals called out for him to throw her to the dogs. The prevailing culture among the British in the Protectorate, staff and settlers alike, was that the savages they had found here were little better than beasts, and that a girl like this deserved neither pity nor protection.

Tolliver had written to his sister that he felt as if his soul had expanded here in Africa. What he had not admitted to anyone, not even to himself, was that in the course of that expansion, his soul had taken on a new shape, new subtleties of color, that dispelled rigid assumptions of his childhood. Vera called into question much of what Tolliver had been taught about the people in this lovely, often violent land. And he had seen that her gentler, more understanding approach was the better one. The people here, while they might seem uncivilized at first, had just as many good and bad points as any Englishman.

Without Libazo's quick thinking and brave actions, those drunks in the bar in Nairobi last year might have gotten the better of the raw, untrained police officer that Tolliver had been. Yet when the generous reward came through, Tolliver had accepted it as if all the credit for the arrest belonged to him. He vowed that he would give a portion of it to Kwai Libazo, who was standing against the jail's ancient stone wall, looking like a mahogany statue. Tolliver looked over his shoulder at him. Libazo's body remained frozen. Only his eyes moved, and their message to Tolliver was an expectation, a plea, a demand that Tolliver prove his basic humanity.

Tolliver met his gaze. If he left the girls in the jail, they would be subject to the jailers' and the male prisoners' abuse. But suppose he let them go, they bolted, and the fingerprints on the murder weapon turned out to be one of theirs? He sighed.

Abrik Singh knocked and entered. "I prepared a cell for them," he said. "Shall I take them to it?"

Tolliver looked back at Kwai. "Sergeant Libazo," he ordered, "take these women to the cell."

Libazo saluted. "Yes, sir. I will guard them personally until Inspector Patrick's report makes our next step clear."

He was being cheeky in the extreme. Tolliver had no idea what the thought processes of a man in love with a prostitute might be. But he conceded. "Please do so."

Abrik Singh made the noise that revealed he was suppressing a gasp. He thinks I am putting the fox in charge of the henhouse, Tolliver imagined. But he trusted Libazo. He shoved away any doubts in that regard.

"You come with me, Sergeant Singh," Tolliver ordered. "I want you to stand by at Inspector Patrick's laboratory for the results of his analysis."

Vera looked up from her gardening and grinned at Tolliver as he came through the front gate. "Have you come home for luncheon? To what do I owe this honor?"

"To the Grand Mufti, I would say," Justin answered, taking her elbow while she rose to her feet. "Whatever else it is costing the crown by way of paying for ceremonies and gatherings, one has to admit that with him in town, ordinary petty criminal activity has sunk to a low point. Hardly a housebreaking or a drunken brawl in the past several days."

She stood up and dusted the dirt off her fingers. "Excuse me, Mr. Dingle," she said to the gardener. "You go on with planting the lemon trees, but once the sun is full on here, you might as well take a break and get out of the heat until later."

Frederick Dingle looked up at her, serious as always. "Thank you, my lady." It was practically the only thing he ever said, except when he discussed which plants would look best where in the garden. One could hardly shut him up on that subject.

Justin held the door for her and followed her inside. She went straight back to the kitchen and scrubbed her hands at the sink. Miriam was filling pitchers with boiled water for drinking.

Justin took a glass from the hutch and held it out for her to fill up. When he had drunk it off, Vera took it from him and did the same.

"It's too hot to eat," Vera said, knowing he would not agree. He ate no matter what. "We haven't much in the house but some Arab bread and cheese."

"I want to talk to you alone. Let's make do with whatever there is. Come with me." He took off his uniform jacket and hung it over the back of a chair and went out to the shady veranda.

Apprehensive about what he would say, she gave Miriam instructions and followed him. She had barely sat down when he started to tell her about the arrest of the women from the souk and the danger they were in. He paused every time Miriam came and went, setting the table, putting down a basket of bread, serving her some lemonade and him a bottle of porter. The policeman in him was ever sensitive to servants' gossip. Secrets got out anyway, but that never stopped him trying to protect them.

Vera was very interested in Kwai Libazo's lady love—not that any proper Scottish woman would think of her in such terms. All she needed to know was that Kwai liked the girl. If there were true affection between them, they deserved a chance to be together.

She straightened her back and looked across at her husband. "Aurala Sagal is such a beautiful name. Why don't you bring her here so she can escape that horrid life? She can help around the house."

His jaw fell. "Are you mad, Vera? I have just told you that she has been working as a—a—"

"Prostitute." She could say it if he couldn't. She knew exactly what the Europeans in the town would think of her if she let such a creature into her home. But they would be wrong. "I want only to protect Kwai Libazo's woman. Wouldn't it be right to help such a girl escape that life? If that's what Kwai wants to do, to help her escape, why should we not aid him?"

He reached across the table and took her hand and kissed it. "My love," he said, "I know that it would not make a difference to you, but I am an officer of the law. And she is a lawbreaker. Besides, suppose it turns out that she is the murderer. That is what I am most concerned about at this moment." He explained that Aurala Sagal's and the other girls' fingerprints were being analyzed as they spoke. "I have asked Sergeant Singh to bring the report to me here. Once it arrives we will know more."

"But you are just after telling me that Aurala and her sister are in danger from the men in their family. If you find that they are innocent of murder and set them free, it could be the same as condemning them to death. Their male relatives will kill them for doing something they have been forced into."

"All the more reason we cannot keep them here." There was fear in Justin's eyes. "What can you be thinking? If Aurala's brothers did come after the women, they would be coming *here* to find them."

She put her hand to her mouth and reached for him. "Oh, my, you are right. I never—"

He shook his head as if at a foolish child, which was what she felt like at the moment.

"Is there nothing we can do?" she asked.

"I promise I will take what steps I can to protect them. But for now, we cannot be sure they are innocent of murder."

Vera knew Justin had the best of intentions, but she was also sure that the police force would not do very much for a girl who had been a prostitute. "Thank you, dearest," was all she said.

Their conversation lagged once their food arrived. Vera picked at a tiny bit of it, but it was just too hot to eat heartily. Justin, always ravenous, wolfed down everything in sight, which made her feel even more woozy.

"I don't know what I will do if we come up empty with these suspects," Justin said as he peeled an apple and offered her a slice. "I don't know anyone who can tell me anything about the

Arab community. Aurala named a score of men who might have wanted to kill Majidi. It's easy to conclude that one of them did it and entirely another matter to figure out which one. We can't fingerprint the entire Arab population."

Vera took the slice of apple and bit off a morsel. She wished she knew people and could explain things to him. Up-country, where she was born, she knew things he did not and could tell him about tribal ways, what to expect in the wilderness. Here, in a city she had only passed through as a child, she was as much of a neophyte as he.

"The front garden is coming along quite nicely," he said, apropos of nothing at all.

"Mr. Dingle is a treasure," she said.

They took in sharp breaths simultaneously. "Mr. Dingle," they said in unison.

"He became a Mohammedan for a while," she said. "He told me this the very first time I spoke to him in the Public Gardens. He may very well have information that could be helpful."

Vera wanted to go with Tolliver while he questioned Frederick Dingle. She insisted that the gardener was too shy and nervous to respond easily to a relative stranger, especially a policeman, that it would go much better if she were there to put him at ease. But Tolliver did not think it at all appropriate for him to involve his wife directly in a murder investigation. He left her sipping quinine-lemonade and pouting. He found Dingle at the side of the bungalow, in the shade, his back against the garden wall. He seemed to be asleep. He was elderly, in his fifties at least, but quite fit. By Vera's reports he was full of energy when it came to gardening, but always quite hesitant and lethargic otherwise.

Unconscious as Dingle had seemed, he jumped to his feet as soon as Tolliver approached. "I—I—" he stuttered, and seemed to be trying to stand at attention.

"My wife is wonderfully pleased with all you are doing. The place already looks a damn sight better than when they moved us in here." Tolliver watched for an indication that Dingle was relaxing. If he was, he didn't show it.

Thanks to Vera, Tolliver knew exactly what sort of question would open him up. "Is it difficult to find garden plants that will grow properly in this climate?"

"Oh, no, sir. The trick is to use the plants that the Arabs have been using in their gardens for centuries. Bringing in typical English plants, as you know, is practically impossible. If you can get them to grow at all, the baboons'll tear them up trying to find out if they like the taste. Except for irises. Now your irises will..." And Dingle was off. He seemed to be dictating a treatise on the use of irises in Middle Eastern gardens.

Tolliver looked for the right moment to interrupt, but Dingle's words poured forth in such a torrent that there was no opening to change the subject. He followed Dingle to the front gate where the subject changed to pest-resistant roses.

When Tolliver finally got a word in edgewise, he blurted out his question with no graceful transition. "Mr. Dingle, I must ask you—did you know the man whose murder I am investigating—Khalid Majidi?"

Dingle's rheumy pale eyes look startled, then fearful. He closed his mouth and clenched his jaw.

"You see, I know that you have been in Mombasa for a number of years. I had heard that there was a period where you practiced Mohammedanism. There are not many Englishmen who are conversant with the Arabs. I thought you might give me some hints that could be helpful."

"You know I am a prisoner in the jail."

"You *were* a prisoner, no?"

"No, still am. I am required to go there at sundown every day. I am still serving a sentence."

This was news to Tolliver, and it was just like Vera not to have mentioned it. Still, no one in the town seemed to treat the man as anything but a gardener. Tolliver was used to

English prisoners being given a great deal of leeway here in the Protectorate. In fact, they were often given charge of native prisoners on work details.

Dingle raised his hands as if to stop Tolliver from saying anything. "I converted to Islam because I thought it would cure me of my alcohol disease. It did for a while, but the demon in me won out again. I am a very weak man."

Tolliver was nonplussed. How embarrassing to hear a man say such a thing. "Yes, well, but you are a wonderful gardener," he sputtered finally. "I am glad my wife has your help. I just wonder if you can tell me anything that might be helpful about which Arabs might have wanted to kill Majidi."

"Oh, sir. I was studying their religion. The scholars who taught me took a very dim view of Mr. Majidi. The mosque was not the sort of place to find out anything much about his sort except that he was not a good man. But I have seen a man who may know. He is also a prisoner in the jail—Mr. Carl Hastings. I have seen him often coming and going at Majidi's shop. It is well-known that he has been selling ivory to the Arabs for some time. Everyone who has been in Mombasa for the past few years knows that."

"Thank you," Tolliver said, trying to sound sincerely grateful. Dingle was right. Hastings knew much more than he was saying. But Tolliver was equally sure that he would not reveal what he knew. "I'll let you get back to your work," he said. As he turned to go into the house to say good-bye to Vera, Abrik Singh approached along the street and called to him from the front gate.

Before he took the four steps to reach Singh, Vera was out the front door saying hello. She must have been snooping near the window. Abrik bowed to her and handed Tolliver an envelope that bore the notification: *Official Evidence, British East African Police, Department of Fingerprinting.*

Singh and Vera watched wide-eyed as he opened it and took out the report. Tolliver smiled into their worried eyes as he read, *"None of the girls from the bazaar."*

Vera clapped her hands together as if her best friend had been exonerated. "Sergeant Libazo will be so pleased," she said.

"Celebrate if you like," Tolliver said. "But Patrick says that the size of the fingertips was very similar. Which means it must have been a woman, and there is not a woman left in town who is implicated in any way."

"We'd better go to Fort Jesus and release those girls. While I am there I will see if I can get anything new out of Carl Hastings," he said to Sergeant Singh.

"Darling," Vera said, "You will protect those girls, won't you?"

"As best I can," he said.

"Sir," Singh said. "D.S. Egerton asked me to tell you that he wants to speak with you as soon as possible."

"Wait just a moment," Vera said. "I'll get my sun helmet and walk with you down the hill. I need to buy some things for our dinner."

"I hope I may come home in time to eat it," Tolliver said.

Kwai Libazo stood in the corridor of the prison at Fort Jesus prison, keeping close watch on the locked door between him and Aurala and the other girls. Whenever he looked through the barred opening into the cell, Aurala was either sitting on a cot with her back against the wall and her eyes closed, or with her head close to her sister's, whispering. He had not left them for more than a few minutes to get water or visit the privy. He had told them to scream at the top of their lungs if anyone but A.D.S. Tolliver even attempted to open the door.

Kwai was very hungry and wondered how long it would be before Inspector Patrick and his magnifying glass would know if one of these girls had left her fingerprints on the marble casket that killed Bwana Majidi. He wished it could be a long time. But he also knew that he could not stand here forever and keep Aurala safe from the other guards. He would not blame one of those girls if she had killed the man who had made them slaves.

He did his best to convince himself that it could not possibly have been Aurala.

The guards had brought him precious little to eat. They insisted that he should leave guarding the girls to them, but he did not trust them. They had talked of nothing but how much they enjoyed "playing host" to prostitutes. These girls had been forced to give themselves to men for money, and the guards would now think it was their right to do whatever they wanted with them. Kwai knew he would want to kill any man who forced himself on Aurala.

He went to the little window in the cell door and looked through. She must have felt his glance because she looked up at that moment and flashed him the warm smile she had given him the first time he set eyes on her. The policeman in him was supposed to wonder if it was the smile of a murderer. He told himself that he was not really worried that she was guilty, but that was not entirely true. After what Majidi had done to her and her sister, he could believe that she would want to see him dead. And he would have to agree. The British might say he was thinking like a savage. Kwai told himself that he, like A.D.S. Tolliver, believed in the rule of law. But he had learned, in less than two years on the police force, that the law did not always deliver his idea of justice. He went back to his post and listened to his stomach growl.

It was midafternoon before A.D.S. Tolliver and Sergeant Singh arrived. "Release them," Tolliver ordered.

Sergeant Singh scowled. "The charges of prostitution, sir?"

"Don't be absurd," Tolliver answered. "We have too many more important matters to deal with."

Kwai moved to the cell and inserted a large iron key in the lock. "Request permission to escort them home, sir." His heart was happy that Aurala would not be tried for murder, but he knew too well what might await her and her sister outside the security of the fort.

"Let Singh take care of that," Tolliver said. "We have other urgent business." He looked into Singh's face and added, "Make sure that you take them safely to their home. And send a constable from time to time to make sure there is no disturbance there." He looked at Kwai who saw an apology in his eyes. "It's the best I can do." Tolliver's voice had taken on an edge of insistence.

Kwai knew what he said was true. And that the sharpness in Tolliver's voice showed he hated that fact.

Kwai was grateful for that much, but he feared it would not be enough. He unlocked the cell and stepped back with head lowered, clenching his teeth on his bottom lip. He held his head up as Aurala filed out. She walked so close to him that her garment brushed the skin of his arm. He almost groaned. He breathed in the scent of her, held his breath, and then she was gone.

"We are taking a detail to guard a special procession at a mosque. It seems the Grand Mufti is getting ready to go back to Egypt and they are beginning the prayers and ceremonies of farewell. It is up to us to add to the honors by guarding every event."

"Yes, sir."

Tolliver lowered his voice. "D.S. Egerton is the one who gives the orders, Sergeant Libazo, and don't you forget it." His tone was uncharacteristically harsh and could only mean that he was just as displeased with the assignment as was Kwai Libazo.

Justin Tolliver watched the afternoon light fade while some two hundred Muslim men filed into a mosque near the bazaar. They remained indoors for upward of half an hour, and then came out, walking slowly and singing, accompanied by flutes and drums. Led by young men sprinkling rose water, they processed around the building and after circling the mosque once, returned inside. The street lamps had come on before the ceremony was over, and Tolliver and his squadron escorted the Grand Mufti and the Liwali back to their residence. Tolliver rode in the horse-drawn carriage with the dignitaries. The askaris ran at double-time behind. D.S. Egerton was waiting to greet the Grand Mufti at the front door of the Liwali's palace.

As soon as the bigwigs had entered the place, Egerton took Tolliver by the elbow. "We have been invited to attend the dinner about to take place."

Tolliver would have preferred to go home to Vera, but he didn't see how he could refuse the D.S.

"Don't look so glum," Egerton said with a laugh. "They will think we don't like them."

Inside, they found that they had been relegated to a separate room, since it was against the Muslim religion for its men to eat with infidels. It was Egerton's turn to pout. Not having understood the taboo, Egerton had assumed that to be polite, they had to break bread with the Muslims. He proceeded to spend the rest of the evening lamenting the fact that they had been lured into the event on false pretenses. Tolliver, bored with the D.S.'s complaining, was nevertheless grateful for the food: grilled lamb and wonderful chewy flat bread. A salad made with oranges, olives, and onion, dressed with olive oil, which was surprisingly delicious. He drank the mysterious pink, frothy fruit juices and thought how refreshing they would be laced with a little gin or mixed with champagne. He suggested from time to time that as the guests of honor were in a separate room, they might slip away, but Egerton preferred to stay and complain.

It was nearly ten o'clock before Tolliver was able to extricate himself. He found the squadron and Libazo waiting for him at the front of the Liwali's palace.

"We have rotated keeping guard and taking a dinner break," Libazo said.

"You are dismissed," Tolliver said to them all. He had hoped to go to the fort and interrogate Hastings, but at this hour the prisoner would likely be asleep. Tolliver would have to keep his questions for the morning.

In lieu of a good night, Egerton said, "I have made an appointment for us to meet with the Liwali at ten tomorrow morning to talk about the guard detail for the Grand Mufti's embarkation for Egypt. Meet me at my office at 9:30, and we shall go together."

Tolliver commandeered a trolley to take him to MacDonald Terrace, and then walked the short distance to the bungalow. He was thinking of a glass of claret, a bit of a Bach duet with Vera, and then her arms.

When he arrived at home, however, he found her sitting with Robert Morley in their front room. The missionary was in tears.

Vera leapt up and rushed to him as soon as he came in the door. "He is devastated," she whispered. "He had a lady friend. The poor woman has died in childbirth. It has taken such a toll on him. He must have cared for her a great deal. He took her to the native hospital, but the doctors could not save her. I cannot persuade him to talk about what will happen to the baby."

CHAPTER

19

There was no music and no pleasure in Vera's arms that night. A glass of claret was the best that Tolliver could manage of his desires. In the end he fell asleep reading by lamplight in an armchair in the bedroom while Vera continued to whisper soothingly to the missionary in the parlor. When he awoke, the clergyman was gone and Vera was snoozing on the divan. He slid off her shoes, and gently, without disturbing her slumber, carried her like a sleeping child and put her into bed, otherwise fully clothed.

Next morning, when a ray of the rising sun woke him, he had not the heart to rouse her. He shaved and dressed, left her a note, and went to have the biggest possible breakfast at the Hotel Metropole.

At the meeting Egerton had requested, the D.S. was officious and went on at great length about the needs of the Empire to no purpose Tolliver could divine. Their subsequent meeting with the Liwali turned out to be truly strange. He lectured Egerton and Tolliver about the Shari'a court under his jurisdiction and the importance of law in the practice of Islam. Speaking in tones Tolliver would have expected from a grammar school master, he informed them of what they already knew: that the Sultan of Zanzibar was still sovereign here on the coast, and that the determination of what was and was not a crime depended on his law, not the British government's. This latter observation was not Tolliver's understanding, but, of course, he could not contradict the Liwali.

The next thing the man said was positively insulting. "You British sail about on ships flying the antislavery flag, but your real aim seems to be to conquer the world."

Tolliver waited for Egerton to object, but the D.S. remained stonily silent.

It wasn't until the Liwali was escorting them to his front door that he mentioned what might have been the actual reason for the confab—that on the very next day the Grand Mufti and his party would be sailing for Alexandria on a French mail steamer of the Compagnie des Messageries Maritimes.

"What was that all about?" Tolliver asked when they were out in the street.

"It was about the need to maintain good relations with the blighters," Egerton said. His voice was dour, but he strode along with such vehemence that Tolliver imagined he was more angry than unimpressed.

Egerton looked around and lowered his voice. "At least the Grand Mufti will be out of our hair by this time tomorrow. That will be a relief. You will accompany me to the farewell ceremony."

As ever, Tolliver knew it was useless to object. He parted company with the D.S. at the entrance to the fort. His mind was swimming with questions he wanted to ask Hastings about who might have mouthed threats against Majidi in his presence.

As soon as he entered the prison and saw the look on Kwai Libazo's face, he knew something was very amiss.

"Gone, sir," Kwai said. "Mr. Carl Hastings has escaped."

If Vera had not been so exhausted by her long, emotional conversation with Robert Morley, which had lasted into the small hours, she might have awakened as soon as Tolliver slipped out of bed. As it was, he was an hour gone before she awoke, still feeling fatigued. It was midmorning before she was dressed and out the door. Impatient with herself, she hurried to the souk. She had a marvelous idea. She smiled to herself at the thought that Justin might have to arrest her for stealing.

The dry season had started before they arrived from Europe and had by now parched the city and made Vera wish for mud instead of grit. Humid as the air could be, there had not been even the lightest shower. Along the dusty streets, she found herself humming a Kikuyu song about beautiful rain.

> *Rain, rain, rain,*
> *Delicious rain, beautiful rain.*
> *Bring us happy mud.*
> *Bring us flowers.*
> *Wed with the sun and bring us food for our bellies,*
> *And laughter,*
> *Rain, rain, rain.*
> *Laughter in the rain.*

When she had dragged her dusty feet to the police building, she found the place in turmoil. Squads of askaris were jogging off in all directions, looking very serious indeed, as if determined to catch a killer on the loose. She looked down at the small parcel she carried and thought she must be wrong about what its contents would tell Justin.

He was nowhere to be found. "They have gone off to search for a missing prisoner," was all the sergeant in the lobby would tell her.

The boy Haki was more helpful. She found him sitting next to the front door as she was about to exit. "The big Englishman has run away from the jail," he told her.

She imagined that they had somehow discovered that Hastings was the murderer after all. "Walk with me to the souk," she invited the boy. "I'll buy you a honey cake." It would be a while, she was sure, before she would be able to speak to Justin, and she had another important mission in mind.

When they arrived at the bazaar, she did not go near the silk shop, but asked the boy to go in and find Aurala Sagal. "Ask her to come to the entrance and speak to A.D.S. Tolliver's wife," she said.

"What about the honey cake?" the boy demanded.

"Get her first and then I will buy you two honey cakes."

It was only a few minutes before he returned with a beautiful young Somali woman in tow. Aurala Sagal was much taller than Vera, elegant and graceful, with big dark eyes that held both fear and curiosity.

Vera gave the boy some coins and sent him away to enjoy his treats. She looked around. There was not an English person in sight. Still, she asked the girl to follow her into a narrow cul-de-sac beyond the butcher's stall. She wished she could sit down with Aurala and drink a cup of tea. What did she care what people would think about her talking to such a person? She was only trying to help a girl escape from what her brutal father thought of as justice. Vera's own father had taught her to care more about what God would think of her than what British society would say. But she could not upset Justin by attempting such a thing. The local gossips would do everything they could to make him ashamed of her. She preferred to accomplish her goal without causing him grief.

"What is it you want with me, lady?" the girl demanded. Her voice was low, but sharpened by anxiety. "It is not safe for me to be out in the streets."

There was no point in beating about the bush. "I want to help you escape from this place."

"I have no other place to go," Aurala said, downcast.

"But I have a place to send you, if you wish to go. It is up-country."

"I would have to leave a friend who—"

Vera held up her hand to interrupt. "Kwai Libazo knows you are in danger."

"You know about him?"

"He is a friend of mine," Vera said. It was not a thing she could ever say to a British person, but in a manner of speaking, Kwai was more like a friend to her and Justin than any British man or woman in the entire Protectorate, except for her father. "Kwai cares very much what happens to you."

The girl managed a wan smile, but her large dark eyes did not soften. "He knows they might come, but he does not know they are surely coming. He wants to protect me, but he must do his work. I do not want to rob him of that. He only wants to be a policeman."

Vera understood very well what it meant to love a man who was devoted to that work. And she saw that this girl was so attached to Kwai Libazo that she would stay near him at the risk of her life. "Kwai Libazo is a very intelligent man," she said. "Perhaps you should tell him the truth and let him help me get you out of harm's way."

Fear, pleading, something close to despair flashed one after another in the girl's eyes. "Will you speak to him, so he does not think I am trying to run away from him? He is the kindest man I have ever known." She looked into Vera's eyes. "I will do what Kwai Libazo wants me to do." Hope had entered the mix of emotions in her glance.

"Very well," Vera said, "I will speak to Sergeant Libazo. For now, stay out of sight. I will make sure he comes for you as soon as possible."

Vera followed a few feet behind the girl, saw her safely enter the silk shop, and then hurried out into the street. She must find Justin and convince him to send Kwai to help Aurala, but as both of them were off chasing Hastings, and the fierce sun made her light-headed, she was afraid she would faint again. She hailed a rickshaw to take her home, worrying about Aurala and praying that Justin and his squad would finish their work quickly.

When she arrived at the bungalow, Frederick Dingle was watering some newly planted passionflower vines along the front trellis fence. "You look unwell, my lady." He always addressed her that way, as if she were living at Tilbury Grange, Justin's father's estate in Yorkshire, and he were one of the gardeners, instead of a convict laborer on the coast of a far continent. "Shall I send for A.D.S. Tolliver?"

She shook her head, which made it swim all the more. "He is too busy," she said. "It seems that he is off somewhere in the town, trying to recapture a prisoner, Mr. Carl Hastings, who escaped the fort."

Dingle dropped the trowel he held in his left hand. Fear shone in his eyes. "Oh, no...He must have...Oh, my." He set down the watering can and folded his hands in front of his chest. "I think I know how he escaped."

It took her a few seconds to absorb the thought. She turned about. "You do?"

"Yes. I may have inadvertently told him how."

"Come with me," she said. Tired as she was, this news energized her. She led Dingle to the end of the street and hired a trolley to take them down the hill, back to police headquarters. She still carried the small package she had intended to take to Justin.

When she approached the Indian sergeant at the desk, he immediately made a wrong assumption. "Has this prisoner done something wrong ma'am?"

"Not at all," she answered. "He has important information about how Mr. Hastings may have escaped."

The sergeant pointed to a bench that faced the front door. "He can wait there. I will take care of this." He spoke in a deferential tone, but it was clear he thought she must leave it him to deal with the situation. Well, she was not about to be dismissed by the likes of him. But he was dismissing her.

"Is Inspector Patrick in his office?" she asked as politely as she could manage. She held up her package. "I want to give him this."

"He is out, ma'am."

She screwed up her courage, determined to put her package into the right hands and to get help to Aurala. "Then I would like to talk to D.S. Egerton."

"He has gone out also, ma'am. He and Inspector Patrick have gone to the Cecil Hotel to an important luncheon with High Commissioner Girouard and Inspector General Hollis."

Her heart sank. If it were up to her, she would barge in on them. But Justin would never live down the fact that his wife had interrupted the most important men in the Protectorate. "Are none of the British officers here?"

"Not just now, ma'am."

Vera then had no choice but to leave Mr. Dingle sitting on the bench in the lobby. She took her burning worries and her little package back home to the bungalow.

Fifteen minutes later, when Kwai Libazo entered the headquarters, he asked at the desk if A.D.S. Tolliver was inside.

"No," the sergeant on duty said. "Do you know where he has gone? Mrs. A.D.S. Tolliver was just here. She brought in this prisoner." He pointed to Mr. Dingle.

"I don't know exactly where he is," Libazo answered. "We separated. Sergeant Singh went to the port, and Mr. Tolliver was going first to the club and then to the house of a eunuch from Zanzibar who was known to have dealings with Hastings. I went to the railway station to make sure Mr. Hastings did not get on the noon train."

"Has he gone on the train? Should we telegraph up the line to re-arrest him?"

"Hastings did not take the train, and no steamers have left the port in the past twenty-four hours. So far as we know, he is still in the town. We do not know what Mr. Tolliver might have found."

Kwai went and asked Dingle what he knew, but the man would not give an African any information. "I must report what I know only to a British police officer," Dingle said.

The rule frustrated Kwai, but Dingle was white. And Hastings was white. If he insisted, it would be the black policeman who would be punished for insolence. He quickly established that there was no white officer in the entire building.

Much as he despised having to do it, Kwai went to the sergeant at the desk and with every ounce of deference he could muster, made his request. "This man has important information for A.D.S. Tolliver. Request permission to put him in one of the empty offices upstairs until I can fetch the A.D.S. here to receive the information."

The sergeant smirked. "This person," he said with a sniff, "is a convicted prisoner."

"You are right," Kwai said, trying to mollify the man. "But whatever else he is right now, he may have the answer to how to find the escapee. Perhaps our best course of action is to keep him out of sight until he can give his evidence."

The sergeant sighed more deeply than was necessary and agreed. Kwai delivered Dingle upstairs, ordered the constable on the second floor to bring the man some water, and then ran out to find Tolliver.

CHAPTER

20

Tolliver left the eunuch Ismail al Dimu's house and emerged, famished and frustrated, into the blast furnace of the street. Al Dimu had convinced him that had he known where to find Hastings, he would have turned him in rather than have anything more to do with him. Al Dimu seemed to have only hostile thoughts about anyone or anything.

Tolliver was contemplating popping into the Africa Hotel for a bite to eat when he saw Kwai Libazo running toward him, the look on his face promising important news. He immediately forgot how vexed and hungry he was. They raced back through the throngs.

When Tolliver entered the room where Dingle was waiting, he did not have to ask the man a question.

"It is my fault," Dingle said, jumping to his feet and speaking without preamble. "I told him about the tunnel."

"Tunnel?"

"There is a tunnel leading out of the fort. I heard about it from a policeman I used to drink with, name of Foran. Anglo-Irish."

"Yes, yes," Tolliver said, unable to hide his impatience. "Please get to the point."

Dingle shrank in his chair. Expressing impatience with him was clearly a mistake.

Tolliver belatedly tried to hide his annoyance with the man's reticence. "Forgive me," Tolliver said. "But we must recapture Hastings as soon as possible."

Dingle's answer came in the halting way he talked about everything but flowers. "Yes, I know, sir. I know, sir, I had looked for the tunnel. But out of curiosity. Never to escape myself. I found it. I told Hastings about it, but not to help him escape. Absolutely not! I told Hastings where it went so he would know it was not a safe route out of the place. Not safe at all."

Dingle's terrified look said it all. The ruins of the little Portuguese church on a cliff had a reputation for being deadly. Stories abounded of its being a breeding ground for every terrifying reptile and venomous insect Africa was prone to produce. Even in the correspondence Tolliver had received, when he was arranging to rent the cottage on the beach at Ras Serani Point, the owner had warned him to stay away from the crumbling Portuguese encampment. He said he didn't want to read yet another one of those notices in the newspaper about the death of some unsuspecting idiot who went up there to paint the view and gave his life to a snake.

"You think he went out that way?" Tolliver's flesh crawled at the thought.

Dingle shuddered. "I think he must have. How else would he have gotten free?"

"I'm afraid you are right," Tolliver groaned. "It's been a mystery to me how he managed to escape. I interrogated all the guards, and they swore to me there was no funny business, nothing about about letting him go." Hastings had last been seen inside the prison the previous night, just before lights-out at eleven o'clock. The guards were lax about keeping English prisoners confined to their cells. No one would swear he had locked up Hastings, but Tolliver believed that no one had purposely let him go. For one thing, the ivory hunter was pretty well stone broke. If he had wanted to bribe his way out, he was unlikely to be able to offer a sum adequate to tempt a man to lose his position and suffer imprisonment himself. "Can you show me the tunnel entrance inside the fort?"

Dingle's shoulders slumped. "Yes, sir, but you must be very careful. No one should ever go through there. No one."

"That's as may be, Mr. Dingle," Tolliver said, "but I shall have to investigate it nonetheless." He sent Dingle to the fort and steeled himself to get on with mounting a search party. If Vera knew what he was about to do, she'd be screeching.

It took the better part of an hour to organize a squad and equip them with lanterns, torches, and weapons. Libazo went back to the barracks to fetch a Maasai sword from the box at the foot of his cot.

When they were ready, they pulled Dingle from his cell and followed him down to the lowest level of the fort. He pointed them to an all-but-invisible cleft in a wall at the end of a narrow passage, behind a couple of bins. As soon as he finished his task, Dingle hurried away, as if terrified they would force him to come along.

Tolliver and his squad squeezed through the opening.

The narrow tunnel was hewn out of the coral rock. Since they could not walk two abreast, Tolliver positioned Libazo just behind him and a little to his left, with a hurricane lamp on a pole held out in front of them, so that the light could lead the way. Libazo balanced the lantern pole on his left shoulder and held his sword in his right hand. Tolliver carried a rifle at the ready.

The place smelled like a grave. The ceiling was so low that he and Kwai could not walk fully upright. Every few paces, they walked into a giant cobweb that shrouded their foreheads and eyes.

When they had moved along for a few yards, Libazo pointed his sword at the ground in front of him. "Stop, sir," he said. "Hold the lantern, if you please."

Tolliver complied. The rock floor below their feet was littered with the rank dirt of centuries.

"A man with large feet wearing stout English boots has passed this way very recently," Libazo said.

"How do you know the footprints are recent?" Tolliver asked.

"There are rat tracks all around here, but there are none on top of his footprints, sir."

They moved forward then, and Tolliver hoped the ominous skittering noises ahead of them were only rats. He wondered how Hastings could have had the nerve to enter this vile place alone. He must have had a lamp of some sort, but still—only a worse fate at the hands of his government could have driven him to this. If he was still hiding here, he could not miss the sound of a dozen men approaching. On a whim, Tolliver called out, "Carl Hastings, if you are down here, we are coming to take you back to safety."

"Is that what we are doing, sir?" Libazo had the audacity to ask. At least he kept the irony out of his voice.

"Shall we just get on with it?" Tolliver pressed forward, but he had hardly taken ten more steps when the lantern shining before him picked up red and black scorpions, at least eight of them, scurrying across their path. He bit his lip to stave off a gasp, but he couldn't stop a shudder. He halted until the creatures disappeared into the gloom ahead. He was glad of his stout boots, but the boys with him wore only sandals. "Bring up more light, a burning torch," he said as evenly as he could. Fire could actually be a better defense than bullets in this dreadful place.

He took the flame from a young constable whose eyes were wide with fear. They were all stiff and sweating despite the dampness of this crypt.

With the torch in his left hand, Tolliver shouldered his rifle and took out his pistol. Maintaining his point position, he moved along faster than before. He had to get his men into the open air, before one of them passed out.

His breath stopped again when he saw a nest of writhing snakes not three feet ahead. Without forethought, he tossed the burning torch into them. He aimed the pistol and hit one as it tried to slither away. Two others twitched in the flames and were still. Their flesh stank. One of the askaris behind him made a noise as if he were going to retch. "Young pythons," Libazo said.

"I hope we don't run into their mother," Tolliver replied. He would have liked to laugh, but he couldn't manage it. Fear knotted the back of his neck. He picked up the torch, which had gone out, lit it off a burning one held up by one of the lads, and moved ahead, hoping the men close around him could not hear the thudding of his heart.

After only another sixty yards or so, the path began to ascend. A weak light glimmered ahead of them, and Tolliver caught a faint whiff of the sea and something sweetish and corrupt. With more desperation than bravado, he quickened his pace.

"Hastings," he called out again. "If you are here, give yourself up." He worried that the escapee was already miles away and wondered if Libazo would be able to follow his footprints once they were outside. Had Hastings gotten out? Would Hastings have tried to make a run for it across land? Away from the coast, in that scorched, uninhabited tract a man alone could not hope to get far without guns, ammunition, and water. And the protection of a large group. There was always the chance, of course, that he had already been whisked away in a fishing boat. To a dhow. He could be well on his way to Zanzibar by now.

Closer to the opening, Tolliver slowed his steps. The smells of sea and rot were stronger. The opening at the end was partially overgrown with some sort of bush, which was silhouetted against the light. Tolliver passed off the torch, holstered his pistol, and took his rifle at the ready. "On your guard, boys," he said just loud enough to be heard.

The exit was a bit narrower than the tunnel. Libazo handed the lantern to the man behind him and closed ranks with Tolliver. They paused to let their eyes adjust to the light. They emerged.

They found themselves within the ruins of the fort-like chapel of St. Joseph. It stood on a promontory overlooking the ocean, less than a quarter-mile from the black-and-white striped lighthouse that towered above the cliff. The chapel's thick walls had no roof. The ground inside was covered with vegetation. Lizards scattered before them. God knew what else was hidden in the underbrush. Gooseflesh crept down Tolliver's back.

The other men had emerged. Libazo gasped. "Sir!" He reached out and brushed a large and hairy spider off Tolliver's sleeve. Tolliver stopped, shuddering, clenching his teeth. Libazo looked him over, and he returned the favor. "Check yourselves, lads," Tolliver said, no longer at all worried that he might give warning to anyone hiding here.

"Look there," one of the constables said, pointing off a few feet to their left.

The telltale sight of khaki trousers and stout boots brought them to Carl Hastings, lying nearly facedown on the ground, half in and half out of an opening in the wall. The sun, still ferocious at this time of day, beat down on his body. A hurricane lamp, which must have fallen when Hastings went down, lay broken on the ground. There was a charred area beside the corpse, and some of his clothing and flesh had burned too. The sweetish stench of burnt human flesh brought bile to Tolliver's throat.

"He must have been already dead when he caught fire." Tolliver was thinking aloud. He bent down. Something had gnawed on Hastings' chin and cheek. Most of the boys were vomiting now. Tolliver had all he could do not join them. He looked at Libazo. Only the stiffness of his stance and the hardness of his stare gave away his inner disgust.

Libazo pointed to the dirt near the corpse's right hand. "Dead or nearly dead, sir. See the claw marks."

Tolliver looked about. "What could have killed him—?" he started to ask.

The answer came in a split second.

A mottled brown snake reared on the other side of the body, not three feet from Tolliver. Its fangs and the inside of its mouth were dead black. "Mamba!" someone screamed. Tolliver's skin turned to ice. From behind him, Libazo swung his sword, slicing the snake's head from its body.

Tolliver leapt to his feet. They all stood barely breathing, scanning the ground around them. And then panting, as if they had just finished a race to the death. It was a full minute before any of them could speak a word. Tolliver did what he would have done to any man who had just saved his life. "Thank you," he said. He gripped Libazo's shoulder and held it for a second. "Thank you."

As soon as he had organized the lads who would stay to guard the corpse, Tolliver started back along the outdoor path, euphoric at the mere fact of being out in the light. But these high spirits faded quickly as he considered the practicalities of his investigation.

The day's shadows were already long. Darkness would fall, in its sudden African way, in the space of an hour. He had left four constables with the body. He had to get some boys back up there soon to move Hastings's remains to the fort. Otherwise, the men left there would spend the night surrounded by creatures that could kill them instantly with a sting or a bite.

And he was no closer than he had ever been to identifying exactly who had killed Khalid Majidi. No one else in the entire Protectorate Administration seemed to care a fig about that. On top of which, he had not eaten since breakfast.

As it happened, what with transporting the body, locating the doctor, and summoning him to examine it before the heat destroyed any evidence, Tolliver barely had a moment to down a tin of bully beef from the barracks stores before he was called to the autopsy. He sent Haki with a note to Vera, not to wait dinner for him. It was becoming a habit he greatly regretted. But that argument over his leaving the force was over. He would see out this assignment. After that he would be done with taking such risks to serve a justice that didn't exist.

It was after ten when the doctor finished his examination and declared that Hastings had died, as they all suspected, from a mamba's bite.

"Well then, his killer has already been executed," Tolliver said.

The doctor turned over his instruments to an orderly to be cleaned. "Since the deceased was a subject of the Crown, you'll have to report immediately to Egerton." He finished scrubbing his hands and dried them. "I saw the D.S. earlier in the bar at the club. I'd tell him myself, but I was up at three this morning, delivering a baby. It's bed for me before I collapse." He picked up his black bag and strode off, looking not half as tired as he professed to be.

Tolliver sighed and prepared to do his duty. The death of an Englishman, even one accused of a crime, was no light matter. Reports would have to be written. The Colonial Office in London would have to locate his next of kin. Personal belongings would have to be inventoried. Tolliver was thankful that his job of work in that regard would end with his report to Egerton.

He found the D.S. playing snooker with some other district officers. Egerton took the news in a corner of the billiard room and invited Tolliver for a drink and a sandwich. It was an offer Tolliver could not refuse. Once they had given an order to the waiter, Tolliver told Egerton about the discovery of Hastings's body and the doctor's conclusion.

"Save His Majesty's government from having to try the bastard," was all Egerton had to say on the subject.

"He and Majidi must have had accomplices in the slave trade," Tolliver offered mildly.

"No doubt. But it seems likely that their operation is done for with both of them gone."

Tolliver attacked the sandwiches as soon as they arrived. "Al Dimu, the eunuch, bears watching," he said between bites.

"I suppose," Egerton replied, taking only a few pieces of fruit, and pushing the rest of the plate toward Tolliver.

"And we have not discovered who killed Majidi."

"No one among the Arabs is at all concerned about that," Egerton said as if he meant to let the Liwali and the Grand

Mufti have the last word. After all he had been through, it galled Tolliver that Egerton might force him to give up investigating Majidi's murder. He thought to protest, but didn't see the use of it.

On the way up the hill to home, he fumed. The D.S. really believed that the British police force should kowtow to the Grand Mufti. But whatever the D.S. said, Tolliver knew he could never give up now. Granted, Majidi was also a murderer. Whoever had killed him had in actuality avenged the death of Joseph Gautura and also extracted punishment for the other hideous crimes Majidi had committed. The snake had punished Carl Hastings for his disgusting part in capturing and transporting slaves. Such rough justice should be enough.

It wasn't. Tolliver told himself that he was a policeman and that he wanted to find the killer in order to serve the rule of law. But he was well aware how strongly his own curiosity also figured in his desire to solve the mystery. He could hear the voice of his mother scolding him for always wanting answers to questions other people wished he had not asked. In this case, he would serve his conscience, not his masters.

As he walked from his front gate to the door, a lovely fantasy of Vera in her harem outfit pushed his other thoughts aside.

He was barely through the door when she came running to him from the bedroom, already in her night shift. He began to unbutton his uniform jacket.

She kissed him. And he was enveloping her in a warm embrace when she pushed him away. "Where is Kwai Libazo?" she demanded.

"Did you expect me to bring him home with me?"

"Don't tease, Justin. Aurala Sagal is terrified. I think she expects those brothers of hers are going to arrive any minute."

"Is it really imminent? Kwai went off duty almost three hours ago." He began to rebutton his jacket. "I'll go to the barracks and—"

She stopped his fingers. "If he is off duty, there will be no need. He went straight to her, I am sure."

He took her hands in his. "How do you know that?"

She pulled his arms back around her. "Because I know love when I see it." She reached her arms around his neck and kissed him.

"Shouldn't we make sure he has gone to her?"

"I have no doubt that he spends every second that he is off duty with her." She gave him a triumphant smile. "Besides, I gave a note to Haki to give to him, telling him what he must do."

"Of course you did." He laughed out loud and went back to undoing his buttons.

The next thing he did put an end for the night to all analytical thinking on his part.

Kwai Libazo and Aurala engaged in no such pleasure games in the dark of that night. Kwai, as Vera implored him to, had gone straight to Aurala as soon as he was released from duty. Much as he desired her and much as she had learned to desire making love with him, their time together was spent only in talk about her leaving Mombasa as quickly as they could arrange it. Neither said what they hoped for: that they would one day be together forever. There were too many obstacles between them and that lovely dream.

"A.D.S. Tolliver's memsahib said she would appeal to the people at the Mission in Nyali to hide you there until she can take you to Athi River, to her father's house, where you can stay in safety." Kwai watched Aurala's eyes as he spoke. Her look signaled fear, something like horror, but she said nothing.

He stroked her cheek. "Tell me what you want to do."

She asked him a question instead. "Do you want me to go far away from you?"

He smiled at her. She might be Somali, not Kikuyu or Maasai, but hers was an African's answer to what he had asked. He chose to make an African's response and answer her question with another one. "Do you want to be my wife?"

"Do you really want to do that?" she asked very softly.

He laughed at their conversation of only questions. "Yes. It is what I want. It is a grave thing for two as different from each other as you and me to marry. But it is all that I want."

Still she looked at him, more with wonder than with either yes or no in her glance.

"Please think about it," he said. "But whatever else happens, I want you to be safe. You can be protected in the up-country where no one knows where you are. My people are near there. Mrs. Tolliver's father is a kind and good man. He will shelter you. I will come there as soon as I can to be with you." He waited while she opened and closed her mouth several times, unable to respond. Perhaps not knowing what her heart wanted her to say. He kissed her hand.

Finally, she found her voice. "What kind of man would want to marry a woman who has done what I have done?" There were tears in her eyes.

He wiped them with his thumbs and caressed her hair with his fingertips. "I could tell you that I am a very special man because I want such a thing. But that is not true. Kikuyu men, Maasai men, and I, being both, do not care that the girl I marry has made sex with someone else. In my village, a man would not consider that any more important than her having eaten a coconut or drunk its milk. The men of my tribes want a woman who will make them a good wife. They do not believe what your people believe, that a girl who has done what you have done should be killed."

She looked down at the floor and fingered the beads around her neck while he spoke.

He went on. "I have spent a lot of time among the English. Reading their stories, listening to their thoughts. They say bad things about women who do what you have done. But they also go to them to pay for sex. And even worse, after they marry, they still make sex with others. For me and you, we do not belong to any of these groups. But we can belong to each other. If I can belong to you and you can belong to me…"

She made a sound, a little high noise that could have been the sound of her heart breaking. But when she looked up into his eyes, he saw that she was giving herself to him. He put his arms around her and felt as if he was her man and also her shelter, where she would live and always be safe.

"What is this?" Tolliver looked down at the large pewter spoon that Vera had placed on the breakfast table in front of him. It lay on green tissue paper from which she had unwrapped it as gingerly as if it were a precious blossom. She stood stiffly beside the table.

"It is something I think will be very important to you." It was almost a question. She looked as if she were teetering between triumph and defiance. "I tried my best to bring it to you yesterday. But I could never find you."

There were times when he wondered if he knew her at all. He folded his arms across his chest. "Vera, why are you being so mysterious? What is this about?" He did not think she was giving him a household gift. Despite the warmth and satisfaction of their lovemaking the night before, she had awoken in a strange, touchy mood.

"What you see there may very well contain the murderer's fingerprints."

"Good heavens. What would make you think that?" He felt that his expression was far too skeptical not to be insulting.

But really. Did she think the murderer was a waiter at a buffet restaurant?

"You don't have to take my word for it. You can take it to your Inspector Patrick and find out." Her hands were on her hips. Their words were logical and somewhat controlled but underneath, it felt as if an argument were trying to erupt.

"Yes, but where did you get it, and why do you think the murderer handled this?"

"I stole it if you must know. From the dried-fruit stall across from Majidi's shop in the souk."

"What? When?"

"Yesterday, but I didn't tell you about it last night because I knew you would get angry. And tell me I was being childish."

"Vera, really?"

"It's what you always say when I try to act like an adult instead of some helpless little girl. This minute you are looking at me as if I put two and two together and made five. I am very good at maths, you know. While Majidi was still alive, I was buying some fruit from that vendor across from his shop." She paused as if challenging him to guess correctly what she had in mind.

He remembered quite well how foolhardy her actions had seemed. He held his temper. "Go on," he said quietly, though he did not approve of the risk she had taken then, nor of the one she might have taken to purloin this thing on the table.

"That boy whose picture was in the paper, who is going to Egypt with the Grand Mufti to study the Koran at Al-Azhar University. His grandfather owns that dried-fruit stall. While the boy was waiting on me, he told me, a perfect stranger, that he thought Majidi was an evil man. There was a distinct gleam of hatred in his eyes. Before I could ask him much about why he believed that, his grandfather came from behind a curtain and interrupted our conversation. I thought about that two days ago. And then I remembered what you said, that Mr. Patrick thought the fingerprints on the murder weapon were small and could be those of a woman. It occurred to me that they might be those of a boy, a boy of fourteen or fifteen, like him." She turned her palms out to him in a gesture of innocence, but then she said, "That's when I decided to go there again and steal this spoon."

"You frighten me sometimes, Vera. You should have told me your suspicion and let me take what steps I thought appropriate."

"I knew what to do," she said. "I'm not an idiot, you know. I selected a few things and watched him spoon them up and wrap them. Then I paid him with a large bill, so that he had to go behind the curtain to get the change. There were many spoons like this one. I took the one I had seen him handle. Then I moved away so that he would have his back to the place where the spoon had been when he returned."

Justin let out his breath with a sound very near disgust. "Suppose you had been caught?"

"I wasn't, was I?" She was fighting back tears. She had hoped, this time, that he would admire what she had done.

"That does not make what you did right." He was not about to give in.

"Very well," she said, reaching out to pick up the spoon.

He caught her hand. "Don't."

She struggled to pull away. He held her hand as gently as he could. When she stopped struggling, he brought her hand to his mouth and kissed it. "You make me so afraid for you sometimes."

"Why can't you believe that I might know something you don't know?" Her eyes challenged him.

"You know a great many things that I don't know, dearest." He had added the last word to try to soften his approach, but it did not suffice.

"What are you going to do with the evidence I collected?" she demanded.

He kissed her hand again and let it go. He pulled out his pocket watch. He was wearing dress whites because of the ceremony to see off the Grand Mufti. "Why don't you come with me to drop it off at Patrick's laboratory? Then you may want to witness the great man's farewell."

"The great man? When did you become so admiring?"

"I didn't, really. The chaps on the force started to call him the G.M. Then that evolved into 'the great man.'" He picked up the pewter spoon with the green tissue paper.

She was putting on her hat inside the front door when she asked, "You do realize that the G.M. is taking the boy with him back to Egypt today?"

"Good grief," he said. "We have only an hour before the farewell parade to the port. The ship sails at eleven."

They caught a trolley at the end of the road. "Fast as you can," Tolliver said to the trolley boy as they shoved off.

"No speed limit, Bwana?" the boy said with a grin.

"Don't be cheeky," Tolliver responded. He put his arm around Vera and held her close as they hurtled down the hill. Game girl that she was, she didn't scream, not even when they nearly collided with a donkey cart crossing at the bottom.

Luckily, Inspector Patrick was in his room at headquarters. Tolliver watched the seconds ticking by on the round clock on the wall while Patrick donned his white cotton gloves and meticulously went about his business, carefully dusting the spoon with his powder, picking up his magnifying glass as if he had all the time in the world. He turned the spoon and dusted the other side. He took out the silver-and-marble box that had been the murder weapon and adjusted the lamp. He looked from the box to the spoon and back and forth, until Tolliver had all he could do not to tap his foot or say something.

Vera made matters worse by making bug-eyed faces and shaking her shoulders as if she were about to explode. She would start to pace if this took much longer.

Finally Patrick put down his glass, took off his spectacles, and announced, "Well, there is only one set of fingerprints on this spoon. Fortunately, the grip is broad enough that there is one very clear thumbprint, just there." He pointed to a spot between the end of the handle and the bowl. "It is an excellent match for the thumbprint on the murder weapon. Whoever used this spoon is your culprit, Tolliver."

Vera applauded, but Tolliver knew it was not time to celebrate. The murderer was about to leave the Protectorate, and he had no idea whether he would be able to stop that from happening. "I haven't a moment to lose," he said. He turned to Vera. "Dearest, I must make tracks. Can you—"

"You run ahead. I will make my own way to the ceremony."

"Are you sure you don't—"

"Go," she said.

He went down the stairs two at a time. He checked Egerton's office thinking to ask if it would be possible to apprehend the boy, but the D.S. had already left to follow the parting procession to the dock. Down on the ground floor, Kwai Libazo was nowhere in evidence.

The streets were thronged with Arabs decked out in all their finery, each one wearing an ornamental sword as well as a bejeweled dagger. A picture fell into Tolliver's mind of him with only his pistol trying to hold off an army of angry Arabs wielding sabers and cutlasses. Trying to make any headway in the crowded street was like trying to swim in a pool where the water was filled with yards of thick brocade. A hundred or so feet from the marquee at the dock, he came upon the end of the formal procession.

Egerton and the district commissioner were just ahead of him. He could have caught them up and told Egerton what he knew. That was what he should have done.

But he knew exactly what Egerton would say about leaving well enough alone and not causing a scandal at this point. Every sinew and bone in Tolliver's body rebelled against that. He would not cause a scene, but he would at least give himself a chance at confronting the killer.

As the British contingent entered under the marquee, he squared his shoulders and, giving an imitation of a man with a special role to play in the ceremony, he followed the Arab high-muck-a-mucks up the gangplank and onto the deck of the steamer, saluting the French officer at the top.

The boy whose picture he had seen taken at the Baranza Hall looked very formal in a midnight-blue kanzu. He sported a square hat that resembled nothing so much as a candy box covered with red silk. His large, soft brown eyes were fringed with thick lashes and filled with fear at the approach of the British policeman.

The Liwali, beside him, put his hand on the boy's shoulder and then spoke to Tolliver. "Mr. Egerton told me that you might try to interfere, Mr. Tolliver," he said quietly. He looked over his shoulder to the Grand Mufti, bidding farewell to a long line of well-wishers. The great man looked, as usual, completely at ease, as if nothing ever disturbed his equanimity. The Arabs were bowing to him and then exiting back down the gangway.

Tolliver turned again to the Liwali and spoke to him in English. "I have definitive proof that this boy killed Khalid Majidi."

"Nevertheless, he is leaving with the Grand Mufti."

Tolliver opened his mouth and closed it again. He had not even considered what jurisdiction he had on land in Mombasa—which actually belonged to the Sultan of Zanzibar—much less whether he had the authority to make an arrest aboard a French vessel.

"I think the boy may have been incited to do what he did by people still living here," Tolliver said, not knowing what he could do about that either.

The boy looked up at the Liwali with a grave expression and said something in Arabic. The two exchanged a few sentences. The Liwali became more and more animated with each retort. In the end, he smoothed the fine wool of his garment with both hands and held up his head, the gesture of a man who seemed to want to make himself taller. He put a hand on the hilt of the jewel-encrusted saber at this side, but it seemed merely an assertion of authority, rather than a threat. "The boy has just told me that he acted on his own," the Liwali said. "His grandfather had told us that he suspected the boy. We thought the child wanted to rid the sons of Islam in Mombasa of the evils that Majidi inflicted, but it is more basic than that. It is something I would not expect." He paused and put a fatherly arm across the boy's shoulders. "In his first sermon after arriving, the Grand Mufti described the world into which our Holy Prophet was born, and his battle against idolaters. Taimur, here, has just told me that every day, in the souk—in fact, many times each day—he gazed into Majidi's shop and saw him, in the back room, kneeling before the safe where he kept his money, adoring his wealth as if he were kneeling on his prayer rug and praying to Allah. The boy became more and more outraged, thinking of the idolaters who had persecuted the Holy Prophet, and how Majidi called himself a follower of Islam, but did so many evil things. Until he…"

The Liwali did not finish. The line of well-wishers was petering out.

After bidding farewell to the last of them, the Grand Mufti approached. He seemed completely serene. "It is so kind of you to come aboard to see me off, Mr. Tolliver," he said in perfect English. He nodded in the direction of the men in white uniforms and linen suits under the marquee. "Your countrymen were kind enough to bid me farewell as I came out of the mosque, and they honor me by joining in the procession to escort me here. But you have done me this special honor, and I appreciate it. I hope that we will meet again, *Insha'Allah*."

Tolliver had no idea how to respond. He bowed and, having no other sane choice, left it at that.

The Grand Mufti then took the boy whom he had chosen for a great honor and moved to the railing to the cheers of the crowd.

"Good-bye for now," the Liwali said to Tolliver. "I am sure we will see each other often."

Tolliver bowed to him too, saluted the French officer who stood guard at the top of the gangway, and marched onto the shore to join those under the marquee. He did not know if he was frustrated or relieved. He was watching the boy who had killed Majidi go free. But Majidi had deserved to die, hadn't he? And Justin knew that if he had been the one to prosecute the case, he would have had to explain Vera's part in gathering the evidence.

He found her—his exasperating and beloved wife—in the crowd of onlookers and took her with him to stand beside Egerton.

Egerton introduced Tolliver to a studious-looking man about Tolliver's age. "This is Bowes. Read Arabic at Oxford."

Bowes shook Tolliver's hand but turned his attention to the Grand Mufti as he began to address the crowd from up on the deck.

"He is speaking the Omani dialect," Bowes said. And then he listened to the Grand Mufti's speech and put it into English at the same time. Tolliver had seen Vera do this with Kikuyu and English. It always seemed like a magic trick.

"In the name of Allah, the Merciful, the Compassionate," came the great man's words in Bowes's voice. "Inspired by God himself, idolatry was first of the evils that the Holy Prophet preached and toiled against. He was born into a world of chaos and licentiousness, where men who worshipped idols behaved like animals. God spoke to him and gave him the path away from such outrages and toward a world of brotherhood and love. The oath of his very first converts began, 'We will not associate anything with God.' They swore this to the Holy Prophet himself. And so we must swear it again today and every day in our prayers. The just, the righteous worship only Allah." The Grand Mufti reached out and put his hand on the shoulder of the boy beside him. "Those who worship riches are idolaters, just as if they had made a golden calf and knelt to it. Be strong in your faith, my brothers. As surely as darkness flies before the rays of the sun, falsehood will vanish before truth." He put his hands together in front of him and bowed to the assembly.

The crowd listening on the dock raised a clamor. The Grand Mufti lifted his hands over his head and continued to wave while the gangway was raised and the French steamer weighed anchor. With billows of smoke rising from her stacks, and with the Grand Mufti still looking toward shore, the big ship slipped away and, surrounded by an escort of dhows under sail, made its stately way out onto the ocean.

Vera's voice was gentle but firm. "It will be only a week. Egerton has said you must stay, so what can we do? I have to go without you." She was packing a carpetbag with things she would need during the twenty-four-hour train journey from Mombasa to

Athi River station, the rail stop closest to her father's Mission just below Nairobi. Her small steamer trunk already contained some of her warmer clothing and many gifts for her father and Wangari, the Kikuyu woman who had been her nanny. She put her hands on Justin's forearms. "For now, let me spirit Aurala away before her brothers find her. I wanted to take her sister too. Aurala at first refused to go without her. But Leylo flatly refused. She gave Aurala only two choices: Go alone or stay behind."

"Do you think Leylo is staying behind to throw the brothers off Aurala's trail?"

"It does not bear thinking about," Vera said with a shudder. "It was all Kwai and I could do to convince Aurala to leave without her."

She put her hand on Justin's shoulder. "And I do want to see Father. It's been ever so long since I left him alone."

Justin's face remained sour. "If I know you, you will be off into the wilderness hours after you arrive." He was afraid he sounded like a petulant child.

She was holding a green shawl and looking at him with an imploring expression. "I promise I will do no more than go out into the Kikuyu reserve for a picnic with Papa. You and I will go up together to visit him at Easter."

A vivid memory of a picnic he and Vera had taken in that reserve together filled him with envy. He wanted to continue complaining, to add that it always rained in Nairobi at Easter. He knew he was making too much of this. She was going on a very short trip for a very good reason. Libazo was going too, "to guard our ladies," as he put it. But since their wedding day, Tolliver had not been apart from her except when he was at work. He had even brought her along on the foxhunt his brother, John, had made such a big show of staging at Tilbury Grange during their honeymoon.

Deep inside, he felt as if he would be bereft without her. What would his days be like without her conversation, without hearing her playing the piano as he entered the front walk? In the months since their wedding he had grown so used to her being always close by. Reminding himself that she sometimes outraged his sense of propriety did not help. Propriety be damned. He knew in his blood and bones that he was always meant to be joined to her. If his male acquaintances—he couldn't call them friends—on the force could read his thoughts, they would think she had somehow unmanned him with her sex. Well, they would be wrong. He never felt stronger, more of a man, than he did with her. Together, they were complete. So what if, in day-to-day things, she did not always obey him. He was certain that she would never bore him. A wave of desire was coming over him. Something for which there was no time; her train would leave in less than an hour.

"I could stand here looking at you forever," she said. But then she turned away and packed the shawl and did up the grip, which he took to the door.

Before they left the bungalow, he kissed her the way he would not be able to at the station.

In the buggy, she held his hand. "Kwai Libazo is meeting us there with Aurala. Wait till you see him."

Tolliver had had to pull strings to get Libazo permission to leave, and it prickled Tolliver's sensibilities that the argument that Egerton found most convincing was that Tolliver wanted Libazo to go as a bodyguard for Vera. Tolliver knew better than to bring up the need to protect a girl who had worked as a prostitute.

When they arrived at the station, a porter took Vera's little trunk. The train was already in the station and beginning to build up steam. The freight wagons were at the front and the passenger carriages at the rear, farther away from the smoke and sparks of the engines.

The condition of the platform did not make it easy for them to spot Libazo and Aurala. The place resembled a disturbed anthill, with people moving in all directions—carrying things away, carting things toward the goods cars, which were being loaded with everything from automobiles to crates holding the china and crystal of newly arrived settlers.

"They are there," Vera whispered as they pushed through the throng. "That's Aurala in red."

Near the end of the train they passed a tall Swahili dressed in a snowy *kanzu*, a dark green vest, and white turban with a length of fabric hanging down over the back of his neck. A typical jeweled dagger was stuck in the sash around his waist. Next to him was his wife, in purdah—covered completely from head to foot in a red *bulbul* that showed only her eyes.

"I would not have recognized Libazo if you hadn't told me," Tolliver whispered to her.

"That's the idea, of course," Vera said, her eyes scanning the crowd even though she hadn't the vaguest capacity to recognize Aurala's brothers or their spies.

Tolliver sidled around the couple and put on a gruff voice. "You should move aside. You are standing in the way."

Libazo put his hands together and bowed. "Yes, your excellency," he said in what sounded something like a French accent.

Tolliver and Vera did their best not to burst out laughing. They stopped a little farther on, near the first-class carriage where Vera would ride.

At that moment, Haki ran up to Kwai and Aurala. He was dressed as a little Arab boy, in a white *kanzu*, a tiny brocade vest, and an embroidered skullcap.

"Here I am, Father, Mother," he said in a loud voice. "The ticket clerk told me that there is no charge for a child traveling with his parents."

"What a clever lad," Tolliver whispered to Vera.

True to his disguise, Libazo took the boy up the iron steps into the second-class carriage designated for the darker races.

Tolliver escorted Vera forward and lifted her into a compartment. He was delighted to find that a man he knew from Nairobi, Baron Von Blixen-Finecke, would be traveling with her. They exchanged pleasantries through the open window while they waited for the train to leave.

Tolliver remained on the platform, watchful for any sign that Aurala's brothers might be in pursuit.

It wasn't until the train was well out of the station that he turned and left, still on the lookout for he knew not whom.

His heart found again that sinking, lonely place it had occupied while Vera was packing.

As it turned out, except for the Sunday of her absence, Tolliver had no time to pine for Vera as much as he had imagined he would.

Within hours of the train's departure, Singh came and told him that Leylo's brothers had taken her. "Word in the souk is that they have carried her to a lonely spot on the mainland and beheaded her," he said with a shudder.

"Do we have the body?" Tolliver asked.

"No, sir. The report said it was done north of the town, up nearer Malindi. At least that is what the traders in the souk are saying. Evidently, the brothers, knowing that Aurala had escaped, continued north, back to Somalia."

Tolliver shook his head at the thought of such a gruesome end for the woman who could not have been much older than twenty, Vera's age.

For the rest of the week, he was occupied day and night. The minor felons and petty thieves of Mombasa had evidently suppressed their temptation to do wrong while the Grand Mufti was in the town. They had now let loose their pent-up urges to garner ill-gotten gains. One of them had had the gall to steal the altar cloth from the cathedral.

On top of all this, every ship from Europe, India, or South Africa brought in new settlers, and it was up to the police to perform health inspections and make sure that anyone arriving who showed a sign of disease went into quarantine.

Without Libazo, Tolliver had to make do with various constables to work on the cases. None of them was at all as helpful as Kwai. Consequently, Tolliver went home exhausted each night, if he went home at all. He was busy, but bored.

Vera cabled him just before she boarded her return train, confirming that she would be arriving on schedule.

He did his best to get a decent amount of sleep the night before her arrival and met her at the train with a lovely bouquet put together by Frederick Dingle, and which Tolliver strongly suspected had been harvested from the Public Gardens.

Justin brought Vera home to bathe and change and then took her to the Grand for a dinner of roast beef and, all things considered, a quite passable Yorkshire pudding, even for a son of York.

He could not bring himself to tell her of the fate of Leylo Sagal. Not just yet.

At the table she was full of conversation and gossip about all that was going on in Nairobi. He sipped a lovely claret while she regaled him.

"Baron Von Blixen is going to try to grow coffee higher than anyone has before. He expects the future baroness to arrive next year when all is ready."

Tolliver cared not for the news, wanted only to listen to her voice and hear her forthright, decidedly un-British opinions, and to smile inwardly at how many people she must have shocked at the dinner dance she had attended at the Nairobi Club.

"I did my best to be polite to District Commissioner Cranford," she said with a wrinkle of her nose. "He made a great show of inviting me to dine at his table. Then he spent the whole evening complaining that the natives are lazy and prone to drunkenness. You will be very proud of me, Justin, that I never pointed out that Cranford calls the natives lazy while he doesn't shave himself or tie his own tie or put on his own jacket, for that matter. He does not clean his own guns or prepare his own food. Those lazy natives do all that work for him."

"You are right of course, my darling, but I am mightily glad you did not insult the district commissioner by telling him so to his face."

"And have you ever seen a native drink as much as an Englishman?"

"Or a Scot, for that matter," he said. His eyes were teasing her.

"Or a Scot." She laughed and raised her wineglass and took a sip. She leaned across the table and whispered, "Let's go home, darling."

He folded his napkin and stood up immediately.

They walked toward the bungalow hand in hand.

"I have another bit of news," she said. "Have you heard anything from Robert Morley?"

"Not a peep."

"Papa received a letter from him. He and Katharine are moving away. He has agreed to take over a mission down in German East Africa, along the Ulanga River."

"Why ever would he?" Justin's mind was on getting home.

"His letter said he had been tempted to sin here in Mombasa and that he must go away. Papa thinks he is punishing himself for something."

"Did you tell—" He caught himself. "Of course you did not."

"No."

"It seems a bad idea to go down there with things being so tenuous with the Germans. I suppose his poor sister is going to let him drag her there."

She drew his arm over her shoulder and twined her fingers into his. "It is so very upsetting. He does not seem to give a single thought to what she might want or not want. He just assumes that she will go along with whatever decision he makes. I have a good mind to tell her to abandon him to his own resources."

"She probably would not take your advice."

"That is exactly what Papa said. And I think you are both right. She seems to resent him some of the time, but I doubt she will ever stop thinking she must care for him, no matter what he does. Sisters are like that."

They walked along, both thinking of Vera's missing brother and the pain of not knowing where he was or how he was.

As soon as they were through the front door, she threw her arms around him. She kissed his ear and touched it lightly with her tongue—the way he sometimes did to hers. "I am about to act like the hussy you have often known me to be."

"Oh, do, please do."

Hours later, she snuggled against him, kissed his shoulder, and lifted her head. In the patch of sky visible from their window, out over the ocean, in the predawn, a few of the brightest stars were still visible.

"Dearest?"

"Mmm?"

"I waited till now to tell you." Her voice was more energetic than he would have imagined.

"What? Not another piece of settler gossip? Go ahead, shock me."

"I'm—I—I hope it will not shock you."

Her tone told him to be on the alert. "Tell me."

"We are going to have a baby." In the candlelight, she searched his eyes for a sign of how he felt.

For a moment he could not react. He had of course imagined that this would one day be the case. He had not expected to be surprised. He had thought, until this moment, that he loved her an impossible, an indescribable amount. That his capacity to love was completely filled with her.

And then, suddenly, a door opened in his heart on a space the size of the Royal Albert Hall.